The Planet of Souls

The Planet of Souls

by Endru Atros

PAPERBACK ISBN: 978-1-7377737-7-1
EPUB ISBN: 979-8-2011728-7-9

***

WRITTEN BY ENDRU ATROS
PUBLISHED BY ROYAL HAWAIIAN PRESS
COVER ART BY TYRONE ROSHANTHA
TRANSLATED BY SZYMON NOWAK
PUBLISHING ASSISTANCE: DOROTA RESZKE

***

FOR MORE WORKS BY THIS AUTHOR, PLEASE VISIT:
WWW.ROYALHAWAIIANPRESS.COM

***

VERSION NUMBER 1.0

Motto for today:

One universal field of intelligence is an immaterial field, it is the Field of Consciousness. It exists at the root of everything - matter, mind, space and time. All the so-called particles in the universe, the forces in our cosmos are only waves in this ocean of existence. Planets, people, trees, animals - we are all just the Vibration Waves of this Unified Superstring Field.

As science progresses, new theories appear regarding the number of dimensions of reality in the universe. For example, superstring theories assume the existence of even several dimensions.

And so, according to this theory, the eighth dimension is truly remarkable because it has different infinities within it. In this dimension there are universes that are completely distinct from ours, with completely different laws of physics.

It is difficult for us to understand it and that's good, because knowledge about them, for most of us, is needless.

Endru Atros

Chapter I

Three Suns

I walked forward shuffling. The cold touch of the water on my feet seemed unreal, but I could feel the slight tickle of the receding wave. But where did this shudder of fear squeezing my temple and this tingling skin on my back come from? The bright night with the starry sky radiated with the pale moonlight illuminating the beach in front of me. Its bright rays pressed into every crevice in the sand and shimmered, as they reflected from the surface of the water, sliding on its back.

"What am I doing here?" Somewhere in the corner of my head, a fearful thought rattled.

Something was pulling me towards the nearby rocks. I tried to resist this force, but my body wasn't listening to me, so I moved in that direction like a sleepwalker, seeing nothing but a bright spot against the dark irregular shapes of the rocks emerging from the water. All around, the dark surface of the sea flashed here and there the seawater foam. With each step I took, the white spot grew larger and seemed more expressive, friendlier, but its strength still held me in its embrace, telling me to get closer. A little more, a dozen more meters and I could already make out the outline of the human figure. Long blonde hair made me realize it was a woman. Due to the breeze sliding from the high hill into the embrace of the sea, her hair was slightly undulating, brushing her bare shoulders. Her face was hidden by a shadow, but the body, dressed in a long, light tunic, shone through the thin material moistened with splashes of water drops torn from the surface of the sea. The waves hitting the ledge dissipated into a mist of salt water, creating a white coat that enveloped her entire figure. But it was not a fish-tailed mermaid, but a young girl smiling friendly at me. Spreading her hands in greeting, she lured me. Coming closer, I looked into her eyes. I had seen eyes like that before. Big black eyes, with oblong dilated pupils were staring at me, piercing my soul to the very bottom.

"Come with me," I heard the melodious voice, though her lips didn't move.

"I'm coming," I said to her against my will. My gaze involuntarily slid down her body, where the plunging neckline revealed the water droplets glistening on her breast. The girl turned towards the sea and started walking confidently. With each meter of distance, she sank more and more.

Having reached the place where the girl was standing a moment ago, I rested my hand on the rough and wet surface of the rock, which beamed with the warmth of the sun that had heated it all day.

"Is this really happening?" the thought ran through me. I look at the figure wading through the water. She went on. This time, helping herself with her hands, she pushed the water away. Her long, straight hair fell to the sea and, wetting its ends, it stuck to her bare back, to, after a while, gently flow from her white skin into the water again and glide on the surface of the wave.

"She has sensed that I'm watching her," I thought as she turned her head towards me, staring at me questioningly. It stimulated me to act.

"I'm coming!" I call to her without hearing my own voice. When she reached the edge of the rock disappearing in deep water, she faced me and waited.

I felt the water flood my hips. The rebellion reflex shook my body. I was about to turn around and head back for the safe sand when something disgustingly slippery crept up onto my leg. It instantly wrapped around my foot. Spirally squirming, it crept upward. I felt a grip on my calf. Suddenly, a strong jerk almost knocked me into the water.

It was a warning.

The girl sent me a graceful smile to encourage me to continue my journey. Now she was walking backwards behind the ledge, looking at me. The moonlight that enveloped her painted a rippling shadow across the water. This shadow spoke to me, reached my consciousness, directed me into her embrace. I felt a tug again, this time weaker, a slight one encouraging me to continue my journey.

"Come, follow me, it's not far," I heard her voice. A few more steps and she disappeared behind the edge of the rock.

Drip, drip - I could clearly hear the sound of falling raindrops.

"It's not raining here," I realized, waking up. "This is another time I have had the same dream since I came here," I thought as I sat down on the bed.

From the moment I entered this house standing on the edge of a small summer town right next to the beach, I had had a nightmare feeling about something that would definitely happen. I just didn't know what, when and where.

For the first few days, during my morning gymnastics, I thought about the girl from my dream. She was very real, almost palpable, only her black eyes didn't match her character or anything I had dealt with so far.

I came there, desiring peace and quiet. I had to finish my novel, just like I had promised my literary agent. Two months earlier, I had sent him the text of an almost completed novel. Almost turned out to be extremely difficult to implement. Inspiration faded along with my thoughts. I missed something. Something bothered me and made me anxious. It seemed to me that it was because of a beggar woman, or maybe a gypsy woman I had met. I didn't know who she was.

Less than two months earlier, Richard and I had been returning from a party at some unrepentant singles club, and it was then that I encountered on the street the old woman.

She was sitting on the wall next to the constantly flowing human figures. It was Saturday, a warm and sunny night, conducive to nearby walks. I noticed Richard walking ahead, reaching into his pocket and throwing the woman a bill into a small black box on the wall, which looked like some music box forgotten by time. In the light of the street lamps, thanks to the sequins adorning its surface, it sparkled with all the colors of the rainbow. I stopped next to her, looking for money in my pocket with my hand.

"No need, I won't take anything from you," I heard her strong, vibrating voice.

She stared at me with black eyes with unnaturally dilated feline pupils whose yellow rims contrasted with their black color. Her long gray hair covered with some colorful scarf fell in disorder over her shoulders. Loose strands which came from under the material covering her forehead, gave her face a strange look. When she turned her head towards me, her hair waved slightly, shielding her neck with large red beads. I looked into the casket, there was nothing there except a black bottom.

"Why don't you want money from me?" I asked.

"You are marked," she replied with a calm voice looking at me with a slight amusement.

"What?" I blurted out.

"Soon," as if without connection, she continued.

"What will be soon?" I asked, and instead of following Richard, I dwelled on the subject, wondering what she meant.

"You'll see her."

She fell silent.

"Who will I see?"

"The girl in your dream. It is your destiny; you will not run away from it."

This time her eyes flashed strangely. For a second, I thought she was young and beautiful. I had never seen eyes like this, never even heard that a man can have such.

My hand digging into a pocket found some note. I jerked my hand and took out the money. I quickly threw it into the casket.

"It's useless. You won't bribe fate," the strong singing tone of her voice made me uneasy.

"What are you still doing there?" I heard Richard's voice in the distance. I started walking towards him. When I turned my head after a while, the wall was empty.

"Have you seen?" I asked him.

"What?"

"The woman who sat on the wall, where is she?"

"She's gone," he replied, surveying the area. The street on either side was empty.

As I got out of bed and prepared for my morning run, my thoughts were analyzing the night's sleep.

"What could that mean?" I thought about the night vision of my subconscious tormenting me.

Sleepy, with doubts, I started my morning gymnastics. I jogged every morning, no matter what the weather. Unless it rained heavily, then I exercised in a gazebo near the house.

I rented this old wooden house for three months from some real estate agency. The whole summer in this seemingly almost utterly outlandish place was to result in completing my novel.

Now I was just finishing my morning run on the beach. I didn't run too far that day. I turned back, running on the wet sand past the waves ending their lives on this patch of white sand. Suddenly ... I noticed her - the girl from my dreams. She was walking on the beach with a stick in her hand, and her dog was running around her, barking madly. The black poodle demanded fun.

"It's her, I'm sure," I thought, amazed at the sight.

I decided to know her.

I jogged towards her. When I was right next to her, I stopped and leaned forward, putting my hands on my knees. Panting loudly, I pretended to be exhausted by intense running.

"Tired?" I heard her voice.

I straightened up and looked at her. Her eyes, just like then, at night in my dream, were shiny, black, large and with yellow dilated pupils. They contrasted with her white skin and long blonde hair. Well, hair can be dyed, but skin not," I thought, staring at her breasts, and hoping he wouldn't notice it.

"I've run a little too far, and I still have to go back," I said to her as I came closer.

She swung violently, throwing the stick far away. The dog ran in that direction.

"Peter," I introduced myself extending my hand to her. I was curious about her hand, that first body contact.

"Krys," she replied, taking my hand with her narrow, delicate palm with long fingers and manicured pearly shining nails.

"What are you doing here?" she asked.

"I run."

"I see, but what are you doing here in these parts?"

"I rent that old house on the edge of the woods, not far from here."

"I know, I saw you there. I asked what you do when you are not running."

"I rest, gather my strength for inspiration that has left me," I laughed shortly. Her hand was still holding me, "too long for the first greeting," I thought.

"Did you know that this house once belonged to my great-grandmother."

"No, how would I know that?"

"You didn't look around, weren't upstairs?"

"Not yet, I've only been here a few days."

"I see," she blurted out.

"You're coming home?" she added, gently running her fingers along my palm.

"Yes."

"Will you invite me in? Someday," she blurted out quickly, as if frightened by what she had said, because it sounded like an imposition.

"I wanted to see the house, I haven't been in it for a long time," she said quickly, explaining herself. "Lastly, I was there as a child, before my family left for the city. Then studies far away from here, you know what it is like with those returns to your neck of the woods."

Only now did she let go of my hand, but so reluctantly, more out of reason than out of need.

I didn't mind her still holding my hand, I felt some physical longing for the warmth of her hand. Strange? I thought for a second about my desire.

"So, I invite you for breakfast and morning coffee," I said quickly, fearing that we would part and never meet again.

"I can only make scrambled eggs," I added with that smile of a little boy. She burst out laughing. Her pearly voice added charm to her entire figure. As she laughed, her eyes narrowed more and became less black, but shinier.

"Scrambled eggs are okay. Do you want to run? I'll run with you," she offered.

"No, this time I will let it go."

"I wanted to meet you, that's why I came to the beach so early," she admitted, looking at me without embarrassment.

"Why?"

"I came to my hometown a week ago. I wanted to rent this house, but you beat me. Inside, on the upper floor, there are prints of my family. Of my mom, grandmother, great-grandmother, and mine too.

Memories," she whispered softly after a moment.

Unhindered by anything, she followed me home, and the black dog puttered between our legs.

I was wondering intensely whether I had order inside for such an early time of the female visit. "But what the hell, I won't drag her to the bedroom, and the kitchen is not that bad, I hardly used it," I thought. The whole way I was rankled by the thought that it was all made up. This dream, the old woman and that girl, was no coincidence, it was a deliberate act. But of who, what, providence or a man.

We went to the house, to the very door, an old wooden one with carved elements on its surface. I opened it and gesturing, invited her in.

She entered cautiously as if afraid that she would fall over on the threshold. You could see the focus on her face. Her slightly narrowed eyes tried to recognize what they had seen long before.

"It looks different now," she whispered entering the living room.

On the right side of the room, there was a kitchen with a large dark mahogany table, and further a study. She looked in that direction. On a large old cherry-tree-colored desk, there were papers scattered, as well as an old typewriter.

"There used to be my grandmother's pantry," she said. "But the floor is the same and the beams on the ceiling haven't changed at all," she added with some strange deliberation, looking around curiously.

"So, watch what you want while I prepare breakfast. Coffee or tea, or maybe juice or milk?"

"Juice, please," she answered me as if to a waiter. It was evident that she was absent.

Krys went up the wooden stairs, and I went to the kitchen. As I turned the eggs in the pan, I heard the shout from above:

"Come quickly!"

Curious about what she had discovered, I walked towards her. "Why didn't I go there earlier?" I wondered as I walked up the narrow wooden steps that creaked terribly with my every step. It was impossible to run there, the stairs were too narrow and winding. When I dealt with all the steps, I saw a small vestibule and two side corridors.

"Where are you?" I called out.

"Here," I heard the tearful voice from the right. I looked in that direction. The walls covered with some patterned material, contrasted with an old motley rug lying on the floor. Everything was slightly dusty. The door was open, so I entered.

Krys was standing in front of old photos hung on a wall, sobbing softly. I stood behind her, put my hand on her shoulder and said soothingly: "it's okay, don't cry."

"I used to play in this room as a little girl," she said, sniffling.

"Gosh!" I exclaimed, looking at an old photo. "I know this woman from the photo," I blurted out. "I spoke to her two months ago."

"I know, this is my great-grandmother."

"Then I didn't notice her ..."

"I know."

"Would you let me have a look around?" she asked.

"Of course."

She went to the opposite wall where there was an old dresser, with an empty space on the shelves behind its panes. She opened the bottom drawer and fumbled in it with her hand, something snapped inside, and the side of the dresser swung open.

"This secret compartment was made by my grandfather, and I helped him," she added seeing my surprised face.

A casket appeared to me. The same or similar to that of the old woman sitting on the wall.

"I have already seen such a casket," I said to her.

"It has belonged to our family for a long time, a very long time," she replied, not surprised by my statement. She picked up the box and facing me, she said:

"We can go to your breakfast now; I think the scrambled eggs are on fire."

"Oh god, my breakfast!" I screamed as I moved downstairs. The smoke from the burning pan was already coming up the stairs.

"Shit, same thing again, I never manage to fry them normally," I thought.

She helped me ventilate the living room, and then she prepared breakfast quickly and efficiently, but without eggs, as I had no more of them.

The casket stood on the table, at which we drank coffee, and I waited for the development of events.

She noticed my gaze directed at the box.

"You have the same one," she said, looking at me with a cheerful smirk on her lips.

"I don't remember having anything like that."

"You were a child, you cannot remember," she briefly summed up the gaps in my memory.

She ate with a slight deliberation, savoring every bite as if she hadn't had anything in her mouth for a long time.

"Where is the dog?" I asked, looking to the sides. "Usually, dogs stand next to the table waiting for some tasty morsel."

"He's safe in another dimension," she said unexpectedly.

I silently directed my astonished gaze to her.

"As a writer, you can imagine such a possibility," she marked her words with a broad smile.

"The beautiful girl is sitting in front of me, with this box of hers in her hand, and she is telling me such a nonsense," I thought.

"I can imagine something like that," I answered calmly.

"This casket has always been in my family. Without it, we will not survive, we will die like all the people on this planet."

"Does it mean that you are not from this planet," I chimed in on her thread.

A grimace of dissatisfaction crossed her face. She leaned in my direction, boring into my eyes with her black eyes, and slowly, clearly, with an emphatic tone meant to show that she knew what she was talking about, she continued.

"You are also not from this planet."

"What," it ran through my head.

"Interesting," I muttered to her, calmly finishing my coffee. "How do you know I'm a writer?"

"Thanks to this." She nodded towards the far wall. On the top shelf of the cupboard, there was my book with my photograph.

"Well, perceptiveness is probably her additional feature next to her exuberant imagination," I thought.

Krys, looking at me, tilted her head slightly in my direction. She put her hands on the corner of the table and continued with a strong, confident voice.

"Life on earth comes from us. It was by accident that civilization arose here. Now we have to live with it and share this life with others. But life is short here, so we use the casket."

I reached for the box with my hand.

"What is it?" I asked, opening the lid.

"For now, it's just a casket for you. For me, it's survival, life, a moment of relief and the joy of existence. Tell me, how old am I?" she asked as if without connection.

"Twenty, twenty-two."

"Yes, earthly twenty-one. Our seven hundred and fifty."

I was silent.

"Nothing is eternal, the stars will go out someday too," she whispered softly.

Once, long time ago according to your time, tens of thousands of years ago, we were doing what is being done on Earth now. Our planet was being destroyed. We were corrected, our bodies. The results were great - initially. When it was realized that the planet was dying and that genetics couldn't be improved with impunity, it was too late. We only have one option left. Another star like ours, in order to survive the period when our scientists fixed what they had broken in us, because our planet couldn't be repaired anymore. We needed time to find it and we were dying out en masse. When we found It, Earth, we split into two populations. The handful that survived moved here. The rest struggled to survive on the dying planet. But nothing is perfect. Here on Earth our biological clock ticked differently. We lived like other people, for several dozen Earth years. It was scary. So, they found a way - the casket. It opens the space between our planets."

I listened attentively to it as if to some radio play.

"The casket curves space, allowing anyone who has it to return to our planet and travel back to Earth. When I'm at home, I live and enjoy what I'm there. But I cannot stay there forever. Science has not completely won over genetics. There is a stain on our lives here and there."

She fell silent.

"What?" I asked, thinking that it would have been good material for a book.

"We have to go back to Earth every now and then so that our material cells can regenerate. We can't do this in our place, because we don't have them there, that's why we live so long. If we don't do this, life is shorter and we die. However, when we are on Earth, time passes for us as it does for everyone on this planet - we age quickly, very quickly. Among us there are those who don't come back, live here and die like everyone else.

"They are Renegades," she added, "but I don't condemn them. 'What does it matter to live a hundred years or a thousand, you have to die anyway' they argue their decision. These rights also apply to you, our rights," she added.

"I'd rather live a thousand years than a hundred," I murmured, expressing my opinion on the subject.

"In my place, people live longer, but also differently. Not as intensely and unpredictably as here, and that's why some of us enjoy life on Earth," she added.

"What are you coming back for?"

"To live. Every few dozen Earth years we have to come back to Earth to regenerate. When our stay on Earth is long, we don't have enough time to come back and we die like everyone else on this planet. The older you get, the longer you have to stay on Earth and regenerate your cells. The irony of fate. If I get old on Earth, I will be such on 'Hope', and that's not nice."

"Is Hope the name of your planet?"

"Yes, and it is also your planet. My great-grandmother, whom you have already seen, is already 87 on Earth, and 2683 on our planet. When you come to Earth at this age you never know if you will be able to return to Hope. Here you get sick, you got run over and that's how you end your life before your mana think about the return. Life here is beautiful though.

Love - great experience, sex - wonderful, nature - divine. You have warm waters, seas and oceans, mountains and skies, and food - is delicious. It's something we don't have. There, on Hope, we don't die 'now', everyone must come back here and die like a human."

"Interesting theory. Are you, Krys, maybe a journalist who wants to get material for an interesting report?" I asked.

"And the great-grandmother, dream?" she answered my question with the question. I was silent, not knowing what to think about it -

complete surprise didn't allow me to think through everything I heard.

"That's why my great-grandmother doesn't want to come back here, but I can, I'm still young."

She sighed.

"As a child, I was on Earth several times, here in this house," she added.

"How is it that no one notices you disappearing?"

"Transfers, constant transfers, and documents and interfering with the information system is not a problem for us. The problem is that our knowledge cannot be transferred to earth."

"Why?"

"We just don't know how it works and why it works, except maybe for a handful of Hopers. It's like teaching an ant quantum physics. We are more spiritual than bodily there."

"How does the casket work?" I asked, curious about her theory.

"It is a transmitter integrated with our spacetime flight station. I just swim in on Hope and I'm already on Earth. Here, whatever you throw inside, after a while it shows up in our place."

"Don't you think it's too small for you to fit in there?"

She laughed as if at some kind of joke.

"You are one of us. Think you want to come back to Hope."

I thought. I can't write that it flashed, thundered, and a fire ball fell from the sky or a spaceship came. Nothing like that.

I was just standing in front of a white undulating surface against which we could see the rest of the living room in which we were.

"That's all?" I asked aloud.

"Do you want to come in?" I heard. "You're not ready yet," she added in a concerned voice.

"How to come back?" the frightened tone of my speech seemed not to come out of my mouth.

"Think."

I was sitting at the table with her again. My hands were shaking with emotion. Now I was definitely not dreaming.

"How did you find me?" I decided to keep playing her game.

"Eyes," she used to say with short sentences. For ordinary people and yourself, they are human, brown. For us, such as you saw in my great-grandmother and you see in me. Thanks to them we recognize each other."

"Does it mean that you see them just like I see yours?"

"Yes."

That was too much for me. I got up from the table and headed for the bathroom where there was a mirror.

I looked at myself. Normal as always.

Krys stood next to me. Her eyes were different, definitely different, large, black with elongated pupils and very shiny.

"You're beautiful," I whispered softly in my mind, more to myself than to her.

A smile lit up her face.

"Nobody told me about it on Hope," she sighed heavily. "There we are all the same," she moved closer to me, touching me with her breasts. Her hand took my hand.

"We are Afterglowers."

"How old am I?" I asked.

"Twenty-five. You haven't been to Hope yet, so time hasn't stopped for you. My great-grandmother and yours are friends - they were friends. As you know, your great-grandmother died, she didn't want to come back to Hope, and your parents, actually only your mother was a Hoper. They didn't recognize the planet of their ancestors and kept you away from it all. It was her will, and as long as she was alive, we respected her decision. Now that has changed. My great-grandmother didn't want to accept it, saying that you have to decide what is good for you."

"Is that why you were in my dream?"

"You were not dreaming; I entered your mind. And the image you saw was your subconscious registering my presence. Would you have let me in if you hadn't seen me in your dream?"

"Probably not, and certainly not so fast."

"Don't be afraid of me. Here I'm just as human as you are and have no supernatural powers. Except for one thing. Penetrating your mind, but it is a mutual feature. You are capable of it, but you don't know how to do it yet."

"I'm not afraid of you, but it is difficult for me to grasp it all right away, to believe what you say."

"Did you know that couples from Hope make trips to Earth."

"Sex tourism?" I laughed at my own joke.

"This too, but paid for with the passage of time on Earth and faster aging. More often they are couples who want to taste this earthly form of being."

"So, you are poor in this spiritual shell."

"You are right, but certainly not less happy, just different."

"Peter, come with me, I want to show you something," she pronounced my name for the first time in a soft, very moody way.

She stood up, took my hand and tugged me lightly towards her. Our bodies met for a moment, too briefly for me to feel her warmth. I put my arms around her waist and let her through. The dog was still gone.

She moved a few steps away from me, looked up at the sky, then came back and took my hand.

"Come on," she repeated, moving towards a nearby grove.

"Where are you taking me?"

"To a cemetery."

"I don't like cemeteries."

"We don't have them, which is a pity. Tell me what do you think about what you heard from me?"

"What the hell, I can come up with such a plot myself," I thought, but said aloud:

"I don't know, I wonder if I have schizophrenic ailments, and you don't exist at all, but are my delusion," I didn't pull my punches, looking at her with great satisfaction. "Maybe she will get offended and disappear," I thought.

But she didn't, she came up to me and kissed me briefly, actually she just brushed me with her lips.

"Is it a delusion? Have you felt it?"

"Nothing at all. You can repeat it," I said, smiling broadly.

She was silent, looking at me with satisfaction.

"You are kidding me. Right?"

"It was sweet, but short, too short."

She laughed, pleased at that answer. She looked at me as if she had been in love with me for years, and I was that dream prince on a white horse. She ran her fingers through her long beautiful hair in a carefully studied motion to draw attention to her. But even without it, I was staring at her and was intrigued by this fleeting kiss. What is this? A move without anesthesia," I thought.

"No, it's something else, I can't define it yet. When I look at her, I feel some inexplicable bond, some infatuation, some magnet drawing me to her," I thought.

"Her singing voice and the touch of her hand roused me from my meditations. She took my hand and, looking into my eyes, she proposed:

"If you want, I will take you to your real world, to your mother's cradle."

"And the father?" I blurted out.

"He's an Earthman. Children inherit our genetics only from their mothers."

"Maybe another time, when I am ready," out of fear, I conciliatingly agreed with her.

We came between the graves. She guided me confidently and decisively. Finally, she stopped at one, rather strange tombstone at this Catholic cemetery.

The large black marble slab had no Christian symbols. The second strange thing was the dates engraved on it. She lived, he lived years - marked with a star, and next to it 2,778 for a woman and 2,699 for a man. Typical surnames, very popular in these parts.

"This is to prove that what you say is not fiction?" I asked slightly irritated.

"No, of course not. Calm down, relax, close your eyes and you'll hear."

"What will I hear?"

"The voice of your relatives, you are one of them, my parents and your mother were "genti" which however, doesn't mean that we are related, it doesn't work like that on Hope."

"Then how?"

"I'll explain it to you later."

We sat down on a small bench next to the grave, she took my hand again. I closed my eyes, calmed down and tried not to think about anything.

After a while I fell into a strange state, as if a dream, because everything around me vanished and a black void enveloped my mind. I heard the sound of the waves and saw a distant point in the dark.

"It's beginning," I thought.

Everything came back immediately. The graveyard, girl, bench.

"Once again," Krys said to me.

I closed my eyes again, this time after a while I saw two figures in the same white tunics as the girl in my dream had worn. Both human beings were approaching me quickly.

"They were, how to put it, as if otherworldly, neither young nor old, neither ugly nor pretty, so unremarkable. The woman and the man stood beside me.

She put her hands on my shoulders and said:

"Hello Geo."

"So, for them I'm Geo," something flashed in my consciousness.

"Your mother was our friend," added the man. "Being 'genti' united us. We supported each other for hundreds of years. Now she and us are gone."

"Your mother fell in love with the Earthman. She loved him, so she stayed with him and was happy. It was due to her decision that you didn't know who you are. Thanks to being 'genti' we can contact now. Help Hope. It needs your help, it needs you. You are the only one of us who has something that no one in Hope has, that we all lack. To live on Hope, you don't have to come back to Earth to regenerate," added the female figure.

"Why me?" It flowed out of me.

"No one knows. Your mother on Hope was a molecular embryogeneticist in the human sense of the word.

"How do you know about it, since I haven't been there yet?"

"From her herself, we were 'genti' after all. You can always come to us here for a meeting."

"Alone too?"

"Unfortunately, not - Iva is the link between us. But you can go to your mother yourself and talk with her if she wants to connect with you."

"How long does it work?"

"In human time, almost eternity. Until our 'genti' runs out. Everything that we can pass on to you, can also be passed on by our daughter Iva, here called Krys."

I felt an embrace in my head and my interlocutors began to dissolve like a fog that lay on the nearby meadows in the morning.

"I need to see a doctor," I thought.

"You don't have to," I received the silent message from Krys or Iva - I was confused about her name.

I opened my eyes.

"You can always come into my head?" I asked surprised.

"No, not always, only when you invite me there. Like now when you put yourself out there to meet my parents."

"That's good. Nobody likes to be watched," I blurted out. "It must be embarrassing to get into someone else's mind."

"You will see for yourself what it is like."

She gently lifted my hand, encouraging me to get up from the bench.

It was hard for me to get up. I was amazed to find that I was exhausted like after some crazy run.

"You've lost a lot of energy, but it will pass. It will be better later," Iva told me.

She was holding my hand as if we had been lovers, not people who had met only a few hours earlier.

The dog was still gone.

"We are 'genti' like our parents," she said to me, turning her face to mine. Her eyes shone with an unnatural glow. She looked at me like a teenager in love, who can look closely at her musical idol.

"What does it mean? In your place." The word 'our' didn't want to pass through my throat somehow. If I had said it, it would have meant that I believed in everything that had happened to me by her affair.

"We are destined to each other on Hope, not necessarily here."

"Who is my father?"

"Nobody. In our place, if a woman wants to have a child, she doesn't have to be with a man like here on Earth."

"In our place neither, but she must have semen, so someone is the father," I added angry that she was evading the answer.

"Unfortunately, a mixed relationship Hoper has not yet been born - we thought so until your mother declared that you are the first Hoper with earthly genes."

"But my father thinks I'm his son."

"Ask your father, maybe your mother told him the truth, or ask your mother, it might be better."

We were walking hand in hand and, surprisingly, I was fine with it, although I still didn't know what to think about it. I leered at her. I liked her, she was pretty, mild and with a great figure that turned me on as a guy. "Hoper or not, I'm not going to give up my habits and stop picking up pretty girls," I thought. The warmth that radiated from her penetrated me through and through. It went all over my body and reached every corner of my skin. I felt a thrill of excitement. She looked at me and smiled as if knowing my thoughts.

"Damn, she's eavesdropping on me." I got scared.

She was silent.

"I had never felt anything like this with any girl I had dated. It was like some kind of higher-level foreplay. Introduction to successful orgasms," the silly thought dawned on me.

She burst into laughter, trying to suppress it.

"Have you eavesdropped on my thoughts?"

"You let me in yourself thinking of me," she replied, "but it was nice. Thank you."

I asked directly:

"Do I need to be careful?"

"You don't have to, we're 'genti'," she repeated.

"Then teach me to understand this 'genti'."

"You have to understand what it is about yourself. But it will come easy to you, I'm convinced of it. You have already understood that 'genti' is a special bond between two Hopers."

"You were in my head," I said. "How do you read my thoughts? You literally read what I think or you only intuitively know what I have in mind."

I was trying to test the water.

"It depends on you - if you let me, I read your thoughts literally. If you want me to know only your intentions, it is so."

"Now I just found out that you like me."

"That's indeed what I thought, but it's good that you don't know exactly what it was."

"Then tell me."

"A bit of courage is needed for that, and I don't have it now. So come on, I invite you to dinner, maybe I will manage to cook something. I have some ready-made products in case of rain and my inspiration."

"I'll help you," she offered.

"It would be good, because I'm a poor cook."

The dog was still neither seen nor heard.

For the next few hours, we didn't return to this unusual conversation.

Iva - she asked me to call her that - quickly realized what I had in the fridge. There was nothing special in it, so she cooked pasta, prepared sauce and meat for spaghetti, and I made a salad. I opened a bottle of wine that I had prepared for the blues during writing, and we sat down at the table.

"Where have you stayed?" I asked.

"In a hotel in the town."

"You can live here, after all, we are 'genti'," I joked.

"I knew you were gonna say that."

"How? - you were in me again?"

"No, finally understand that I enter your mind when you invite me, never otherwise."

"That's good."

"And how can I get into yours?"

"Identically, only when I invite you. With one exception."

"This is the second time I hear about this exception, maybe you can explain it to me."

"When you or me are in mortal danger, then 'genti' allows a direct warning."

"That's good too," I said with satisfaction. "Did you know that such a story, I was able to come up with myself? After all, I wrote a few books."

"I've read all of them."

"Now I knew you would say that before you said these words." I was amazed. "Has 'genti' told me that?"

"Genti is a state of spirit, mind and it doesn't tell you anything, you yourself knew that I wanted to say this, as you know that when we are together, we don't want to part."

"I also without 'genti' can be with you," I joked.

"You're not ready for this yet. 'Genti' is a powerful force and you must be able to control it."

"To be with a beautiful girl, I'm always ready to learn," I continued.

She smiled and touched my hand.

"Let me in and I'll explain it to you."

"Strange, because so far it was girls who have always let me in," I replied, laughing at my own joke.

"It can also be so, but it's without 'genti'."

"Maybe later," scared, I crawfished. She was silent only to change the subject after a while.

"You need to find your casket. Your mother hid her somewhere."

"Maybe she destroyed it if she didn't want me to use it."

"It cannot be destroyed here on Earth."

"Will you help me look for it as I helped you?"

"Of course, we are 'genti'," she replied, looking at me with her narrowed pupils. "Why does she mention that 'genti'? I like her and that's it. I also like the story that she spins," I thought. I couldn't get it, maybe because I invented various strange events myself and my mind didn't want to accept that this time it was I who was an extraordinary event. Only these eyes didn't allow me to forget even for a moment that there was something that proved that what she said could be true and that I could be one of Hopers. "Or maybe she has contact lenses," I thought.

"I don't," she said from above a glass of wine.

"What don't you have?" Just in case, I asked, although I immediately sensed that she knew what I was thinking about a moment earlier.

"Contact lenses. You got thoughtful, you relaxed and you let me in for a moment."

"Yeah, I know, we are 'genti'," I said in her direction, a little irritated.

"This is what it is all about," she emphasized softly.

"Why can't I come into you?"

"Because you are still bothered by the doubts, you don't believe yet, you don't know how to be 'genti' yet."

"When I am, will you tell me this?"

"You will know for yourself when you first enter me. "

"Can it be precipitated?"

"It can."

"How?"

I saw a blush on her face. She blushed from her thoughts. "What has she thought?" I was wondering. And then I saw her thought for a second or two, I saw it or how to put it differently, I was in her. "That's why she blushed. Nice, but is it possible that she thinks of making love to me. Maybe I have delusions," I thought.

"You don't have. I did think so, but I'm pure. I was waiting for you because we are destined to each other. However, moving from thoughts to action is not easy," she added. "And now, let's go to the hotel."

We went out, leaving the casket on the dresser. The drive to the hotel took us half an hour, then the return and we were back in the living room. She prepared a room for herself on the second floor, she found sheets, towels and after a while she came to me. I was sitting in my armchair and staring at the TV set, but I didn't know what it was showing. My thoughts were stuck in recent events. I analyzed everything from all sides and it didn't seem to me that I was crazy. "Or maybe she is crazy?

And the casket, cemetery, dream, the old woman and my mother. Yes, this is a way out, I have to check if I can make contact with my mother. We always had good relations.It's really happening, and I'm up to my ears in it," I thought. I felt her hands on my shoulders. She began to gently massage my neck. I tilted my head back, succumbing with relish to the light pressure of her hand. It started to be nice, too nice and I didn't know if it was a caress or a massage that made me want her. Relaxed, I turned off the TV and placed my hands on her delicate fingers. I closed my eyes. I was opening up, I felt that I was opening myself completely to her.

"Come, come into me I'm your 'genti'," I sent the message to her.

"I am."

"Are you an angel who came to save me or a being destined for me by Our Creator?"

"I am Iva - I've been always with you even though you didn't know it."

Something was filling my inside, but it wasn't quite a physical sensation, just a nice, slight tingling all over my body, or maybe it happened only in my mind. "What does it matter?" I thought.

"Come with me, I will take you where you like to be the most."

It was brightening in the living room; I opened my eyes and saw my 'Island Paradise'.

There was a white yacht near a beach, with a girl lying on a deckchair. Iva quickly zoomed the image of this figure. "This is my dream?" I thought for a second.

"Is it 'genti'?" I asked. "Is it you on the yacht?"

"If you want it, it will be me. Only you decide about it."

"Be with me," I thought, and as if due to the use of remote control that changes the TV channel, we both stood at the stern of the yacht.

Something wasn't right, however. I looked at it, but I didn't feel it. "I'm coming back," I thought, and we found ourselves in the living room right away. We sat on the couch, holding hands.

"Were we on Hope?" I asked in a slightly trembling voice.

"No, to be 'genti', you have to open the box. It was just your dream. I showed it to you."

"Iva, I'm impressed, but now I'd like to be myself, at least for a while."

"Alright, you have already assimilated a lot, great-grandmother was right - you are an extraordinary Hoper."

"What does it mean?"

"There are more Hopers like you who grow up and live outside their planet, I would say that there are a lot of them. Some people don't know who they are, others don't want to know it, and most don't know how to be 'genti'."

She got up from the table and stood in front of me. Beautiful, slightly excited by the situation, she looked like an unearthly phenomenon.

"You are the exception. No one has ever been able to enter the mind of the other genti in such a short time. The best ones take weeks to do this, and some months.

This meeting at the cemetery was a test for you and me. If you were one of the many, you wouldn't have seen anything there and you would have found me crazy."

She looked at me and hesitated, but continued after a while.

"I'm happy and thank you Geo."

She came over to me and kissed me on the lips. This time a little longer, but I didn't have time to kiss back, because as if scared, she pulled away from me.

"It's the wine," she added to excuse herself.

"Does that work for you? Then I'll pour more," I joked.

"Pour, I will gladly drink, after all, we have something to celebrate."

I opened the second bottle and poured the wine into glasses.

"To us and our 'genti'," I said. "But I would like to spend the rest of the evening with you like a normal guy and a girl who are on Earth spend time in a nice atmosphere."

"I don't know if I can. I got to know life on Earth only as a little girl, the rest is learning from other 'genti'."

"Really? So, it's great. I will teach you and you will teach me. Where do we start?" I asked.

"Do you want me? I mean, do you want to make love to me? Am I asking right?" she unexpectedly asked this very personal question.

"Yes, but girls usually don't ask such questions on a first date."

"No, why?"

"Because they are ashamed. Although they may think so sometimes, they don't admit it."

"So, we have a date?"

"It depends on us. If we want, it will be a date."

"Let it be so. Will we make love after the date?"

"If you like, we will be."

"Gosh, how intense and sincere she is," I thought. I was surprised.

"Have you made love to an Earthman yet?"

"You are not an Earthman, and I'm pure, no one has made love to me. When I was on Earth, I was a little girl, and on Hope, I am destined to you, we are 'genti'.

"Does it mean that on Hope, you can make love only to me?"

"In fact, yes. There is one more way, but I'm ashamed to talk about it."

"Her statement interested me, but I decided pass this thread of her confession over in silence. I turned on the music. Slowly, without taking my eyes off her, I got closer.

"Will you dance with me?" I asked.

"Gladly."

She surprised me again, I thought for some reason that she couldn't.

She danced beautifully, lightly, with grace and sensitivity. Hugged, like two lovers, we devoted ourselves with pleasure to this earthly entertainment.

"Do people on Hope also dance?" I asked, holding her hand as I walked her to the table.

Iva took a glass of wine in one hand, a bottle in the other and walked towards the sofa, saying:

"It will be more convenient to talk there."

She sat down comfortably, taking a sip of wine, then replied:

"No and yes. You cannot compare life on Earth to life on Hope. It is completely different there and we are different. But now I don't want to talk about it - okay?"

"You're right, it's a lovely night, beautiful girl. I invite you for a walk along the seashore."

"You're kind, I'll be happy to take a walk."

We joined hands and headed for the beach. The moment of silence and self-reflection didn't last forever.

"You know Geo, I've known you for twenty-one years. But now I realized that I didn't know you trully. I dreamed that you would come to Hope, that you would be with me and our 'genti'. I missed you and cried for you. I was unhappy. When your mom died, I decided to act and came here. Now I know that it is worth being on Earth."

This confession was like a summons, so I hugged and started kissing her. We lost ourselves completely in our kisses. I never thought that I would kiss a girl like this one day. We collapsed on the ground. Embraced like two wrestlers, we didn't want to break away from each other.

"Geo," she whispered, "take me home," or she said at home - I didn't hear well enough, but it was one thing, because suddenly we got up and, holding hands, we ran towards the house.

When I undressed her, she pleaded?

"Geo, I don't know anything about earthly love, teach me."

"Just like I don't know anything about love on Hope," I replied.

Chapter II

Iva

In the morning I woke up very early. I was delighted after that night. I think this is how the state in which I was now is defined on Earth. Geo was still asleep.

"How can you sleep so long?" I was surprised. "Should I wake him up or let him stay a little longer in this non-being? Let him sleep, it's so nice to look at me in his male edition. How will He take it when He finds out that He and I are one?" I wondered.

I have to change, or in fact, I have already changed my mind about Hopers going to Earth in order to experience carnal pleasure, physical love, enjoy food, earthly view and male company. I love being a Hoper, but now I also love being an Earthling.

Four months earlier, my great-grandmother's genti had unexpectedly signaled the loss of her friend, Geo's mother.

There was a change - I received a message - 'Your Geo is free; he is no longer protected by his mother and her decision not to interfere with his consciousness.'

I was very happy, but also sad, on the one hand, we lost her 'genti', and on the other, I was able to get Geo back. I had suffered for so many years because of his mother. It was she who had denied me the right to her son, to his 'genti', to happiness and love. "I'm pure and not besmeared by other genti, but how long can I endure?" I thought as I tried to get the casket.

I quickly got a permit to stay on Earth. The order was strictly followed, but Geo's 'genti' wasn't on Hope yet, so they assigned the box to me right away.

... I am lonely, very lonely suspended in space, waiting for my male company. One hundred and fifty Hope years ago, I got shocked.

"Iva, when you finally understand that Geo is lost to you," my great-grandmother's voice filled my interior. I immediately closed access to my consciousness. "No, that's not true. I know we'll be together," I thought. I knew about it from the very birth, but a spark of doubt appeared in me.

"Sorry, Tora - great-grandmother is very intense on this point. She's not a person, because we become a person only on Earth."

"I know, I know, your 'genti' is convinced that you will meet. But you know it doesn't mean anything. Until Gala, his mother changes her mind and returns with him on Hope, you can't meet."

"True, such is the law on Hope."

I knew about it, but I dreamed and was afraid that He wouldn't have enough time, that He would pass on like every human being. Meanwhile, his mother passed away quickly, unexpectedly within two Earth months. Diseases, the plague of earthly creatures didn't concern us, but only on Hope. We don't get sick, but we also die. We used to be like them. They are us. - Now in their place we are like them.

Convoluted? - no, time is convoluted, and basically it convolutes like a spiral of DNA. How to explain to him who I am, who He is, who we are and why 'genti' in our lives is so important? Should I throw Geo in at the deep end? And if he doesn't endure, he doesn't want to be a Hoper and, like his mother, he chooses a short but intense life? I will follow him, I will be with him forever, whether it will be a hundred of their years or hundreds of ours - no, not so much, They and We don't live on Earth so long.

Geo woke up and looked at me. His dream thoughts reached my consciousness. "She is wonderfully beautiful," he thought, looking at my figure standing by the window. My naked body filled the window space with a bright glow, casting a shadow on the floor.

"I'll talk to Geo about it," I thought further.

"What are you going to talk to me about?" I heard his thoughts before he realized he knew what I was thinking.

"Genti works," I thought. I was glad. Without turning to him, I sent him the message - "about our world. About Hope and life on our planet." He took it exceptionally calmly.

"Alright, but now come to bed, because we haven't finished yesterday's lesson," he joked in his mind as he continued the silent dialogue.

Lightly as a feather, I started to glide towards him on my toes. I liked yesterday's lesson. I knew it was just an introduction, a prelude to what awaited me, us. I was ready for any lesson, for all the lessons of the earthly world.

"He's drooling over me, he wants me." I was glad to discover his thoughts. I slipped under the sheets, lying down next to him. His naked body, ready for love, triggered in me a surge of lust, euphoria of desires to satisfy myself and him.

When, after a few spasms and loud moans, I fell on pillows, I saw myself with Geo on Hope.

"Come inside me," I asked him softly.

"Literally or figuratively?" he asked. "Because if literally, I don't have the strength, and if figuratively, I'm already inside. Surprised?" he asked.

"Can't you always be literally in me?"

"What does it mean, always? I can always, but not now. Now I need to regenerate."

"You don't have to; you are the exception."

"There maybe yes, but here sex can last a long time, but not always."

"Does he always have to talk in riddles?" I thought.

"No, Iva, it's not a mystery, that's just how the male organism works on Earth," he added. "And what is it like in your place, our place on Hope?" he corrected himself quickly.

"See for yourself, come I invite you to our 'genti'. I will take you to our Island Paradise."

I got up and took my time to get the casket. On the way back, I was glad to look at Geo, who was staring at me with a lascivious insatiable gaze. I sat down beside him, I opened the lid of the box, then placed both hands over his eyes and opened up as widely as I had never done to anyone.

We sailed.

"This is what I'm here? This is what we look like?" he asked with a frightened thought.

"Don't be afraid, you are with me, we are 'genti'."

He bridled as if he had wanted to escape, but he couldn't anymore. We were now united; we were flowing onto his white yacht anchored in the Island Paradise.

We fell softly to the deck.

"Are we on Hope?"

"Not yet. You're not ready yet."

"Where are we then?"

"In our 'genti'."

"And why do we look like earthly spirits?"

"It will pass soon, you will see."

By the time I finished thinking, I was already myself. Almost myself.

Geo sat down on a deck chair.

I knelt down beside him, taking his hand.

"It will pass, only at first you see yourself like this, with time the transition to genti will be as quick as the blink of an eye."

"That's good, I didn't enjoy this trip."

He looked at the beach.

The white sandbank stretched as far as the eye could see, to disappear only somewhere at the end of the bay where the yacht was anchored. A little above the beach, there was a wall of dense green trees, bushes and flowers of various colors, with difficulty breaking through the grasses suppressing their desire to soar towards three suns. Farther, you could see low hills with white ribbons of water flashing in the light and falling down the valley. The beach was empty.

"We are alone," he said, "and naked," he added after a moment, looking at me.

"That's how we went on this journey." I put my hand on his stomach and with my fingertips I was gently making little circles, going down.

I was curious what sex looked like there. I had gotten to know the earthly one, but not that on Hope. I had listened and watched other Hopers do it, peeping them, but I hadn't experienced it myself, I had had no one to make it with. Geo hadn't been there. In my lonely genti, I had thought about sex, but it had been a different vision. The yacht is Geo's genti. My vision had been a crystal hall shimmering with all the shades of our suns.

"I'll wait," I thought, seeing Geo's amused expression.

"If you want to get dressed, then look inside our closet, there you will find everything you need," I thought to him and for him.

Geo got up, looked around curiously and went downstairs.

"I have to see the yacht," he called without turning his head. He didn't understand yet.

"Come see our bedroom," he called from downstairs.

The huge motor yacht with three decks hid many beautiful places. I made an effort to create it for him. I wanted him to be happy, so genti provided me with information about the most expensive luxury yachts on Earth.

"Where's its crew?" he asked.

"They have time off," I said quickly, not wanting to scare him. "And do you want to have company?" I added. "Mine is not enough for you?"

"Iva is enough," he thought softly about me, "but who will run this colossus?" he worried unnecessarily.

"Here, Geo, we can do anything.

And the dog is still gone," he sent the message, thinking of the black poodle.

We heard barking.

The dog was running on the beach and baying in our direction.

"Why the dog?" I asked.

"I don't know," I thought on the basis of associations. "On the beach, I met you with your dog."

He froze, got motionless - something dawned on him.

"Will everything I think about materialize or is it a coincidence?" he sent me his observation.

"Anything you want and what won't be against mine, our genti."

"So can we talk, because somehow I haven't got used to this silent exchange of words yet?"

"Understand, here in our genti we can do anything. We can talk, but why should we if you hear my thoughts?"

"It's not the same for me. I have to get used to this new situation. Explain," he asked in his voice. "Was it me who brought that dog?"

"Yes, but you didn't put him on the yacht, but on the beach."

"Does it mean that if I think about something and want to have it, my wish will come true?"

"My and your wishes will come true only when it concerns us."

"Then let's go eat something. I invite you to breakfast."

"Just don't fry eggs anymore," I laughed at the memory of the burned pan.

"Oh no, I will think that the table is set and everything is ready to eat."

"Don't make fun of genti - it doesn't work that way. Genti is not a maid who prepares a breakfast for you."

"Too bad," he pretended to be worried. I closed access to myself. "How to explain to him that food doesn't look like it does on Earth?" I thought. "Neither sex nor anything he knows so well." He came to me, I felt his concern, he was lost. So, I took his hand and we went down the gangplank to the living room. Here we sat and, holding both of his hands and looking into his eyes, I said in an undertone:

"You get used to living on Hope. The price for this is longevity."

"The price for what? What are you hiding from me?"

"I'm not hiding but dosing you the opportunities offered by genti."

"What's wrong with me, what's wrong with us, right here, where we are?" he asked looking piercingly into my eyes.

"Do you want to come back?"

"No, I want to know everything - please tell me."

"Not everything can be told. You have to absorb the rest. When we find ourselves on our planet, you will gradually absorb the knowledge we have."

"And what won't I absorb now?" he asked in a low voice.

"There is no such a body on Hope. There is also no taste of food, because we don't need meals. Although we eat, it is a tradition, and only for those who enjoy it, or those who travel to Earth."

"And love, what does love look like? I mean, how do people make love on Hope? In the same way as we did yesterday, today?" he corrected himself.

"I don't know Geo, I've never had sex with anyone on Hope."

"But you probably know something, heard something, you saw something."

"Yes, but it is different for every Hoper."

I got up, I walked to his back, I wanted it to be like the day before in the old house. I started massaging his neck. I focused, thinking hard. I closed my eyes and felt desire. I felt his hands on my fingers and a pretty mundane question:

"I feel nothing - what's going on?"

"The desire is gone."

"Is it that bad?" My thought reached him.

"What is that bad? - explain to me," he asked.

I sat back down next to him. I hugged him, saying:

"Here and on Hope, if you want something, you have to think about it - you understand?"

"I understand," he said but after a moment he added: "No, I don't understand anything."

"Okay, I will explain it to you that way:

"Do you want a ball?"

"No, why would I need a ball?"

"This is just an example."

"Okay, I want."

"Just think clearly and exactly what kind of ball you want, small or large, dotted or spotted. It's best to imagine it, thinking what it should be like, so that it goes to you, not to the beach or somewhere out there."

After a second, a small tennis ball rolled to Geo.

"You see how simple it is?" I was glad.

"Is it the same with food here?" he asked.

"Are you hungry?"

"Actually, no, I don't even want morning coffee."

"But I want orange juice," I said, curious how he would handle this task. "Give me it, please."

After a while, the juice began to trickle down onto the living room floor. It flowed from the non-existence of our space under the ceiling.

"Stop it, Geo."

The stream disappeared and a glass of juice appeared on the table beside.

"Now, it's good."

"Drink it," I asked Geo.

He picked up the juice and began to drink.

"I don't taste anything, it's flavorless."

"Think what it should be like."

"It's good now."

"He put down the glass which disappeared immediately. "Where is it?" He asked like a surprised little child.

"You have stopped thinking about it."

I leaned down to him, embraced his head and kissed him, for a long time passionately putting all my thoughts into it. I thought about the taste of the previous day's kisses. I opened my eyes and saw Geo's surprised look.

"Think Geo, think about how we were fine yesterday," I whispered to him, pulling away for a moment.

I could feel his hands wandering over my body. I was naked. "Okay Geo, think this way, we want each other like that," I thought. Our thoughts were tangled like our hands.

However, not everything went as it had done the day before, we were not yet able to align our thoughts with our desire.

Geo was fast, too fast, I wanted more caresses and affection. But here He could do it always and was always ready, so He made love to me whenever I wanted it. Geo was inventive and I liked his ideas. "A wonderful feeling, and although it takes place only in our heads, it gives us a lot of joy and satisfaction."

That's what it seemed to me then, now I know that I was wrong, because from where a Hoper is to draw patterns when he or she wasn't on Earth. Finally, having satiated our cravings, we tore our thoughts away from each other, and Geo asked:

"How is this possible? My character looks like me, but he is fleeting, he has no mass, only this kind of holographic image makes me realize that it is Me and You. It seems unreal to me, but it is absolutely true. How does it happen? We don't have material bodies, yet when I touch you, I sense your body, your warmth, I hear your rapid breathing and feel the touch of your hands."

"And what is our bodies' matter? I answer - it is properly arranged atoms, they still exist, but are kept in our genti."

"Why?"

"So that we can live longer.

And reason, awareness - It's something fleeting and permeates the universe, so our genti materialized our consciousness to the form in which we are now," I explained it to him in an earthly way. "We are the mind, consciousness in its pure form."

"I want to swim in the sea," he said happily, smiling broadly at me. "It is possible?"

"Anything is possible, but it could be a shocking experience for you."

"Why?"

"You can't control genti yet. You could go deep under the water and start thinking about breathing, that you would run out of air, and the water would rush into your lungs and you would start to sink. You would be in no danger, but it wouldn't be pleasant if you lost consciousness."

"And what would happen next?" he asked, interested.

"Nothing, genti would send you back to where you came from."

"You will find yourself on Earth in the old house and I will be with you." He looked at me with interest that had a spark of contrariness.

"I want to try swimming to the beach. The dog is waiting," he laughed at his excuse.

Now I knew Geo was the exception among the Hopers.

"Then chase me!" I screamed, bolting to the upper deck. I was running fast, and when I fell from the deck into the water, out of the corner of my eye, I saw Geo jumping after me without thinking.

He was brave. He dived quite deep, I was right above him, and He, showing me a broad smile, grabbed my ankle and pulled me down. As I swam past him, he grabbed my waist and pulled me against him, then kissed me. When it seemed to him that he wouldn't have enough breath, he let go of me and sputtered up. When I appeared next to him, he rushed to me with his thought.

"First come, first served," he said and moved to the shore, doing the crawl as if he had been at a sea on Earth.

"He's wrong, he won't win with me, because here it is not the strength of the muscles that decides but the mind," I thought and was already lying on the sand.

After a while, he appeared next to me on the beach. He was panting as if he indeed had put a lot of effort into the swim to the shore.

"It's a hoax," he muttered, dissatisfied with my victory, standing over me and spraying droplets of water at me. "It's amazing how quickly he assimilates 'genti' - great-grandmother was right, he is our hope," I thought.

As he settled down next to me, I cuddled up to him and, hugging him, I whispered:

"But in this, you are the winner."

The dog was running around us, demanding the play.

"Come inside me," I said in an undertone. "I desire you." As the three suns were coming down behind the moon of Our Hope Station, we returned to Earth to the old house.

"How long have we been away?" he asked surprised, looking at the clock.

"According to the clock on the dresser - half a minute," I replied, thinking about my, our biological clock.

Chapter III

Meeting

Geo and Iva quickly prepared for the trip. Here on Earth, it was not enough to think, you had to go to get where you wanted. And the way to the city where Geo's parents lived was about a hundred kilometers of earthly roads. He called his father first thing in the morning.

"Dad, I will come to you today with my friend. I would like you to know her," he announced his and Iva's visit.

"I'm glad, I'm waiting for you," Norbert, Geo's father replied.

They packed the dog and, having gathered their things, got into the car and set off.

Iva relied entirely on Geo. It was he who decided how and which way to go to the place where he had spent the happy days of his childhood and all the holidays of his youth.

A little away from the city limits there was a cemetery where his mother's grave was. Driving on the wide and a little busy expressway stretching along the coast, they felt a special bond between them.

"Watch out, some madman will come out from behind the trees," Iva warned him at one point.

He slowed down and moved to the side of the road. The car, driving zigzag, only covered them with dust, rushing down the road as if there had been no one else on it.

"How did you know that?"

"You will also know when you absorb knowledge on Hope. It's genti," she added.

"Do you drive a car?" he asked.

"I haven't tried it yet, and I don't have your driver's license, but I can do it for sure.

"How do you know you can if you haven't driven a car yet?"

"If you can, I can too." She paused, wondering whether to tell him now that He and She were one thing.

"No, I won't tell him now, he wouldn't understand it."

"I know, I know, 'genti'," he anticipated her further dilatation.

They drove up to the old cemetery and, in silence and concentration, walked along the alleys towards the great cross. He stood over his mother's grave.

"Fresh flowers, probably from my father," he thought. "A grave like all the others around. The inscriptions on it are also ordinary. Would mom want to contact me?" He was very nervous. "And if not, then what?" He had been here many times and had spoken to her many times but only in his mind. He had complained how hard it had been for him to live without her, how much he had loved her, and how much he had missed her.

"And if she doesn't answer me, it will mean that I am schizophrenic. Anyway, when I get in touch, I may also be it," he was torn by changing moods.

"You're not Geo. Concentrate."

Iva stood half a step behind him, encouraging him.

He calmed down, concentrated and sent a message to his Mother:

"I'm here, I'm waiting for you, please come, I already know about everything. Iva is here. Talk to me, it's all so strange. Help me believe."

"Beloved Peter," the message rattled in his head.

He recognized her voice - it was strange, he heard nothing, it all happened in his head. And yet, yes it was definitely Her. She appeared to him, but she was different. She wore a white tunic and had blonde hair as well as eyes like Iva's. He had never seen such eyes in her.

"Why eyes?" he flashed the thought to her.

"I had an operation allowing me to wear special contact lenses right after you were born," she replied to him.

"Why didn't you tell me about Hope?"

"I wanted the best for you. I wanted you to stay away from Hopers, but I was wrong in thinking that Iva would forget about you. Good thing she's with you, she's a good girl. Stay together."

"Now I can't protect you anymore, but I know that since you are here now, I was able to overcome the evolution. You are the exception among Hopers.

"What does it mean? Mom."

"Iva will tell you everything. My genti is weak, I haven't used it all your life," she managed to say when her glow began to fade away. She had both hands stretched out towards Geo.

"Where is the casket?" Iva managed to asked.

"Geo knows. We played together there," they heard her weak signal before she disappeared.

"Don't go, Mommy!" he shouted loudly.

Iva held his shoulders and shook him slightly.

"Come on, I sense the danger."

"What?" He looked at Iva with his already conscious eyes.

"Dalmek, a genti spy from a Customary People's Clan."

"What's happening?" he asked looking around. The few trees growing among the tombstones didn't provide any cover for anyone. "There is nobody here," he said, surprised, looking at Iva keeping an eye out.

"They want the casket. Turn yourself off," she said in her normal voice, blocking access to her thoughts.

He put flowers on the grave, looked around again, but saw nothing suspicious.

"Where is he?"

"You won't see him. Dalmek is a spy consciousness. A being without body and glow. Pure energy penetrating the consciousness of Hopers from other genti."

"Are they dangerous?"

"No. They won't hurt us, but they steal information that interests them. This Dalmek wants to find out where your casket is."

"What should I do?"

"Do you know where the casket is?"

"No."

"So, open up, and when you sense that he has crept into your consciousness, destroy him. Send him into non-existence. He will not come back from there. You have the power, I believe it," she incited him.

Geo took Iva's hand. He focused; he was angry that some Dalmek disturbed him when he contacted his mother. This anger grew in him with every moment.

"There he is," he whispered in his mind to Iva.

With all his awareness, he created an energy within himself, with which he surrounded this bluish 'spark' in the shape of a ball. Trying to escape, it bounced off his envelope like some electron in the nucleus of an atom. When he sensed that it wouldn't escape him, he squeezed it like an apricot squeezes its pit and threw it into the space of non-existence. It was such a strong energy that it threw Iva away from him a few steps away. Amazed and delighted at the same time, she exclaimed to him:

"Geo, that was amazing! How did you do that?"

"I don't know," he replied, "I was angry and it seemed to help me." Exhausted, he sat down on some wall. "Nobody in our Clan has such power," she whispered. "They already know about you," she added.

"How?"

"You've just sent them a signal, wiping out their spy."

"Is it wrong?"

"No, that's okay. We will have a little peace; they will not send another Dalmek to you. He is too valuable."

"Why did he come here if they hadn't known about me before?"

"He had been with your mother and had been waiting for us. This is why your mother didn't answer directly where the casket was."

On their way back to their house by the beach, they drove to Geo's father.

He lived in a neighborhood of white houses with small gardens. He didn't look surprised to see Iva in the doorway.

"Hello," he said with pleasure, looking at the pretty girl with long blond hair, who, holding Peter's hand, entered his house.

When they settled down comfortably in the small patio, Norbert, leaning over aromatic coffee, unexpectedly said:

"You already know about mom and Hope?"

"Yes, and how do you know I know?"

"Your mother told me that when you come to me with the beautiful blonde named Iva, you will already know. There is also something else in case you want to know if I'm your biological father."

"And are you?"

"It's impossible," said Iva.

"Peter's mom assured me that she has my genes," he turned to Iva. "Not all of them, but he does. Before his birth, she disappeared from time to time. Now I know she came back to Hope. She did research and she found out something, because she assured me:

"Norbert, honey. Peter is your baby. I was able to link some of your DNA bonds with my genti. He is a different Hoper. The first in our long history. He is the link that returns to the roots, to material existence. But he is much more of a Hoper than an Earthman. However, I don't know what will happen when he returns to Hope and I'm afraid of it, so I won't tell him who he is. He should have a child with some Earthling, maybe he will be the first Hoper to whom an inhabitant of the Blue Planet will give a baby," she convinced me.

Iva, surprised, listened to this.

"It was always said in our Dissenters Clan that Geo's mom made a breakthrough with her baby. However, no one knew what this breakthrough was about. Now I know it was true. Geo has amazing genti, he has power," she confirmed Norbert's words in a firm voice.

Iva felt comfortable in this company, but she was troubled by Geo's mother's prediction. "How is that? So Geo can have a baby with an Earthling? And what about me? About my child?" she wondered but she had to stop, as Geo looked into her eyes meaningfully. "He penetrates my shell," she thought. "He knows what I think even when I'm closed to Hopers." But Geo didn't know, rather guessed that Iva might have been dissatisfied with this prediction.

"Are people jealous on Hope?" He asked.

"Like all people on Earth, we have the same vices. Jealousy, hatred, dissatisfaction, there is just no aggression and violence. There is also the other side, more widespread one - friendship, love, attachment to the clan, to your genti.

You are me and I am you," she added eloquently, looking into his eyes.

"Your mom told me one more thing about the box."

"Have you ever seen it?" he asked his father.

"The only time she told me about Hope was when she showed me the box saying that this was her way to Hope, but only for Hopers. Then the casket disappeared from our house.

'Geo knows. We played there together,' he quoted her words. Do you know what she meant?"

"I don't know, Peter. You played together in different places, what could she mean?" he wondered. "Most often she played with you in our garden. But she also took you to my mother's, and your grandmother's house. Maybe that's what she meant."

Geo wondered. When he was 10-12 years old, he stopped playing with his mother. They spend time together, and often, but it couldn't be called the play. So what?

"Iva, can you help me go back in my mind to the age when I was three or four?"

"I can't Geo. I don't have such abilities."

"Wait, Peter," his father said. "Once, when you were a little child, your mother used to go with you to your grandmother and there you often played with her in the attic. You really liked these hide-and-seek games. Once you got inside an old chest and closed its lid. We couldn't find you. We were very concern then. Only after an hour did you start tapping to let us know where you were."

"This could be it," Peter decided.

After staying a little longer, promising that they would visit him again soon, they drove away looking at Peter's father waving his hand.

Peter's grandmother was an old woman, but still agile. She was bustling in her curtilage. She lived with her granddaughter, his father's brother's daughter and her two children lived with her. The old woman was pleased with their visit and immediately invited them to a late dinner. Peter, taking advantage of the fact that both ladies were busy bustling in the kitchen, went to his grandma's attic. Looking at lumber, he remembered happy moments from his childhood. Hide and seek and counting one, two, three ... ten and then the shout - 'Ready or not, here I come!'

Without difficulty, he found the trunk as well as the scarlet casket beneath a pile of strange old items. He went downstairs with it.

"Grandma, this casket was left here by my mother - do you remember?"

"Yes, Pe," she spoke to him in a diminutive way, "I also remember what your mother said to me when she hid it there. 'Give it only to Pe when he asks for it, and to no one else.'

"Can I take it?"

"Of course, grandson, it's yours."

The idyllic evening ended late and they still had to return to the beach house. When they passed the town and were a dozen kilometers away from the house, Geo unexpectedly asked Iva:

"I'm tired, could you drive now?"

"Alright, although I don't believe in your fatigue," she replied with a laugh.

To Geo's surprise, Iva drove the car steadily and calmly.

"Unbelievable," he wondered. "For a novice, you are great. And not only in this," he smiled at her making this allusion. When they stopped at the old house, the dog jumped around the car and announced his joy with joyful barking, running around the trees.

Chapter IV

Hope

There was a conference for all genti at the Customary People's headquarters. Manta, the clan leader, thought about the origins of their contemporary form.

... The planet of the three suns and two moons on the fringes of the Magellanic nebula was in crisis. Since they had begun their journeys to the Earth seventy thousand years earlier, it hadn't been so restless and inconsistent among Hopers as it was then. The Three Suns planet several times larger than Earth was torn by disputes about the future. Only by eliminating anger, aggression and physical violence, no wars broke out there. However, it doesn't mean that there were no arguments, malice and attempts to dominate one another. Theft also flourished, but not physical one, as there was nothing material there except domes and the Moon Station, but theft of knowledge about life in luxury, prosperity and love, that physical, not the abstract one. Stealing thoughts and the pleasures that came with it was the order of the day. Whoever had more power, the energy of his or her genti, could bask in luxury and enjoy the views and things that were inaccessible to others.

Centuries ago, when their population began to die as a result of genetic error, their consciousness had at its disposal only what they had been before. However, these were not pleasant memories. Their planet was dying, deprived of everything it once had had. It was a huge gray desert where everything they had created fell to dust after centuries of use. Their longevity was for them a joy of life and a curse of existence.

When their biogeneticists announced that they had discovered "GENTI" on the moon, the joy of Hopers knew no bounds.

Everyone wanted to take advantage of the opportunity to extend their lives. Back then, they lived about 150 years, but that was the end of their possibilities. Genti gave them the chance to live up to three thousand years. The price, however, was to get rid of the material body.

The general referendum of the Three Suns granted everyone the opportunity to take advantage of this way of life. The name of the Three Suns planet was changed to the name planet of Hope.

However, so that their population wouldn't disperse in non-existence, domes were created on Hope. Hermetic territory where they indulged in the joy of living in a new, non-material world. Three huge domes and ten small ones were created, just in case of some unpredictable extreme situations. Such scattered domes gave a chance for some of them to survive and renew life on the planet in the event of a cosmic catastrophe. The space between the domes was barren soil and megacities or processing plants. Now everything turned to dust before their eyes. Cities collapsed after hundreds of years. The barren soil regained its former character by being overgrown by known and unknown species of plants. Evolution was doing its job, and with the release of certain species of animals specially selected for their suitability for renewing life on the planet, the true evolutionary struggle for survival began.

They didn't interfere with this world, living beside and looking at it with the help of densely placed visors.

Ninety percent of Hopers used this way of extending their lives, the rest were scientists who, aware that not everybody could get rid of their body shell, devoted themselves to science.

But only for a while. As they approached the end of material life, they passed into a state of Hope non-material form.

What was needed for this was the casket, the invention of their genius scientist Pol de Gar. After the first voyage of the material inhabitant of the three Suns to the Blue Planet, it allowed him or her to return under the Dome, and thus become an Afterglower.

Before, however, they procreated children, which replaced them in this strange way of evolution.

Material Hopers had the right to children, but only women, because in their material world they were the ones who decided about the child, and they didn't need a male Hoper.

"A strange feeling," he thought as he looked at Iva. "There we are material, here we are Afterglowers. How is this possible?" he had wondered about it for some time. The Afterglowers themselves couldn't reasonably explain it to him, and Iva took it so obvious that she didn't convince him of her theory.

"On the Planet of the Three Suns," she explained to him, "everyone wanted to live longer and longer. I think this is the eternal desire of every intelligent being in the universe. Our scientists followed the path of genetic changes in our bodies. But some mistake was made and the Great Extinction began.

Every inhabitant of the planet who was born with genetically made changes began to age rapidly after 50-60 years of age and died. As a result, only those who were too old for genetic changes survived on the planet. It concerned the population from 120 years old onwards. They could no longer have children, and it seemed that they would all die out and the entire planet of the Three Suns would be depopulated. Our scholars didn't know why this happened, but they suspected it was due to the degradation of our planet.

As you know, it started the great exodus and the search for a new planet to live. When it seemed that all Hopers would die, they found the Blue Planet in the solar system - the Earth, as they called it, on which they could continue to live.

Our best scientist, Pol de Gar, discovered a way to warp space-time, thus making it possible to travel to the Blue Planet. The casket is a device used to bend this space-time, but only towards the Blue Planet.

Why there? Are you wondering? Because our automatic galactic ships discovered this planet as the first one on which we could live. The spacecraft were not able to transport all the inhabitants of the Planet of the Three Suns to the Blue Planet, so the discovery of Pol de Gara saved us from total destruction. The first to use the casket worked on the possibility of fixing what was broken in us.

What a euphoria prevailed on our planet when scientists discovered that curved spacetime corrects our genetic mistakes and allows us to live almost forever. Therefore, space-time domes integrated with the Moon of Genti were built on the planet of the Three Suns. However, we don't know who and when created the Moon of Genti. However, in order to live under a space-time dome, we have to regenerate on the Blue Planet, which is why we always return to it and die there. It's simple, on Earth, as you call the Blue Planet, we are like Earthlings. Someone who is 2600 years old on Hope must regenerate and return to Earth. There they are 100 or more years old and before they regenerate their cells, they will die as a result of some disease or accident.

The euphoria of being an immaterial glow faded after the first few thousand years. Everyone already knew everything and had nowhere to draw further sensations from. The memory of prosperity and having a pleasant time had long since disappeared in them.

However, this was not the worst. The worst took place after the next several thousand years, when the second mass extinction of the entire population of the Three Suns began.

The small population of the material inhabitants of the Three Suns made their descendants too closely related. They couldn't and still can't have offspring with the inhabitants of the Blue Planet - but as your mother said you are the first Hoper with earthly genes.

So, the molecular bonds of the Afterglow Hopers disintegrated as did their material bodies.

Seventeen thousand Hope years ago, was built the SRS - the Special Relay Station which enabled them to rapidly move to this planet. There they renewed themselves in their material bodies, which had both good and bad sides. For several thousand Earth years, only a handful of Hopers could travel to the Blue Planet, and some members of the Dissenters Clan started a new evolution here. Enchanted by its green forests and blue waters, they didn't want to return to Hope. One such a Hoper was the embryogeneticist - your mother, Geo, who for one hundred and fifty years was a scientist in material form, and after a thousand years of immaterial existence, she went to Earth to regenerate her body and stayed here until her death.

The Senior Lady of the Customary People's Clan gathered all the distinguished Hopers around her. Their headquarters for conferences was the largest Dome on Hope, just beyond the Lunar Relay Station. Several hundred thousand Hope figures flashed their glow as they gathered in their semicircular auditorium housing their entire gathering. A special semicircular caps hanging over them was used to automatically collect and organize the information sent. Otherwise, no one would have been able to control the chaos that arises when everyone sends their thoughts to everyone.

The huge semicircular dome covered the participants of the conference. Only the Senior Lady of the clan and twenty of his closest genti sat beside it without the caps over their heads. The slightly beige caps floated freely over each participant. When they genti sent out some information, the color of the caps also changed. To bluish when it was related to a topic discussed by the assembly. When, however, there were other but related considerations, the color changed to slightly orange, and when completely irrelevant ones, then the caps pulsed with red light. All other glows except blue and its hues were blocked.

The family Senior Lady looked at the dome glowing with all the colors of red.

"As always," she thought.

"Our genti lost a Dalmek today," she began. "As you know, he was destroyed by Geo, the son of our best embryogeneticist, who chose the Earth for her home. We all know how it ended for her.

It is not normal that one genti, without the additional help of other Afterglowers - the power that we all have on Hope, is able to acquire such a skill. He is assisted by his other half, Iva, but it is also unlikely that they could do it as one. Even if all of us gathered here concentrated our genti into one energy, we couldn't destroy the Dalmek, but only weaken him. As you know, such power gives an absolute authority on Hope, therefore we can't allow Geo to return.

There weren't any of our gentis there so we don't know how it happened. Our team of scholars suggests that earthlings have invented some kind of consciousness enhancer and Geo uses it.

Our job is to prevent this from happening. I'm asking for suggestions on how to do this. The subclans are to merge into one genti to avoid chaos," she concluded.

"Now there will be an intersection of ideas and proposals, and the caps will pick up the converging positions and present them to the general assembly." The caps above the participants shimmered with all the colors of red and shades of blue to dark navy blue. They swirled, constantly exchanging information with each other, but with time the red faded until only blue remained.

The conclusions were ready, it was enough to present them to the audience.

"Destroy the Relay Station," the Senior Lady of the Family read the first collective thought.

Genti's suggestion - you are putting your longevity at risk.

"Destroy the caskets of the Dissenters' Clan," this is the second message.

Genti's suggestion - the casket can't be destroyed on Earth.

"Take control of the Relay Station to control the transformation of the Hopers going to Earth."

Genti's suggestion - This means domination. You will have all the clans against you.

"Declare Geo our Senior and submit to him."

Genti's suggestion - This means permanent change on Hope.

Once all the caps were glowing blue, the High Assembly of the Customary People's Clan made a decision:

"We can't allow the Dissenters to dominate. In order to maintain our current status quo, we must control travel to Earth. Once we control who and how long can stay on Earth, we will gain power over all other Clans. To this end, we decide to take over the Relay Station on the Moon."

"Why do we need such power? It is impossible to fulfill," swirled the message from the opposition in their own clan. "The material scientists won't allow changes to the functioning of the Relay Station," was their thought.

The caps lit up with all the colors of the red again, only to transmit the blue light of the message after a while.

"Change the rules for using transformation to Earth."

Genti's suggestion - appoint former scientists from the Relay Station to the task.

After long disputes, four Hopers were appointed to carry out the assigned task. It wouldn't be easy, because material scientists were not susceptible to their genti. Their only advantage was the knowledge of all the stages of the Relay Station operation, which they acquired while working on the moon in their previous material form.

The Clan's dome connected to their moon through the energy flow produced by Central Genti. Each of the domes had its own separate energy channel. It was this way that the power of genti flowed to them, and it was this way that the immaterial Hopers entered after the finished regeneration of their bodies on Earth.

However, there were rarely trips in the opposite direction, i.e., from the dome to the moon. These were only the sentimental initial journeys of scientists who had changed their material bodies into genti consciousness in the recent past. Something drew them into that life. Some didn't manage to finish a research, others left their offspring there, and still others felt that they had lost something irretrievably and irreversibly, but most of them were unable to find themselves in the new reality. They had to wait several hundred years for their first visit to Earth. It was they who most often stole the consciousness of those who had been there and had had in their genti images of earthly reality.

It was difficult, however, for the Senior Lady of the Family to select a few volunteers for this mission. Most were not interested in the internal affairs of the Customary People's Dome. Some would have liked to change the contemporary dome to the one more suited to their beliefs, but this could only be done when returning from the Blue Planet. Others were so packed with information about a great life that they didn't want to do anything else but take advantage of these opportunities.

After much deliberation and persuasion, four volunteers agreed to compete with Geo. They were to find his genti on the Forbidden Second Moon and prevent him from returning to Hope.

To increase their chances against Geo, they decided to divide the mission into ways to reach the Genti's Moon. Brit and Rai would hijack the galactic ship named Afterglow and reach the Moon of Genti on it.

Seta and Tybein would set off on the space shuttle to the technical First Moon, from which they would try to reach the Genti's Moon through the Caps located there. Admittedly, there were those who claimed that no one had succeeded in it yet, but as the Council argued, the Afterglowers from the Planet of the Three Suns may have not remembered it. In the times of the Great Extinction, those who had remembered could have died and thus not managed to pass on their knowledge of the Caps to anyone.

The Senior Lady of the Family issued the permit and immediately the four young Hopers set off to the Central Space Station from where they were to get into the orbit of Hope, to one of the shuttles on this route.

Thanks to the miniature capsules inside the shuttle, they would make this journey in quite comfortable conditions. Brit, the eldest of them, felt like their leader and led them by informing the rest of them about the ways to survive the journey:

"Your consciousness will be dormant until you reach the orbit of Hope. It is too dangerous to leave you in a state of full consciousness. You could end up outside the ship and be lost forever. Nobody has been able to return from non-existence yet. Only in the orbit of the moon, you can return to your Afterglow form."

The entire station on the Technical Moon was covered by one great dome. How, when and who had built it, none of them remembered. Neither the Hopers living on Hope remembered it. The great extinction caused that only the history of construction and operation, recorded on the storage media embedded in the Central Genti of the Moon, remained, and from this they drew their knowledge. However, they were not able to see everything. The previous technique had used record methods that they couldn't fully understand.

"How do you know that we will be able to penetrate the Central Genti of Hope, where all the consciousnesses of the Hopers are located?" Seta worried.

"Exactly," Tybein said, "it might be practically impossible, after all, we're constantly being targeted by Lunar Genti Guardians."

"No, I worked in a power generating center," Brit tried to explain to them. "There are zones where practically material Hopers cannot get in. Even wearing protective suits, they keep off these rooms as much as possible. Excess energy destroys their cells, which makes them age faster. So, they avoid it like the plague."

"But the aging on the moon is more rapid than on Hope," Seta added.

"Therefore, quickly enter the Caps and from there head towards the Forbidden Second Moon to the Central Genti of Hope - you will avoid all the dangers from the material Guardians of the Lunar Genti."

"It's easy for you to say it - you yourself will be stuck in the ship protected by the dome," Tybein said sarcastically.

Their shuttle, which followed the magnetic trajectory generated by their planetary system, carried them into the Hope orbit. Having two moons, it made the most sense to find a means of transport that would use their own magnetic field and the gravity of the two moons. A space station-built centuries ago was seldom used by materialists, who made up less than a few percent of all Hopers. The entire journey by the shuttle to the station was automatic, without the need for piloting or supervision of material pilots.

In the orbit, the galactic 'Afterglow' was already waiting for its passengers, most of whom were ship's crew.

Two material technicians handling Domes and other related devices, a small group of environmentalists studying the restricted zones on Hope as well as two pilots made up the entire crew of the galactic ship.

As material Hopers, they had no physical contact with them. Nevertheless, they greeted him through the internal communication system. There was no friendship between them. However, the mutual need for cooperation made their journey bearable. The Afterglow - the lunar cargo and passenger vehicle, was a relic of their past. For a long time, nothing had been produced on Hope. All the technology was transferred to the Technical Moon, where all construction, technical works and the acquisition of new technologies had been carried out for centuries. The remnants of the era of lofty ambitions of the inhabitants of the Three Suns had served them perfectly so far.

There were many research stations, spacecraft, open-cast mines and relics from the time of the great extinction, and ninety-odd percent of them remained empty and unused by anyone.

Automation designed for the expansion of space in search of a replacement planet had so far worked flawlessly. Most of the ships were idle. Thanks to the brilliant invention of Pol de Gar, they learned to bend space, and that with the help of a small amount of energy provided by the moon. The entire intergalactic station was protected by a dome that allowed the Afterglowers to stay on it. The powerful engines of the idle intergalactic ships were used to provide energy to the entire station. Energy that was needed not by them, but by the material scientists working on this station.

"At least that's what they're good for now," thought Brit.

In times of the great extinction, they were built quickly and numerously with the hope of saving the inhabitants of the Three Suns.

"Hopes were futile, efforts of scientists useless," Set interrupted his thought.

After exchanging their observations, they headed towards the only oasis of peace for the Afterglowers on the shuttle - to the Thought Renewal Room.

They couldn't demonstrate their abilities there. They were limited by the space of the small dome of the orbital station. Their ideas had to be as limited as possible and couldn't go beyond it. Each exit outside the dome ended in non-existence. Those who left never came back, so no one really knew what was there.

Having settled down in the niches of peace and quiet, they waited for the start.

The psyche of the Afterglowers was their biggest problem. Having no material bodies, they didn't get sick, they were in no pain, and they weren't hungry, thirsty or tired. Unless they evoked such feelings in themselves. In themselves, they could, in others, they didn't have such possibilities. Many of them would have been happy to inflict pain and suffering on some other Afterglowers. Such desires still lingered in their darkest self of Afterglow consciousness. They survived their way to the orbit of the Technical Moon by entering a state of Afterglow hibernation, and only the magnetic impulse generated by the center of vigilance over their peace awakened the dormant Afterglowers.

"Here we are," Seta shared the news with others. "Now only the identity check and we will be able to start our mission," she added, looking at the rapidly approaching orbital vehicle. It would help them reach the moon. In the orbital control hall, the paths connecting all the domes of Hope to their moon crossed. Nobody knew any other possibility of landing on the moon.

Control was limited to the entry of the vehicle into a parabolic tunnel connecting their orbital vehicle to the lunar base control point to which they had to flow through the tunnel for Afterglowers. There was no other way for anyone. They didn't have to go through the tunnel like material Hopers, but they couldn't penetrate the dome and find themselves at the base. So, they headed towards the electronic gate, where every passing person had to stop. Then, based on the permits entered in their awareness, the permissions to stay in the base were checked.

The senior of the House of the Customary People's Clan issued them convincing permissions by sending the appropriate authorizations to the Central Registry of base controllers, so after a while, using their rushing thoughts, they get into the Hall of Tradition.

The huge space of the hall was cluttered with all kinds of mementos of bygone eras. From traditional objects from their first space expeditions to the most recent ones from their journeys to Earth. There were also presented chronological events from the life of their planet. They were not a trip group of bored Hopers looking for ideas to be used during further life in imagination. They had a specific purpose.

There was a technical passage leading from the room to the part reserved for technical staff of the station. Tybein shared all the information with Seta. From there, they could penetrate the power system.

None of them had been there before, so their knowledge of what the individual modules of the lunar base looked like was zero. Thus, they couldn't imagine where to go, so they moved through the corridors not much faster than their material counterparts. They jumped over long stretches of corridors, imagining their ending. It was not very safe; however, a moment of inattention and distraction was enough to make their trip end in one of the many unknown corridors more suited to their ideas. All the intricate dome-making 'machinery' was not their invention. This huge object had stood there as long as their records could remember. It had stood, but it hadn't worked because centuries earlier the material inhabitants of the Three Suns had been unable to start it. Nay! They hadn't even known what it had been installed for.

They had been taught the theory of the evolutionary duplication of their species for centuries. From simple creatures that they had been millions of years earlier, they came to the end of their evolutionary possibilities. The system of values and expansion ended in a great catastrophe. The planet was extinct, all its inhabitants died out, almost all of them, because at one time in the era of crazy experiments they had learned to leave their embryos in a state that allowed their future rebirth.

When life on the planet of the Three Suns was reborn again, nothing was like it had been before, except the moon with its ability to recreate their lives once again. This was the fourth stage of this revival. The stage of cosmic expansion and the great extinction stopped by Pol de Gar and their second life after being material. This is how, in a nutshell, the Hall of Tradition presented their hitherto existence on the planet of the Three Suns.

Now the two daredevils, Seta and Tybein wanted to reach the source of Genti, its heart, which radiated awareness to all Afterglowers. So far, no one had managed to get there. But the former daredevils were material Hopers who were limited by their material body.

So, they were walking, or basically moving forward, passing all the technical rooms. They used the memory of Seta who had spent many years there. It quickly turned out that her knowledge ended at a gate that no one ever opened.

The gate in front of which they found themselves wasn't some ordinary material cap, but a heliocentric circle shimmering with an incomprehensible symbol that pulsed with a pale-yellow color. Its color changed immediately when the material people approached it, but it didn't react to their arrival.

"What now?" Tybein emitted the fearful thought in their direction.

"I don't know, no one has managed to penetrate this circle, we tried everything. We studied this phenomenon with all possible methods, and nothing. We tried to stop, turn, change the rhythm of this matter, but it didn't react to anything. We drilled the rock on the sides to get into it from a different angle, but no matter which side we did it from, it always faced us.

We threw objects at it, special devices went inside, it didn't react to anything. It devoured everything, then spit it out like feces - a pile of powder and nothing else. Several material volunteers tried to enter it in suits or in specially constructed vehicles, but none of them ever returned."

"That's all you know Seta?" Tybein sent her her concerns in a slightly nervous tone.

"Me and many scientists, after discovery of Pol de Gar, believe that this is an entrance to another world. Something like the curvature of galactic space-time creating corridors to those who built these devices," she added. "It's linear time distortions."

"You don't remember much," she sighed approvingly.

"Our memories of these caps have been lost," Tybein said, recalling the known obviousness about the time of the Great Extinction.

"What's next? - who is to sacrifice and check if Afterglowers can penetrate to the other side," they wondered. According to the recommendations of the Council, it was supposed to be Tybein. Her genti was best for it. So far, she had managed to return from the most unlikely places she had imagined. She had something that others missed. She dragged behind her an IT thread. Something like a 'spider's thread' thanks to which she came back. It was a trace of consciousness that existed within her, whether she liked it or not.

"What should I do?" Concerned, she sent the full of anxiety question to the Council.

"Go inside first. Nowhere else, no matter what you see there. Then come back and give us your information."

"But how am I supposed to get back?!" she blurted out.

"We don't know how, but you will come back, we know that you will come back," they encouraged her. "We'll divide it into stages. When you come back," they stuck to their wording, "the second stage will be Seta's entry. Then you will take the next step. What step it will be, we will decide when you are inside," the Council explained its strategy of small steps.

Tybein sent them an impulse of a warm smile and a fearful look. She focused and ... disappeared.

They waited anxiously. After a long moment, Seta passed on to them:

"It's okay," she thought.

"Why do you think so?"

"She would already be spit back out like some lost electronic wreckage," she explained.

But no one spat her out. She showed up alone and, in addition, smiling.

"It's wonderful there," she told them very excitedly.

"And what's there?" they all asked simultaneously.

"Another world," she replied mysteriously.

Now it was the turn of Brit and Rai. They were already getting ready to hijack the 'Afterglow'. The galactic passenger and cargo ship Afterglow regularly traveled to the First Moon of Genti.

No one had ever flown to the Forbidden Second Moon. Why? - nobody knew that. However, as it was written in the memories of the Hall of Tradition - it was dangerous, but technically possible.

Chapter V

Return

Geo and Iva were just getting ready for a transfer to Hope, when they both felt an unpleasant impulse. They looked at each other.

"What was that?" Geo asked, looking at the focused face of his girlfriend - now that was what he thought about her after all they had lived together.

It felt like a warning, but he couldn't think against what. He looked questioningly at Iva, waiting for what she would tell him. She stood immobile listening to her genti.

"We've received a warning from our 'genti'. We are in danger."

"What?"

"I don't know, the impulse was too weak. We'll find out the rest on Hope. Come on," she added, taking his hand.

"What about my casket?" he asked, looking at his mother's casket standing on the dresser.

"Nothing, take it with you."

"How?" He looked at her in astonishment. Her eyes were serious and her face was focused. She thought intensely.

"After all, I will be only a glow there, so how will I hold it in my hand?"

"You don't have to hold it. The casket will be with you in your consciousness. Like mine when we were in the Island Paradise."

Geo felt an inner peace. He wasn't afraid, he knew that he was going home. He had by his side Iva, whom he trusted. He also felt that someone else was with him. Some part of his consciousness told him that his mother accompanied and protected him.

They entered space-time, holding hands. After a while they appeared under the Dome of the Dissenters. Iva headed straight to their dome, where the Senior Lady of the House of the Dissenters and a whole galaxy of brilliant Afterglowers were waiting for them.

"Welcome," the Clan's Senior Lady greeted them. "The matter is serious and jeopardizes our efforts to keep the balance on Hope," she began without preamble.

Geo was acting like a purebred Hoper who couldn't be surprised by anything. Together with Iva, he took a place under an umbrella at the Clan Council. Here, too, the system of values worked, depending on the topic discussed. They all sat at the round table like King Arthur's, but it was Geo's vision.

Iva saw them on the podium of the Amphitheater she had seen in the town where Norbert had lived. However, the way people saw the gathering didn't matter, the only important thing was the exchange of the thoughts between them. The Senior Lady of the House sent the first message:

"The Caps of Consciousness were violated, which in the Hall of Tradition was marked as a great danger to our planet. What the danger is, we don't know. The symbols and messages concerning the Caps of Consciousness are not fully understood. "Please share your questions and observations."

The Dome's umbrellas turned red, then an orange color dominated them until they all glowed blue. Who violated them and how? What can be done to prevent danger? These two thoughts dominated all the others. This is how the system of values worked there, and although another thought might have been more accurate or revealing, perceptive or selective, it had no chance of being present at the meeting of the Council.

Genti replied with the thought:

"Two Afterglowers from the Customary People's Clan entered the Consciousness Caps and didn't come out of there."

"We should send a chase group after them in order to prevent domination or catastrophe," said the Senior Lady of the Family. "Their main goal will be to guess how it happened and what it is for," the laconic and concise message of the Senior Lady of the Family was the effect of the Umbrella of the Dome, which formulated the will of the general public. It had nothing to do with the real state, logic of events or intuition, perceptiveness or knowledge. It was purely and simply a result of all the thoughts gathered here.

"Will it work?" Iva wondered. "Who is it supposed to be?" this question was also already in line with the will of the general public.

Genti replied:

"Geo, Iva and Tora - our specialist in the history of the Hall of Tradition. Geo is partly an Earthman and has something no one has. He has the power. Iva, because she is his genti and they are one. Tora - because she is a historian from the Hall of Tradition."

"Good luck," said the Senior Lady and disappeared.

But Geo wasn't so optimistic about this mission. He was interested in Hope, he wanted to know all the secrets of this planet. Terribly disappointed, he said that he couldn't really get to know his planet. Everything the domes hid under its caps was unavailable until you were invited. And you only saw what others wanted you to see. The world beyond the domes was invisible to the Afterglowers. They could watch live coverage of what happened there, but they couldn't participate in it.

They played what they had seen even with details, but it was a bit unreal, but safe. The material world beyond the Domes was a very different world, where evolution recreated Hope not always as intended by their original inhabitants.

Their scientists had long known that there had been a phenomenon called dark matter in their galactic system. The star of

Sedah concentrated dark matter particles to form a galactic disk around their Forbidden Second Moon. Every time the planet of the Three Suns passed through the invisible disk of dark matter, severe perturbations were generated, causing disturbances in the comet belt known as the Albaid tail. This comet was the remains of a torn planet that fell out of the gravitational attraction of their second sun during the formation of their star system.

Cyclical hooking on the belt of dark matter caused the precipitation of the rain of comets and the bombardment of their planet with meteorites. Each such event, intensified by the blows of real cosmic giants, sometimes reaching a diameter of several Hope kilometers, resulted in a complete annihilation of everything that lived on it.

After the next hundreds of thousands of years there was a rebirth of life, but in a different form. Evolution never repeated what it had already produced. Therefore, on the planet of the Three Suns, in the event of a cosmic cataclysm, there were mechanisms for the rebirth of their species.

The memory of all these events was kept in the Hall of Tradition. This was the fourth rebirth of this planet. However, their prototype had never been reborn on it, which could prove that they were visitors from other planets - that's what claimed prehistorians.

"And the Earth?" Geo thought. "What about their inhabitants, are they also a plague brought by the aliens?" Amused, Iva followed Geo's reasoning. She had been over such a path of reflection for a long time. Now that she was with Geo, her mind was occupied by one prime thought.

Baby!

Who would Geo have a child with? She was not half Earthling like Geo. She also knew that Geo could have a child, but only on Earth, so she was tormented by these doubts. She carefully hid her thoughts from him. Was it jealousy? - such jealousy didn't exist on Hope, the more jealousy for a child. 'No, it's impossible,' any Hoper would have thought.

Iva, however, knew that Geo was a freak of evolution, the next link, and his children would be a chain in this new evolution. But of Earth, Hope or both planets?" she wondered, looking at him.

She didn't even know how wrong she was.

They were on the yacht in their Island Paradise again. The dog was lying on the bow, staring at the water with bored gaze.

"I miss the Earth." Geo looked at Iva. He knew what she would tell him.

"I can't come back now, it's too early for regeneration. And now we have something to do here," she changed the subject, reminding him of their mission.

Iva began to pass on to him the information she had about the Hall of Tradition and the two Moons.

"Stop it," at one point she received the signal from Geo.

"I already know everything."

"How?" Surprised, she turned in his direction. She was just lying on a deck chair with her face exposed to sunlight. The wide smile on his face made her realize that he really knew, and more than she did. Geo immediately gave her an image of the Caps of Consciousness.

"I don't know, but I do," he explained calmly. He was already getting used to the new way of acquiring knowledge and information. "We can get there without a spaceship and travel aboard it." Not realizing that it might have scared her - he asked with the calm thought: "Do you want to try?"

"I'm afraid, and what will happen if we find ourselves in non-existence and never come back here?"

"I know exactly where we are to move."

"Do you want to go beyond the Dome? Nobody has ever managed to come back when they got beyond her protective umbrella," argued Iva.

"We will not go beyond the Protective Dome. We'll be inside all the time."

"How is this possible? There is no Dome in outer space, that's why they are artificially produced on board the ship."

"I know, I know, but there is something that apparently no one has considered before."

"What?" she asked with a hint of doubt.

"I underestimated him again," Iva thought as the transmission from Geo reached her. "Indeed, so far no one has thought about it," she immediately provided the information to the Senior Council. The mental vibration of dissatisfaction, she took as a symptom of their weakness.

"Geo is different," she retorted, "you forget that he's more than half an Earthman and takes a different approach to many of the brassbound views of Hope. I trust him, you know well that we are one and I will go with him - give us the permission," she asked although Geo didn't even think about asking for it.

"Be careful," came the answer.

"Okay, Geo," she directed the stream of her thoughts to him. He looked at her, surprised that also there some permits were necessary.

"It's not necessary, Geo, but if you have them, you can count on the powerful support of the entire Clan. It is important and helpful, and it can be even invaluable in our mission."

"If you think so, then you are probably right," he agreed with her, but more under the influence of intoxicating moments spent on the yacht than because of the belief in the correctness of her reasoning.

They decided to act immediately. In order to do this, they had to change the dome in which they were now to some other.

Therefore, Iva took Geo by the hand and together with Tora, they moved first to Earth, and from there immediately to the receiving station of the smallest Dome of Hope.

"Why did you choose this dome?" Iva was surprised by Geo's decision.

"Because it has the weakest relay signal, so we will have to use the least energy to overcome it. In it we have to go up against the stream, to the place from which it flows down to Hope," he explained to her.

"How do you know all this?"

"I don't know, but probably my mother told me about it. It was she who appeared to me during this vision."

"It makes sense, her genti is with you and protects you, us," Iva said with satisfaction.

Geo still didn't fully realize what that genti was. His genti, of Iva, Council, mother and of other Hopers. However, he managed to get used to the thought that their genti helped and that it was worth using it.

Several material Hopers from the Protection Station of this dome stared in amazement at the shadows. There was little intimacy between them. They considered Afterglowers useless shadows, but tolerated their presence because they realized that they would become such shadows themselves someday.

Geo looked for a while at the circular cluster of electrons several meters in diameter, flickering with white light. This stream, moving from non-existence, fell directly into the cap capturing this beam of focused electrons. The cap several thousand kilometers high spread this beam across the surface of the Dome in the shape of a huge inverted bowl that covered the surface of the planet. "The Dome under which we are now is the smallest of all the domes, but even so, all Earth's Europe and half of Asia would fit underneath it," Geo thought.

He was standing with Iva and felt no power, no impact of the stream on their Afterglow consciousness.

"This is a highly condensed stream of energy," he sent the message to Iva and, unexpectedly even for himself, he put his glowing hand into it.

He felt nothing. He pulled it out and looked at Iva in amazement. "There must be something up there that this stream produces."

She nodded to show that she agreed with him.

"Wait, I'll be right back," he sent her the thought.

This worldly way of thinking amused her. "He's like a child who plays with unknown toys," she thought.

Geo fully went into that stream. He could feel its strength. It was pressing him into the cap, but nothing else happened. "And what now?" he thought. He tried to get up. Nothing, he didn't even budge, pressed into the ridge of the cap.

"Iva," he said after leaving the stream. "I'm doing something wrong. Help me," he asked.

She already knew, after all, she was Him.

"We have to concentrate our genti on the vision of getting up where this stream is produced."

She knew that the whole council held other thoughts, concentrating only on strengthening their genti. The three of them entered the middle of the stream. White electrons flowed around their glow like a stream of water that passes by a stone on its way.

"Now," the thought of Iva and Tora dawned on him. Nothing happened. They stood as before. It pissed him off terribly and unleashed power in him. The light of escaping electrons flashed, and a little bewildered, they found themselves in a huge circular room full of devices unknown to them. Nothing there was even similar to what was on Hope, let alone the Earth. Some strange structures with bizarre shapes, mostly spiral and fibrous, ran from top to bottom and across this room.

A cave or hall, carved or otherwise deprived of the contents of the lunar rock, shone with all the colors of the Three Suns. There was nothing material there. The streams of light crossed circular electron clusters, flashing from purple to orange. Some with a diameter of several centimeters, others a few meters. Nothing permanent, nothing material, but it worked. They overlapped to form screens of various points changing their order as in a kaleidoscope. They looked to the left, right, around, but there was no sign of the end or the beginning.

"It seems to cover the entire moon," Iva noticed.

"There is the Focal Point," he showed her the white light pulsating with a steady rhythm. "It's like a lighthouse," he thought.

"It lures us to itself - it wasn't there a moment ago," Iva told him.

"Let's move in that direction, we will see what it is," he flashed his thoughts to the girls.

They wandered between all these productions of various forms of energy, afraid of finding themselves in the wrong place that could annihilate them or disrupt this million-year-old system in which they were. Although they were moving quickly, the light was at the same distance all the time. Were it not for the views on the sides that changed along with the road they traveled; they would have thought that they were motionless.

"Mirage?" Iva whispered.

"No, it is a light leading us to the right place. I think what we are dealing with here was prepared for the fact that someone would get here someday."

With each passing moment they approached the white light flashing with an even rhythm. However, it is not known why they felt as if they had been covering not Hope distances but time, which changed the environment around them. At last, all the spirals were gone, and a straight cavernous corridor appeared. At its top ran a sinusoidal pulsating beam of violet electrons.

Now they were jumping over every straight stretch of the corridor in their minds. And they still had a feeling that it was endless. When it seemed to them that they had already circled around the entire moon, they suddenly saw the Cap. It seemed unreal in this electronic world of the lunar interior. Its surface shone with intense light towards them. In the solid rock surrounding it on all sides, it looked like a pass leading to an unknown land.

"Is it a cap leading to Their or Our World?" Iva blurted out.

"To all worlds," he replied, looking with astonished gaze at the cap visible in the distance.

"I think so too," Tora returned his thought.

The cap sparkled with the symbols of the Three Suns, changing colors when they approached it. They felt no anxiety or fear of the next obstacle they had to overcome.

"Come on," Iva sent the signal and, taking his hand, she got inside with him. A slight tingling felt on the entire Afterglow silhouette made her realize that the Cap was someone's real tangible awareness and deliberate action. They felt no movement, but knew they had had to travel a considerable distance. The moon's genti shifted their consciousness to a little Hope cap.

"It's trying us," Geo thought to her.

"Describe what you see," he wanted to check if their Afterglow senses perceived the same.

"We are at the crossroads of the space station. We are standing in the semicircular dome with a dozen or so corridors, each with the different entrance structure. From sinusoidal to spinning circles and other weird symbols. The last on the right is fundamentally different from the others. All its surface is yellow, and the shades of this color change from time to time, disappearing in the center of the gate as a red point."

"I see the same. What do we do?"

"We need to find the key to these Gates. They lead somewhere, to some specific place."

"Turn around and look back," Geo asked.

Behind their backs, the cap through which they had entered differed from the image that had appeared to them before. The entire surface was shimmering with the color of blue pulsating from the center to the end of its surface with circles, which spilled like waves on the still water when you throw a stone into it.

"The same signs are in our Hall of Tradition," said Tora, their traveling companion. "However, we don't understand their purpose," she added.

"Do you know what they mean?" Iva asked.

"Not all of them, but we were able to associate some of them with specific places in the universe, but only because they contained several other symbols of the planetary system that we could read."

"Show the ones you know."

"This one is Mars from your solar system." She pointed to the red caps filled with white symbols of the hematite atomic system. "Those green symbols are Eroposus in the Tyrion Nebula 6472. A planet similar to our Hope but without an atmosphere like ours. I think Pol de Gar was right," she added as if without connection.

"This Circle, or perhaps the name of the Gate would be more appropriate, with longitudinal lines moving from bottom to top, is symbol of two Earth-sized planets orbiting two opposite suns. Both were taken into account for settlement, but the lack of the possibility of a safe flight to their solar system by the then spacecraft discouraged scientists from further research."

"What difficulty did they encounter?" Iva asked curiously, facing the screen, then she looked at a fragment of the star map.

"It was necessary to get through the then unknown structure of the remains of some cosmic catastrophe littering this area. The phenomenon itself was quite known, only their properties were insurmountable for us. Then," she added, "now we know more about it."

"What was that? - is," she corrected herself.

"This phenomenon consists in the breakdown of any material that contains carbon particles in its material form. Being in the impact zone of the anti-carboner, it absorbed all carbon atoms, which led to the disaster and the collapse of our research vessels. Now we know how to protect them with a special protective field."

"So, what do we do?" Iva flashed the impatient thought after, according to her, too long Tora's speech. "Will we get into any of them?"

"We're going back to the Hall of Tradition," Geo decided. "We need to know the entrance leading to the Genti of our Hope."

"You're right," they agreed with him.

The way back was quick, they could move using their genti. They discovered something their scientists had long suspected existed, but had no evidence to support it. Now they had the evidence, but they didn't know the places to which the Caps led.

In the Hall of Tradition, with the help of Tora, they quickly found a piece of history and knowledge that Hope had on the subject. There wasn't much of it. Seventeen holographic symbols, only five of which were described by the star map. Using her genti, Tora visualized the map of the universe and the five places on it. It meant nothing to them, the places weren't too far apart, but there was no point of reference to associate them with something. Geo wondered. His knowledge of astronomy was zero compared to that of both girls, but thanks to it, he wasn't burdened with any thought patterns. He put all the graphic symbols of the Cap on Tora's holographic image.

"Do they share a common symbol?" he asked everyone a question. All four felt the support of the Senior Council, but that didn't help.

Finally, Geo understood.

"These are puzzles!" he exclaimed happily.

"Puzzle? What's this?" both girls asked simultaneously.

"We have to treat them like a jigsaw puzzle with different pieces having common sides, and not look for a common point of reference for every of them. Here everything is one and when put together, it will form a whole," he explained to them the essence of playing puzzles. The puzzle of all symbols will create one picture. Go ahead," he turned to the material scientists.

Now, they stepped into action and, with the help of a Hope biogenetic computer, whose heart was the bonding of their own DNA, they quickly combined all the symbols into a single whole.

"It's impossible!" the common thought ran through all the Afterglowers.

It didn't concern material people, so their shouts of amazement disturbed the silence in the Hall of Tradition.

The solution was amazingly simple, so simple that it's weird they hadn't figured it out sooner. They were stuck in the solution, literally standing inside it.

The image that emerged after assembling all the puzzle pieces of the symbols of the Caps wasn't completely understandable. There were empty spaces in it, places for other symbols they hadn't yet discovered. But even so, what appeared to them was amazing. The universal signs of molecular bonds with which they were equipped and from which the universe was built had been transformed into holographic views, signs and symbols understandable to them.

The entire screen of the upper side of the three-dimensional message showed them the distant sides of a universe that was known to exist but whose structure they didn't know. A series of colored lines ran from several planets hidden behind unfamiliar structures in star systems towards a central point in their solar system. However, somewhere in the middle part, lower left one, and on the whole right side with a few exceptions, an image was missing, and the screen pulsed with white light at these points. These were the places of corridors undiscovered by them, leading to the Caps, which were somewhere in the abyss of the lunar mechanism.

"When we find the Caps, the puzzle will show us all the missing pieces."

"What is it?" the material scientists who took part in this discovery or arranging the image from the known elements whispered among themselves.

"Any space-time corridors? Maybe tunnels leading to those places that are white empty spaces in the universe."

"It's rather impossible for anyone to get there. The distances between individual points are unimaginable even for us."

"Maybe they bend the space and go there like we do to the Earth?" said Iva.

"And energy? Here it would take the energy of several suns to open the space between them."

"How do you know they don't have a better way?"

"They do," Geo said unexpectedly.

"What?" the inquiry signal sent by the Hopers dominated the other doubters' messages.

"They have Genti - they control the universe as we control our planetary system. These paths are for all those who in their evolution reach the level of a Homoafterglower's immaterial existence."

"How do you know that?" the wide stream of consciousness cut through the Hall of Tradition. It was like an accusation of using a fabricated theory.

"Thanks to their genti - I just made contact with the first non-hope genti of the galactic system." Geo responded with a strong impulse and pointed to the not-too-distant Green Dwarf galaxy marked as a small dot on the left side of the screen, quickly pulsating. There was silence in the Hall of Tradition.

"These are genti corridors?" Iva, surprised, said first.

The huge space of the Hall of Tradition was dominated by all Hopers free from material activities and a small group of Afterglowers. The Hall of Tradition in which they were, was divided according to their evolutionary stages, starting from the formation of the first communities to the final stage of the great 'poor versus rich' war - as their historians called it. A war in which everyone was a loser, because their planet was so damaged and degraded that it seemed impossible to continue living there. Cities crumbled to rubble, forests and jungles ceased to exist, there was no life in the seas, and the bottom of the oceans was covered with scrap weapons, with which they had tried to annihilate one another.

The handful of surviving inhabitants of the Three Suns living underground and at the bottom of the oceans couldn't create a new civilization, so at the cost of many sacrifices and efforts they moved to the moon to start rebuilding what had been destroyed.

The era of the Great Rebirth of the new Hope population re-inhabiting the Planet of the Three Suns from the moon, this time devoid of all the evil qualities of their previous inhabitants, lasted for hundreds of years. And it was this space of the Hall of Tradition that was best documented. In the center of the dome, the era of the great extinction, and at the end, their epoch. The time of the formation of Afterglowers, their journey to Earth and sheltered life.

When you wanted to learn more about the past or see more, it was enough to direct the stream of thoughts to a given object, place or part of the planet that interested you, or touch it, and it materialized on a scale adjusted to your expectations. After that, everything was also simple. You chose a structure, a spaceship, or a single object used by the Hopers, an animal, a bird, or a plant, it didn't matter. It was displayed to you in four dimensions and then you could rotate it, open it, change its scale or choose the fragment you were interested in and study its structure, destiny or watch it come into being, live or die.

"How does it work?" Iva asked, curious why Geo had picked up the signal and she hadn't. After all, they were one and according to all the existing rules, she also should establish direct contact.

The Green Dwarf carefully revealed information about itself. Now she also knew what the Green Dwarf told Geo. She received transmission directly from Geo.

"First contact from this part of our world," Geo repeated his thought aloud.

Special devices installed in the Hall of Tradition made it possible to process the thoughts of the Afterglowers into the speech of material Hopers or directly telepathically convey to them the thoughts of those Afterglowers who wanted or had to communicate with them, and there weren't as few of them as it might seem. Very often, Afterglowers for various reasons, wanted to communicate with material people in order to draw from them the knowledge about the time when they themselves had been material scientists and conducted various research.

"They are also, mainly they," he corrected himself, "are rightful inhabitants of Hope."

"How long ago did you reach the state of genti and who were you?" the question came from the Green Dwarf.

There was a slight agitation in the room. Geo shut off communications.

"What do you mean, who were we?"

The Senior Council recommended extreme caution. This question proved and suggested that life in the universe was not uniform but could take many forms, and They knew it. Geo flashed to them the chemical formula of their Afterglow existence in the two states of consciousness, the Material and the Afterglow ones.

The Green Dwarf's abilities surpassed the Hope's genti. In their holographic image, starting with the dot that signified the Green Dwarf's place in the universe, a stain began to spread. First it grew slightly, blurred, then it moved to the center of the Hall of Tradition and took the form of a spherical four-dimensional image. The inhabitants of the Green Dwarf appeared.

"They look almost like us," there were heard the hushed voices of the material scientists.

Almost, however, didn't mean the same.

Their material appearance resembled more a developed species of a Homohoper in his or her original state of life on the planet of the Three Suns.

In the evolution of their planet, after the Hopers locked themselves under the domes in their third stage of rebirth, when their planet evolved to perfection, life outside the domes evolved in other forms. A species of primitive mammals developed there, endowed with a small brain disproportionate to the broad, flat face and large bulging eyes. They had no natural enemies whom their material scientists had eliminated from the existence of this planet. This caused them to stop developing at the level of their five-year Hopers. They were not motivated to attain a higher degree of consciousness, and they put all their energy into expanding the population, which grew rapidly. When they ran out of opportunities to use the planet's natural resources, only then did they experience species competition. However, it was too late for their brain development and technological advances, which for them stopped at the stage of foraging and clubs. They died out along with all the lateral lines of mammals.

After a hundred thousand Hope years, the planet was engulfed by a catastrophic plague, a disease brought somewhere from space. The pandemic decimated the development of all vegetation, turning what existed into rotten pulp, which was eaten by bacteria brought from space. They, living in symbiosis with the rotten pulp, turned into the eternal fossil of coal. It was in the past, but the Green Dwarf

Remembrance Hall had preserved the image of those Homohopers who resembled this failed prank of evolution with their appearance.

The Material Green Dwarf, in its material existence, had a dark green complexion, and its head, making up three-quarters of the entire figure, was supported by four pairs of legs protruding from its lower torso. Two of them took turns constantly supporting its head so that it wouldn't flop during the movement.

To Geo, the figure resembled an old painting hanging on one of the walls of his father's house - the figure of an old man supporting his chin during a short nap at a table. At least that's what it looked like in the holographic image everyone was looking at right now. However, as they understood, it wasn't a natural color, but a spectrum of light emanating from their stratosphere, which, next to the sun, emitted this color from the nearby - for Hope distances - Green Dwarf planet.

The entire torso of an inhabitant of the Green Dwarf rested on two short legs so that their silhouette looked like a bent very old material Hoper who, refusing to accept immaterial existence, decided to end their days in the material form.

Only this face and intelligent and loving gaze made them feel that it was their kinsman, different from them in appearance resulting from the natural environment in which they had lived, but coming from the same species of homo protozoa.

In the Tradition Hall, there was the rest of the Green Dwarf presentation taking place. But it was quite rudimentary, and so fast that only a few material scientists understood it.

Rapid graphical information and formulas of mathematical rules for a moment filled the entire lower part of the spherical picture. Then only the visible material silhouette of the Green Dwarf froze as if waiting for an answer.

Geo, pushed by some inner force, approached the sphere and put his hand to its surface. The green inhabitant pulled out, or in fact slipped out an oval cylinder, changing its shape to that of Geo's hand, and put it against his hand. Then swiftly curled it in a gesture of Hope goodbye. Touching his body between the two protrusions supporting the head, just above the eyes, he made a slow movement and, pulling a process with three legs, he turned it towards them.

"It symbolizes a pure heart and friendly intentions," Iva sent the signal to all gathered.

Geo felt an enormous surge of energy and heard the thought of the Green Dwarf inhabitant.

"You will be the only Hoper with our power and knowledge."

The ball spun and instantly turned into a green flashing dot that faded out after a while. The Hopers, amazed, stared at Geo.

"What's going on?" He sent them the worried signal, surprised by their curious glances.

"You have a greenish glow," Iva stared at him in amazement.

Geo's glow was shimmering with a pale green color penetrating into his pale beige form. He felt the knowledge of the Green Dwarf's genti overwhelming him.

"They are many hundred thousand years ahead of us," this was the first message he shared with all the Hopers. "But beside that, they don't differ much from us, not counting their appearance," he joked.

The material people were interested in the technical knowledge of the Green Dwarf, and the Afterglowers, in his genti.

Geo already knew the answers to his questions.

"Travels thanks to the warping of the space of our Relay Station?" he spoke to the audience. "Yes, they can be improved, but for greater intergalactic distances, it is not possible. Cell regeneration - there is a way to do it, but without traveling to Earth, it won't be very effective."

Geo was surprised that all the information obtained concerned only the Green Dwarf. No hints regarding any other corridors permeating the universe. Other worlds or civilizations. He already knew the answers to his questions, but he was not willing to share with them the knowledge he had gained. Disease, violence, wars, hunger, poverty, overpopulation are symptoms of the Earth's baby, and the inhabitants themselves had to deal with it.

They had to deal with it themselves and move to a higher stage of evolution from where the path led to genti. Without it, they wouldn't have survived on Earth as a species. No one would have been worried about their evolutionary failure, because the Hopers were also Homo sapiens, but at a different evolutionary stage. However, the knowledge and information gained related only to the Green Dwarf. There was not even a scrap of information about the other paths of genti that permeated the universe. Now, however, they knew why genti could successfully navigate through space in real time.

There was, however, genti which, in order to survive, must have spread through the cosmos and been the source of other lives, seed or salvation for beings who had evolved to be able to make such journeys. Only this, or so much Geo learned, but there was no indication of how to achieve it, or where that genti was. But Geo, with the spirit of Earthly detectives, began to put the pieces of the puzzle together.

He was going to share his observations with Iva and he felt more and more this special bond with her, and not because she was his girlfriend, but because they constituted a whole, they were one, not only when they made love, but especially when they were genti.

"Inform them of one more important message from the Green Dwarf."

Iva stepped forward, facing the crowd, and like a clan leader spoke to them firmly:

"In order to benefit from communication between two planets, both sides must want it. If you go to their genti without their consent, you will get there, but won't leave their world. It may well be that where you will go, there will be no genti left, nothing but an extinct or abandoned planet where you will be stuck with no way to return. That's why mutual communication is so important before traveling in the genti corridor.

The speed of light is limited, you can determine it, you can measure it. Genti is a thought, awareness. It is not subject to any restrictions. It is, exists at the moment. You will think and you will be, and the way, time or space doesn't matter. There are no restrictions for the Genti Awareness Corridors. Unless they arise from consciousness itself."

The Green Dwarf broadcast triggered an inter-clan exchange of information. Fear, uncertainty and surprise dominated. The fact that there had been life in the universe had been known for a long time, but finding out that this life had been at a higher level of evolution and treated them disrespectfully, was a real surprise for them. Until now they had met only themselves, and at a lower level of evolution, so they were not used to such treatment.

"How is that?" the same thought flashed in all clans. "They don't come, don't introduce themselves, they don't explain, but just endow one of us with all their knowledge of the rest of the Hopers without thinking at all." It was outrageous to some of them.

"Why?" they asked Geo.

"Because we are too different. Hope also doesn't talk to the Earth and their inhabitants for the same reasons."

Geo, impatient with the excess of questions, information and envious comments received from all clans, decided to close the topic.

"End of broadcast," he sent them the message.

Geo and Iva were perhaps the only Hopers who didn't consider anyone, a little bit because Geo didn't know the local customs and the hierarchy of dependence on the Clans on Hope.

All three left the Hall of Traditions to search for more genti corridors, where they hoped to find the rest of the caps matching the white spots on their map of the universe.

Chapter VI

Mars

The Red Cap on the Holographic Screen in the Hall of Tradition lured Geo and Iva with its clear symbolism of water.

Water, liquid crystalline water, fresh, salty or without various mineral additives, is quite popular in the universe material that creates life. "There is water, there is life," their scientists said.

The atomic formula of hematite, symbolizing red, completed the information. They had no doubts that it was a symbolism of Mars, a planet in Earth's solar system.

The road ahead of them led to Mars, and yet they knew there was no life there. The history of the planet of the Three Suns showed that various forms of life, apart from intelligent beings who could create more complicated ways of making their lives better, could also destroy and annihilate everything that lived. These beings were created by evolution going in different directions, not necessarily the same as those of the inhabitants of Hope. Sometimes it was impossible to recreate life on the planet of ancestors, who had destroyed its structure so much that even time couldn't repair it.

"We have to check it out," Geo shared his curiosity with everyone. Others hadn't even thought of that.

"What can be checked there? There is no form of life," they replied with the consistent message.

"There is, I have weak contact - and it is a cry for help."

The image that Geo showed them shocked everyone present in the Hall of Tradition.

The buildings, the clusters of the inhabitants of Mars, deceptively reminded them of their own forms of existence from the heyday of the Three Suns. Then the image showed them short snapshots of an encounter with a hostile alien from an undefined part of the cosmos that initiated their evolutionary adaptation to the new situation. Both the hostile arrivals and themselves were separated by the sudden and unexpected bombardment of meteorites that wiped out everything on Mars, and the impacts of space giants caused the poles of Mars to shift and the atmosphere to escape into space. The situation was worsened by the sudden and unexpected extinction of the Mars core, which led to a slow disappearance of their magnetic field as well as protection of the Mars shell from cosmic bombardment of solar particles.

"How long did it last?" everyone wondered.

"Did they manage to escape?" No, they couldn't, they didn't have where or on what. It wasn't a civilization aimed at conquering space. They had no spacecraft or other means allowing to leave their planet. Only few of them survived who, having taken refuge in the natural depressions of Mars, tried to survive.

This civilization didn't know any space or combat technology, they lived in symbiosis with the Martian Afterglowers that came from an undefined part of the cosmos and were a separate species on Mars.

The Afterglowers survived. Unable to take refuge underground, they used the corridors and, leaving the remaining Martian materialists on their own, escaped from Mars. There was no time to take the Martians together. They didn't believe they could survive.

But Martian materialists adapted thanks to the unusual structure of Mars hiding a ring that entwined the entire planet with corridors. Two siphons at the south and north poles of Mars with the trapped atmosphere inside allowed them to live. They focused all their knowledge and skills on adapting to the prevailing conditions. But with each Martian age, their atmosphere shrank, and it was impossible for its resources to be renewed in a way that would have enabled their survival measured in hundreds of thousands of years.

"We need immediate help," was their last message. "We are unable to open the Cap through which the afterglowers escaped from Mars."

"Let the Council decide," the signal was sent to Hope. The three most important Hope Clans long deliberated unanimously.

Finally, after a long wait, the news arrived:

"The only Hopers that can go in are Geo and Iva, but they themselves have to agree to this mission."

"I understand why me," replied Geo, "but Iva?"

"She can also materialize there. You are one genti. Geo had had glimpses for some time that He and Iva were one. However, he couldn't define what this 'one' was.

"I'm curious about this journey myself, so Iva and I agree to this expedition. We know where the Cap and the genti corridor to Mars are."

"We don't have much time, so we set off immediately," added Iva.

She grabbed Geo's hand and they entered the moon corridors. Quickly following the path, they knew, they moved towards the bifurcation of genti corridors, where the Gate to Mars was located. They found it easily and, holding hands, they walked through it.

The Cap leading to Mars immediately transported them to the end of the corridor, where they were surprised to see the same Cap with the same Martian symbols. They crossed its pulsating circle without fear. They got surrounded by a magnetic glow, something like the northern lights they had seen on Earth. Here it shimmered with all the colors of red. They were material, and their faces and hands glistened with blue sparks crawling over their skin. When they brought their hands closer to each other, they jumped from hand to hand, emitting a gentle crack. Their whole bodies were overwhelmed by an unpleasant feeling of gravity, but not such known to them from Earth, but the one resulting from a horizontal vortex squeezing their bodies like pincers. It felt as if they had been in a wind tunnel with two powerful forces of gravity acting against each other.

"We are the same as when we use our box," said Iva. And although her voice was a few tones higher, Geo recognized it easily.

They were alone. They were standing against a red rock, and there were no structures or other signs of any civilization around. The horizon in front of them was only visible to a limited extent. They were standing beyond some plateau with the huge red rock behind their backs disappearing somewhere above. The strange structure of the atmosphere charged with

Martian ions allowed them to see only the nearest several dozen meters, but it was possible for them to breathe, although each breath had a taste of something unknown to them. Geo, who once had dived into an ocean, realized that this was some kind of a mixture due to the high pressure that prevailed here in these Martian corridors. "Where's the Martians?" he asked Iva. But she didn't have to answer, because in the distance they saw a red flash, like that of a horizontal lightning bolt, which was rapidly approaching them.

They stood motionless, uncertainly awaiting this strange phenomenon approaching them at breakneck speed. The red ball turned out to be some kind of vehicle, or rather, in earthly understanding, some animal.

"What is this?" the inaudible message received from Iva made him realize that their genti also worked there.

It is unknown why he thought about the dog. The loud barking of the black box enraged the Martian earthworm - because of such a being, although on a much larger scale reminded him this strange creature. After a while, its front part noiselessly opened and four dark-red creatures with a humanoid appearance, although a different silhouette, emerged from its interior. They looked a bit funny; their bodies were flattened unlike their earthly figures. Geo and Iva stood still. The series of crackles coming from inside them was completely incomprehensible to them.

"What now? How will we communicate?" Iva asked.

"I don't know," he answered.

However, the gestures made by the Martians were understandable to them. They were inviting them inside their worm. The first one to get inside this bug was their poodle. His joyful barking was heard from within.

"Let's get in, it's safe," Geo muttered, turning to Iva. He took a few steps ahead as he passed between the Martians. They stood erect, and their hands facing the bug, urged him to come in. He had to bend a bit to get inside from which the smell of rotten apples spurted in his direction.

"What associations," he thought of this strange way of communication. "Probably this living creature stuffs its body with some local treat and transforms it into energy necessary to move."

Iva followed him. Inside, a series of articulated segments pulsed with red light. The poodle, charging at his leg, lay down without fear on one of the thick rugs specially prepared for them. They sat next to him. The Martians stood on the sides, clinging to spider-like supports that sprouted from the worm's floor. The spider-like red clamping rings looked like bones scraped from flesh that have not yet faded due to lack of time. Anyway, everything here was red or had a shade of that color and, as he noticed, it was mainly related to the red structure of the place in which they found themselves. The vehicle moved at astonishing speed. They felt it, but couldn't see anything, there were no windows, and everything around it was lit by a red glow. The faster they moved, the greater was the glow coming from the ground. They clearly felt the change in pressure as if they had been plunging into a water to a considerable depth.

"Do you have contact?" Iva asked, looking at the Martians eloquently.

"No, none, not even our genti can break through from within this creature."

After a long moment of such silent driving, the vehicle stopped and its front parted. All of them single file went in unison out of it. The poodle ran ahead, wagging its tail happily. The bright red glow of Martian lighting greeted them in a huge hall with high ceilings and a sloping floor at the end of which one could see a podium illuminated by flashing blue sparks. Four Martian creatures, distinguished by their dress, had their hands joined in a gesture of greeting. Big, little, children, elders all greeted them, with hope looking at the first arrivals from the genti corridors since the Cataclysm. They had always known they would come; they just hadn't known when.

The room in which they were reminded them of their Hall of Tradition. In this enormous grotto, a series of unknown devices shimmered with a metallic glow. There were enormous control panels by which Martians stood. Huge pipes spirally going upwards fastened some machine structures and other devices with loud humming indicators and protruding semi-fluid screens in the shape of a gouged-out eye. It all shivered, flashed, giving the impression of not a material structure, but rather something like a holographic image. There were also huge red screens with a map of the universe and lines of connection visible from the surface of Mars. One of them, thick and red, ran from Mars to the Blue Planet - his Earth, and several other points, towards the universe shown on their maps. Each point was a cap leading to another world - their hope for rescue.

Suddenly, out of nowhere, they heard a metallic voice speaking in the Hope language.

"Welcome, representatives of the Three Suns."

All the Martians present began to greet them, bending their flat silhouettes and swaying like leaves in the wind. These words were accompanied by a slight shaking of the whole grotto. It made no impression on the Martians.

"They are probably used to it," said Iva.

She watched her surroundings closely. She noticed that not all of them greeted them with joy, and some even made hostile cheers and waved red holographic banners with white color predominating on their surface. Geo sent a message to the Hall of Tradition where Tora, with the help of the Council, searched for a solution to the symbols on the other two corridors that Geo and Iva had noticed after landing on the inner surface of Mars. Meanwhile, Geo was invited to visit one of the three cities, and Iva talked with Martian scholars. The dog ran between her and Geo, nervous about their separation. Their cities were clusters of holes drilled in Martian soil that served as their homes, halls, schools, and galleries.

"How big is your community?" asked Iva, interested in the size of the population for which they needed to find a place to live.

"Two million. Of these, almost half are at the other pole of Mars."

Geo quickly received an information from the Hall of Traditions about the possibilities for the Martians to be evacuated.

A quick analysis of their life needs gave them a chance to find a suitable place for them. Several planets known to them met these conditions. The only question was how to get them out of there and transport them to one of those planets.

As they discussed, Geo realized that time was short and that the Martians' move to another planet should have been completed as soon as possible. Due to the forces of gravity inside the planet, their bodies were subjected to lateral pressure and adapted to life by taking on a flat shape. The lack of sunlight and the internal structure of the atmosphere they absorbed, as well as the interaction of magnetic forces, colored their bodies shining red.

Geo and Iva were asked to enter a council chamber, where representatives of the inhabitants of the south were present. Two clusters of life were concentrated in the southern and northern parts of the planet.

"There aren't many of us left," a female figure began the speech.

"Who is it?" Iva asked a guard standing next to her.

"It's Wapa, our savior, our medium, our scientist."

"Our only hope of rescue are the 'genti' corridors. We have to leave the planet within a few Martian decades," Wapa explained to them.

"How long is it?" Iva asked again.

"Four rotations of Mars around its axis."

"So, we don't have much time," Iva sent the info to Geo.

"Our Martian technology doesn't allow us to travel in space. Admittedly, we can and have the ability to come to the surface of our planet," she made a spectacular pause to continue in a dramatic voice, "but what for? There are no living conditions there. This is also where our survival possibilities end. Look," she turned to Geo and Iva.

She switched on an ionic thought liberator, and a mock-up of the system they lived in appeared. They both immediately understood that the Martians had no choice but to evacuate from this planet. A corridor of liquid magma was forming in the core of Mars, which, making its way to the surface, would have to break through to their inner ring. It would then spread out in a wide stream, poisoning the remnants of the atmosphere closed in their corridors. While corridors weaved around the planet, life was possible only at the north and south poles of Mars. Only there, the rock-free vault reached several dozen kilometers. Their scientists calculated that the amount of magma that flowed in the corridors would destroy the entire supporting system of the planet's inner layer and cut off the south from the north, and at its narrowest point it could penetrate into the upper layers of Mars. This would disrupt the entire system of gas exchange between the two poles, which was the basis for generating and purifying the atmosphere they breathed. A magma breakthrough outside Mars and the eruption of gases would end their world.

The terrifying vision of a catastrophe caused by a lack of air after the outer atmosphere of Mars burst into their corridors appeared to them. "Nobody will survive then," she finished her short presentation.

Geo was moving confidently towards the platform. When he stopped next to Wapa, he spread his hands up and spoke:

"How long will it take for the inhabitants of the north to travel to one of the corridors on your side?" he asked with concern, thinking about the size of Mars. His words were translated immediately.

"Using our worms, about one decade," said a hitherto silent representative of the Supreme Council of Scholars.

"Are there more corridors?" He asked looking at Iva, not at the silhouette of Wapa standing next to him. It was as if Geo had been paralyzing her with his figure alone. She couldn't understand how a man in the leadership hierarchy could be higher than a woman.

"We don't know," Iva replied, feeling that an answer was expected from her.

It was normal on Mars. Women ruled there, they were able to better adapt their bodies to the conditions prevailing inside Mars and thanks to them their species survived. And it was not about some scientific wisdom, but about the mere possibility of bearing children.

"Can you imagine the flattened bodies of pregnant women?" Geo's thought reached her.

She couldn't. She had never been pregnant and wouldn't give birth to her, their baby in the traditional Martian way - but she suppressed that thought in the depths of her consciousness so that Geo couldn't know it.

The visor activated again and the two caps of the gates appeared to all present. How different, however, in its form and structure.

One of the gate caps was the Earth direction. It flashed blue light and rippled with a sea shade of turquoise. Its main motif was the chemical formula of water, but not the one written in the periodic table, but one broken into atomic bonds that flowed down from top to bottom imitating rippling.

"We will check the second one right away," Iva announced to the Martian Council.

This cap was characterized by a different form of existence. It didn't flash, wave or represent any chemical or graphic symbols, it only absorbed the light. It was strange and a little scary at the same time. You could see how the red light of Martian lamps was absorbed into the cap. When Geo got too close to her, his greenish glow seemed to break away from his figure to flow into the cap. A thread-thin beam of light from his silhouette turned towards the cap and disappeared in it. This optical illusion was ordered by the High Council of the Hope Clan.

"I'm not so sure about that," Geo sent them his doubts.

At the same time, in a cautious voice he turned to Iva:

"I have an assurance from the Green Dwarf that this corridor is safe for Martians and that they can start evacuating to this planet."

"What is this planet?"

"A young planet that is inhabited by extraordinary creatures, but the evolution has never been able to develop there life forms of intelligent beings like those of Hope or earthly beings. It is a planet of light and shadow with a clean atmosphere and undeveloped with any unnatural structures. Once, hundreds of thousands of years ago, the Creators of Genti resided there for a short time."

"How will we do it?" Iva asked.

Her worried voice didn't go unnoticed by the Martians.

"What's going on?" asked the Senior Lady of the Council. "Will we evacuate to Earth where the Martian afterglowers escaped?" she asked Iva. Unfortunately, that wouldn't be desirable. Earth civilization on the level that exists now would cause your destruction. They would treat you as alien invaders who need to be destroyed," replied Iva.

"Then let us introduce our situation to the earthlings and ask for permission to come."

"I'm afraid it wouldn't do any good, and besides, how are we supposed to do it without revealing ourselves and the information we're hiding from them. There is no time for that anyway. It would take too long and you must evacuate now."

"Give the signal for evacuation immediately. Everyone from the North Pole is to start coming here," Geo chimed in, looking at the black poodle huddling against his leg.

As if to confirm these words, the floor trembled beneath them, and the fragments of red Martian rock began to fall down on them. Sulfur-smelling smoke slowly emerged from the side crevices of the cavern in narrow red streaks. The warning tones of the Martian alarm rang out from all levels of their hall.

"Start the evacuation. Give the order for everyone to start moving towards the luminous cap," that's what Geo called their way to a new life.

The Martian security guard efficiently formed a row of residents consisting only of women and children. All, keeping admirable order, stood in front of the arriving worms. The crowd of male members of the Marian families lined up according to the classification they had trained for many generations. Not for the first time in their history, the lives of them and their relatives depended on efficient evacuation from endangered places. Sometimes it was an earthquake caused by the impact of a large object on the surface of Mars, and other times a magma leak into the caves and chambers of their underground world from which poisonous vapors and gas penetrated into the places they inhabited.

The guards efficiently chose individuals qualified for evacuation from the male crowd and introduced one representative of the male Martian population of their species to the line beside every tenth woman or child.

"It's for the safety of all of them," Iva thought.

She was so busy with the Martians that she overlooked Geo's actions. She didn't see Geo approach the Cap and, putting the dog under his arm, enter the luminous rim of the space-time corridor leading to an unknown planet.

"I'll send the dog back when it's safe," she still managed to pick up his thought.

A long unit of Martian time passed in which the cavern was filling up with more and more Martians. The worms transported frightened and confused inhabitants of Mars to the grotto again and again. Only the shocks, repeated in ever shorter periodic intervals, made them realize that the situation was serious. There was, however, no panic, no pushing or trying to get closer to the Cap.

Wapa's loud announcements regarding the beginning of the evacuation made everyone realize that this was not an exercise but a fight for life.

"When will we go in?" only this question was directed to Iva, who stood in front of the luminous cap and waited for the signal from Geo. "I'm not picking up anything. What happened? Maybe He can't go back from there. The Green Dwarf said that if the planet is not inhabited, you may not come back from it. Why did He take the dog?" she wondered.

Suddenly, with a loud barking, the black poodle jumped out of the cap. A strange creature flew behind him. It looked like a giant butterfly with four wide wings from which emanated strong light. She felt the contact coming directly from this strange creature.

It was Geo who was sending her the message. This great-butterfly served as a relay of thoughts and images. "Images of the present and the future," she understood it as soon as she saw the gorge and Geo looking at her through that living relay. But the images began to flash, changing their color to the luminous glow of the night illuminations. It was the influence of a cold dwarf star and nearby moons affecting the atmosphere, something like the Earth's auroras.

"You can't have anything that has any metal in its structure here. No metals, it's life threatening," Geo's message reached her.

She immediately conveyed it to the Senior Lady of the Martian Council. Although the inhabitants of Mars didn't take anything larger with them, almost everyone wore some ornaments. Iva wasn't sure if some of them weren't made of metals, especially since there were probably no other minerals inside Mars. People started to get rid of various things by throwing them to the wall of the cave.

Geo's long absence bothered her. Now she had to act on her own without his support and the power he had. Motioning the law-enforcement Martians standing next to her, she gave the signal to evacuate. She wasn't sure of the words of Geo which tried to convince her:

"You are to open the Cap and interact with it with your afterglow awareness. Then material Martians will be able to move down the Genti corridor. On the other side, I will open the way for them to the surface of their new planet. Begin the evacuation," Geo's message came to her.

"Now you are going inside," Iva announced in a loud voice, casting anxious glances at the gathering Martians.

The evacuation began. The Martians, running in two ranks, entered the Cap.

"Do you know what awaits them there?" the Senior Lady of the Family asked, having stood next to Iva.

"No, I don't know. But I know that if they don't do it, they will die here for sure."

The entire evacuation was visible on the large screen which showed the worms still arriving with newcomers from the other hemisphere. It was much worse in the other hemisphere. According to the Martians, not all of them would be able to get there, because some of the corridors were blocked, and some of the Martians, fearing going into the unfamiliar world, stayed in their place, hoping to survive.

Within a short time, most of the Martians entered through the gate of light. They realized that their only hope of rescue was crossing to the other side of the unknown world. Suddenly, the Cap closed, and several Martians who ran into it, bounced off its wall, bumping into the next evacuating women waiting for their turn.

Iva lost contact with Geo.

The great-butterfly next to her went out like a broken flashlight and lay, looking at the cap as if it had been a way to salvation. It folded its wings, nestled its tentacled head against its left wing, and froze.

"This is probably the essence of these journeys," I managed to flash my mind towards Iva when I landed on the other side of the corridor in no time. Here I crossed the borders to this unknown world without fear. Standing on the other side, I was surprised to find that the ground on which I stood, glowed with pulsating light, but its structure was as hard as our earthly rocks. I looked around with my head up.

I saw the blue sky and two fiery stars that were close to each other - when it comes to the plane on which they could be seen, but in fact they must have been separated by a large distance from each other, because it seemed to me that one of them was a real giant, and only because of its distance from the luminous planet was as big to my eyes as that smaller sun shining intense warm light towards me. An atmosphere was like that on Earth, I could be calm about that. I already knew from the Green Dwarf that all genti corridors were connected only with those planets that had the same atmospheric composition as that on Hope.

There, however, nothing was the same as on Earth and on my planet. The sky was blue, but on its eastern side, high in the atmosphere, were visible luminous streaks of a faint orange color, which moved across the sky like wind-blown smoke. I didn't feel any gust so I didn't know if these streaks were moved by the wind or they were a phenomenon created due to completely different causes.

A wall of glowing green standing near me lured me in that direction with its luminous greenish glow, every now and then changing its shade from intense fresh green to the color of a rotten green apple that fell from the earth's apple tree. I was in a deep and wide ravine of a dry river, the remnants of which were visible at its bottom. The old river carved a huge ditch in this rock structure, almost the same as I saw on my school trip to a gorge.

I was standing on a rock ledge suspended several dozen meters from the bottom of this trough, and above me stretched a vertical rock disappearing somewhere in a luminous green, so high that it seemed to touch the bluish sky.

"There will be a problem," I sent a message to Iva, expecting an immediate response. Not hearing her awareness in myself, I turned towards the Cap gate from which I had just came. It glowed the same red and had the same symbolism as the cap on our Hope moon - it was a corridor to Mars, but there was no other Gate next to it, but a pentagram.

You could see some drawings shimmering with a red color, visible on its rock surface, or rather on some material screen floating in front of the rock, because the screen was a few centimeters away from it.

I started with the bottom right corner in which all the information on Hope was exposed. After touching its surface with a finger, I saw the huge, bright, multicolored figure of the great-butterfly. Its colorful abdomen seemed to call my gaze. When it rested on it, it immediately unfolded its four colored wings and began to flutter. From this movement a luminous thread was formed, running to the next cap symbol and linking the Luminous Planet with Mars. This thread went further, symbolizing the connection between our two worlds. When I realized this, the great-butterfly as if knowing it, spread its wings and flew into the cap. It looked like a primitive screening of a demonstrative movie for those who couldn't think like the cap builders.

I was to let the butterfly into the corridor, and it would keep me in touch with Iva. "Who leaves such information and where is this great-butterfly?" I thought. Amazed, I looked around, searching for this strange insect, because its sight reminded me it.

Led by some hunter's instinct, I turned my head towards the glowing green brush and then I heard it. A cascade of sounds flooded me with its strange singing tones emitted by these creatures. I knew it was the flutter of the great-butterfly's wings that was heard above my head. Near me, a few of them quietly flapped their wings, devoting themselves to some dance known only to them.

I slowly raised my hand, fearing that if I had done it violently, they would have run away but they didn't pay any attention to me.

Apparently, they didn't recognize any threat in me. I had to spread the fingers of both hands wide to grasp one of them by the yellowish wide body visible just behind the wings. The great-butterfly reacted with a quick movement of its wings. It folded them into a funny roll, forming two cylinders shimmering with dark green colors, tightly adjacent to its body. The rest, spreading their wings, immediately fled to the upper layers of the brush. Holding it in my hand carefully so as not to hurt it, I put my hand in the Cap and opened my palm.

"We are ready to evacuate," I heard Iva's voice in my head.

"Wait for my sign," I replied. Looking down, I wondered how so many Martians would descend to the bottom of the gorge. I didn't see any stairs or any other way to bring them down the canyon. I looked at the screen again. It changed color and pulsed intensely, so without hesitation I touched its bottom again. A grid of greenish rungs got unfolded in it, leading from the foot of the cap to the opposite bottom of the ravine. Only the flashing structure of this descent and the white dot at the beginning of this construction seemed to convince me that this was not the end of the transmission. When I stopped my eyesight on the screen, the chemical symbols of all the elements on this planet were displayed instantly. The knowledge acquired from the Green Dwarf made me realize that there were no metals known on Earth and the planet of the Three Suns there. It was such a convincing sight that I sent the impulse to Iva without thinking:

"No metal objects can be taken to this planet. Here, the life and structure of nature don't tolerate metals."

"I understood, hurry up the ceiling is starting to collapse," Iva sent the urgent signal. She feared for the Martians, for herself.

There, the forces of nature didn't give them much time to evacuate and Iva was afraid that not all of them would manage to move to the new planet.

Meanwhile, under the influence of my movements on the pentagram, the reconstruction of the image into reality began on the slope of the canyon, and the mesh of the structure, unfolding, fell to the very bottom of the ravine. It leaned softly against its floor and began to stiffen from the bottom up, turning into stairs with handrails. The matter from the ground in a spiral motion entwined the structures of the stairs, climbing upwards and creating a greenish structure of the local tree stand, dominant wherever my gaze rested.

"Bring them here," I sent the signal.

After a while, a group of frightened Martians appeared on the landing. I put the first young Martian at the entrance to the ravine.

"You are to direct everyone to the stairs, let them go down and make room for the next ones," I gave him the order and started to walk downstairs, leading the women and the children behind me.

When we reached the bottom, there was a clear taste of the atmosphere of this planet a little more infused with a scent unknown to me. The air was saturated with something that strengthened us. You could see the haggard and maladjusted to the gravitational pull of this planet Martian bodies gain vigor and vitality. There, at home, they had been able to barely tear themselves away from the floor, and here the children, with joy as well as curiosity of new things only given to them, jumped up and moved quickly across the area. Amazed parents tried in vain to calm their offspring. Not being able to understand this phenomenon themselves, they raised their heads and looked anxiously at the starry sky. This was the first such fundamental difference they noticed on this planet. In their place, they couldn't see the sky, only the red rocky vault and the sparks caused by the magnetism of Mars. Nothing but the strange and infused with the smell of sulfur atmosphere in which they had lived so far.

"Water, where is the water?" came the cry of thirsty Martians.

"I had no idea where the water might have been, but intuitively I knew it was there. Water, air and soil were friendly to people and Martians.

A dozen or so young Martians stood beside me. Out of this group, I picked out the three least scared.

"Select a scientist and a few brave ones to join the group and go on a scout. Go forward in this ravine and seek water."

They walked very lightly, and although they had some trouble maintaining an upright posture, they boldly went on the reconnaissance in search of a life-giving drink.

"The gorge is very wide here, and its steep rocky side walls are covered with something like our earthly vines," I thought, looking at the green vegetation. However, my gaze was riveted by the multitude of large great-butterflies hanging on its slopes. I looked at the stairs. The dense crowd of Martians glided uninterruptedly down the ravine, and the cap kept spitting out more of them. The evacuation was well organized and there were no signs of panic or scuffle. "That's already a few thousands," I thought, looking at the great group of Martians helplessly crowding in one place.

"And what's next?" I wondered for a moment. "After all, they have no useful items for life or for getting food and drink." But, as is the case with the human species, Martian children solved this burning issue of eating and drinking. A few unruly kids, fascinated by the unknown world, with curiosity and carelessness given only to those who don't think too much about what they do, began to climb the nearby rocks. Thick and heavily twisted branches of the herbaceous plant were used by them for climbing. They only stopped when the leg of one of them came across a thinner branch of this greenish plant, which, unable to withstand the pressure, broke, and a white liquid began to flow out of it with a strong stream. Immediately several great-butterflies moved in this direction. They sat down at that spouting fountain and began to eat its juice. One of the boys, standing quite far away from the nearest great-butterfly, broke the thin branch sticking out of the whole tangle with his hands, and when the same white liquid emerged from it, interested, he dipped his finger in it and licked the white liquid at the tip of his fingertip. He smacked, grasped the end of a twig happily, brought it to his mouth, and began to drink it like water from a garden hose. Having satiated his thirst and hunger, he screamed loudly:

"Good! How good it is."

His mother, frightened by his gesture, tore him away abruptly from the plant substance.

"Leave it!" she screamed, "It can be poisonous."

"I guess it isn't," I thought about the Green Dwarf. "If that was the case, I would probably know about it."

The little boy sat down on the ground and cried. The screams of the women watching the great-butterflies eat distracted me from the flow of Martians continually descending to the bottom of the gorge. One of the great-butterflies spread its wings wide and slowly began to set them in motion. However, not to fly away, but to give them its message.

It was telepathy - the same that I had gotten from that great-butterfly I had sent to Iva.

Its message was a thought, pure awareness transmitted intuitively and expressionlessly. It consisted of an image that opened to them in the form of a hologram arranged on its wings.

Each slow movement showed a different picture. An image of something that once had lived and ruled on this planet. However, these were not green men from the vision of an Earth UFO, but figures with a human silhouette, whose only thing that differed from the Martians were wings. The image, however, was so indistinct that it is not known whether they grew out of their bodies or were an artificial creation.

You looked at these images like at freeze-frames in an old terrestrial photoplasticon, where at the touch of a button the frame in the window you looked at was changed.

The first image was probably a figure of a former inhabitant of this planet. The second swipe and you saw a leaning figure drinking the white liquid from a broken branch. The third swipe was a cascade of water luminous stream falling down from a mountainous terrain to the very bottom of a great reservoir. The fourth strike of the wings was a blurred image of misshapen figures. The great-butterfly froze, and after a while it curled its wings and got motionless again.

That thought was like a sudden flash: "There must be some relationship between what appears on its wings and the thoughts of the Martians standing before it. It reacts to thoughts that are directed towards it. When they are consensual, the answer is shown to them, and when they are not, it is unable to convey to them the messages that are coded in its brain by those who wanted their memory not to perish. Or maybe they still live here," the apprehension tugged at me.

"No, it's possible, they would be here already," I thought. The evacuation had already lasted several hours, and someone with such an advanced telepathic technique would have already known about it. The news of the vision on the wings of the great-butterflies spread quickly among the Martians. There were more and more people who wanted to try the white liquid. The news that the boy was feeling well after eating, didn't, however, convince everyone to consume the juice from these strange plants.

Geo decided to go back to the Cap in the hope of meeting Iva.

Their task was already done, the rest belonged to the Council of Martians and their citizens, they should have taken care of discovering all the secrets of this planet and worried about how to provide the Martians with basic living conditions. But it was not easy, none of them knew this planet. It was so different from what was familiar to them that they couldn't switch to a different perception of the world. Geo moved briskly towards the ledge, intending to quickly return to Mars.

When he got there, he stopped at the rock screen. He intuitively sensed that all the answers were encoded in his memory.

"Iva, I'm coming back, stop the evacuation," he sent the thought to her. He was not sure if it was possible to travel both ways at the same time, he preferred not to risk the Martians' lives, he knew thanks to some strange conviction that he was in no danger.

"You can now enter the corridor," he received the signal from her. He instructed a young man standing next to him, how to use the screen and the great-butterflies. Then he quickly entered the cap. Iva was waiting for him with a black poodle lying at her feet.

"The great-butterfly on this side will replace Iva and will open the Cap until everyone evacuates," Wap informed.

"The Council of Elders asks if they can transport the worms," she replied with the question.

"Sure, they can, but what for?" he replied irritated. "There is a completely different ecosystem out there, and worms are not a species found on this planet. There may be more trouble adjusting them to the life there. However, let them decide for themselves," he concluded.

"We come back, we are no longer needed by them," he turned to Iva. "The cap will close by itself when magma floods all the corridors.

"How many more residents will have time to evacuate?" he asked Wap.

"Certainly not all of them. Some of them refused and don't want to leave their home. They fear the unknown world," she replied, looking at Geo with evident reverence.

"What's it like there?" Finally, one of the Council of Elders members who decided to stay dared to ask.

"Beautiful, but different. Everything you, Martians need to live is there, and maybe even more, because spiritual food is not alien to the inhabitants of this planet."

The entire vault shook again and small rock fragments fell down, injuring many people crowding in front of the cap.

They stood before the red symbols of Mars, knowing that none of the surviving Martian creatures would be able to leave this planet for several hundred thousand years.

"Of course, if they survive," Iva burst into his thought. "How will we return?"

"The Martian corridors are all blocked," Iva worried, thinking about which way they would return. She was afraid they would be stuck there or in the non-existence.

Geo sensed her unease and rushed to explain.

"I have an information from the Green Dwarf. In our corridors there are branches connecting roads somewhere in space so that you can travel between planets just like in our terrestrial subway stations."

"I know what a subway is," Iva replied.

"So, lead us.

Take us to our corridor," Geo demanded. "We have to go back; you can do it on your own. We will try to visit you soon."

They jumped into the worm and with two Martian coachmen, they moved towards the Hope cap. The road was no longer as smooth as when they had been going in the opposite direction. The bug maneuvered, constantly slowed down, or took sharp turns. When one of the Martian coachmen finally stopped, he said in their direction:

"Run! Quickly, you don't have much time."

The bug's nose opened and they immediately felt the stench of gases, and the sight that appeared to them didn't make them optimistic.

A red cloud of dust filled the entire chamber, limiting the view to a few meters. When they got outside, the bug immediately set off on its return journey.

"Lead us," Iva called to the dog.

Loud barking and the black wagging tail indicated them the direction. Following the loud barking, covering our mouth and nose with our hands, they slowly entered the great cloud of dust. After a while, the Cap loomed in front of them, so without thinking any longer, they went through its gate without fear.

They entered the corridor. Crossing the circle of the cap turned them into Hope figures. Iva swam with thoughts together with Geo as if they had been holding hands. She knew that He knew more than her, for he had the knowledge of the Green Dwarf, which for incomprehensible reasons was unavailable to her. She trusted him immensely, they were one, after all, so she felt his, their genti, which he used to find the right way to return.

This time the path leading to Hope wasn't easy. After a while they found themselves in front of the Gate with unknown symbolism. "We've entered a different corridor," Geo said.

"I don't feel anything, I don't receive any impulse from the Hopers," confirmed Iva. "Let's get in. We can't be stuck here, nor can we go back to Mars. They must have transported us to the different cap."

"Probably yes, for the Martians it doesn't matter what cap it is. How could they know it was a significant difference for us."

"We're going in," said Iva and went first. The bright glare of blue lightning blinded her sight. She looked at Geo. He was standing next to her, shading his eyes with his hand.

"Where are we?" she asked.

"I don't know - it's one of those planets about which nothing is known in the history of your Hall of Tradition."

They stood on a large rock platform, and below them stretched out a valley. And it wouldn't be surprising if it weren't for the colors of large trees and lush vegetation. Everything in front of them was of a color of a pale blue glow flashing to the rhythm of zigzag discharges crossing the sky. Each of these lightning bolts, hitting some point in the valley, produced a circle at the point of impact that quickly spread into a cascade of fluorescent reflections imitating strange geometric images. Figures, lines and wavy sine waves familiar to them, as well as images with an unknown spatial structure. It was a peculiar dance of strange colors moving to the rhythm of thunder echoing from the rocks below them.

"What is it for?" Geo muttered.

"I don't know and I don't want to know for now," added Iva after a while. "We have to go back."

"Yes, you are right, but how will we find the way to the correct corridor," Geo asked, looking at Iva. She was more experienced as a Hoper, and although she didn't have all the knowledge Geo had acquired from the Green Dwarf, she had the gift which was the experience in traveling through a space-time corridor.

"Some Hoper was already here," Geo said, more to himself than to Iva. "I know that, I feel an impulse, some information thread. It could be one of the Hopers who found themselves in the non-existence and landed on this planet. We will come back following this trace."

"Sit down, rest, I'll try to find something," Iva asked. "It will only take a moment."

"No, we can't, the longer we stay here, the harder it will be to leave. Look what's going on down there," Geo said, pointing to the right side of the valley.

Iva looked and got amazed. The swirling circle of blue fluorescent light was approaching rapidly the place below them. The lightning striking it seemed to direct this whole mechanism in a remarkably logical and coordinated manner. It was as if a flock of light had been driven at them with some blows of a whip.

"You're right, let's get out of here," she exclaimed in a slightly frightened voice. Without thinking, they got inside the cap.

They entered the luminous corridor fearlessly, and immediately found themselves in a bifurcation twisted into a shape of an afterglow DNA spiral.

Geo thought hard, trying to imagine the path connecting this planet to the corridor leading to Hope. A clear impulse from Hope allowed him to find a solution. "It's that simple," he flashed the thought to Iva. "Think of a place we've been before, of our beginning on the Hope moon."

Iva knew what this place was. A wide circular room with a series of corridors leading to different places in the universe. It was the beginning and end of all corridors and, as they understood, the beginning and end of each journey in the Genti corridors.

Their instant exchange of thoughts resulted in the decision to return to Hope the same way they had come here.

"We have to report back to the Council, and then return to Earth," he directed to her his desire to return to the planet of his youth. She felt his concern and fear that there would not be enough time on Earth to see her father and people close to him. He didn't know how much time had passed on Earth. Time there in the universe is a relative term depending on who you are and where you are. It apparently didn't exist, wasn't felt by Hope figures. Only the material Hopers counted the days and years, longing for the time when they would be able to assume the fleeting, Hope silhouettes.

This time Geo clearly and without hesitation directed his consciousness towards the bifurcation of their lunar station. He knew what way he had to go. The impulse from the Green Dwarf was directing him to the correct path of the corridor. He realized now that the corridors had forks, relay stations, and waiting rooms. He didn't understand how it worked but he relied entirely on the guidance he received from the Green Dwarf. It didn't take long for them to return, and soon they were on the Hope moon. Directly in front of them, there was a corridor, through which they had already gotten to the Great Hall of Tradition.

Chapter VII

The Casket

The Great Hall of Tradition was filled to the last seat.

"So many Hopers have come here for us," Geo thought. "All the material workers of the moon waited for our return."

Holding his hand, Iva walked along the crowd of material Hopers that parted in front of them.

The Hall of Tradition greeted them with thunderous applause - the material people applauded, and their modern Hopers, having focused their appreciation for their achievements, sent them a single commendatory impulse of approval accumulated by the dome of the Hall. Geo and Iva simultaneously directed their consciousness on the map of the universe, looking on it for Mars and a new planet, which now became home to its inhabitants. The white thread that ran from Mars to the distant stellar galaxy designated as the Planet of the Butterflies confirmed their victory. It opened a new path for communication with another homo sapiens living somewhere in the universe.

"They are Us, we have the same DNA," roared in the hall.

The thread connecting the new planet to Mars pulsed on the great table of the universe.

"This is a sign of a new settlement, of a new era of Martian civilization," I received a message from Iva. "It won't be easy for them; they can't use our genti's corridor. As you can see, we have no connection with this planet," Iva noticed.

"We don't have it now, but it doesn't mean we won't be able to have it in the future," I replied.

"I know, the Green Dwarf," she correctly diagnosed my guess.

On Hope - formerly known as the Planet of the Three Suns, this name was still sometimes used by very old afterglowers - a temporary Council of Unity was established to unite all Hopers and their material inhabitants for new calls and give meaning to their continued existence.

"Opening new corridors and using timelines is getting to know yourself from different dimensions of this time. Those from the distant future and perhaps ourselves from the past. Time in the universe does not always passes at the same pace. Planets, moons, and stars share non-linear relationships, which means that time goes by differently on each planet, and its flow cannot be compared to the passage of time on Earth or Hope.

We have our space-time corridors and Hope timelines which we can use. However, there is a danger that not only we can use them, but also other life forms that are at a sufficiently high degree of evolution," Iva sent the message to all the Hope Clans.

When they returned to Hope the same way, they had gotten here, an excellent group of Hopers from all Clans of the planet awaited them.

"The universe is full of Hopers at different stages of evolution," Geo thundered with his thought as he sat in the place of honor among the fourteen permanent members of the Great Council of Unity - representatives of all the Hope Domes.

"I believe it was from Hope - Planet of the Three Suns that life spread throughout the universe. Now it is only up to you and us, it depends on whether we want to get to know other worlds. Our worlds," he added.

"And that is the purpose for which it was worth becoming a Hoper. Our and your goal is to save and help another homo sapiens. Those who need it and will ask for such help. And we'll start with my father's planet, and although he was not a Hoper, I carry his genes. It was for him that my mother decided to sacrifice her longevity and did what seemed impossible, created me - a new species of a Hoper," he finished his speech with the earthly custom, standing up and raising his hand in a gesture of victory.

The dome above them got covered with a blue color, and almost everyone in attendance approved his message. The Great Conference of Hopers ended. Slowly, everyone was going back to their daily activities. "What am I supposed to do now?" Geo asked Iva.

But Iva was busy transferring to the memory of the Great Hall of Tradition the new memories they had acquired; about everything they had experienced on Mars and on the way back.

Having received his impulse, she turned in his direction and looked at him. She quickly created an intimate corner for him in a remote part of the Hall, and in the center, she placed a large white sofa.

"Rest while I finish mine, our transmission, and then I will take care of you."

She looked at him, trying to go deeper into his consciousness. For a moment she wondered whether to postpone the IT transfer to their Central Database. Geo looked at Iva again.

"Go, I'll wait for you here." With a gesture of his hand, he encouraged her to continue the transmission that she had just started.

He fell onto the sofa, turned off and fell into a reverie.

"Her cat's eyes are looking at me with some elusive delicacy, trying to break into my head," he thought.

What I intended, why I didn't let her in, why I wrapped myself with a shield protecting my thoughts, she was worried due to the lack of communication that had lasted throughout my stay on this strange planet. "I know, I know that You know more than I do about Hope, but I'm worried about you, I want to protect you, and at the same time I miss our open minds, and what I miss most is love, that physical one, this hot closeness of our bodies united by one desire."

He remembered her perfect breasts modeled after the pictures of girls on the covers of colorful magazines moving to the rhythm of the worms' mad ride.

Iva's white skin was without any blemish. Covered with a light fluff on her shoulders, it seemed not to take part in the eternal struggle with the passing time. She was all the time in the period of demonic bloom, in the era of luring him with her perfection, promising to give him whatever he wanted.

"It's time to go back to Earth," he thought, sending to Iva his memory of the night spent with her in the house by the sea. He couldn't notice that she blushed with joy, but he read her thought.

"... so, Geo and I are the unity of undisturbed perfection, of striving to unite in this earthly physical love, where I can be for him what he wants me to be."

He noticed that her desires were dangerously evolving towards becoming an Earthling.

"Were these earthly desires the cause of renunciation of the Spirit Being which they were on the planet of the Three Suns?" Geo thought of his mother.

Having ended the transmission, Iva walked over to Geo, sat down next to him, and took his hand simply, softly and submissively, out of the need of the moment and the longing for the warmth of his body.

"Now we can come back, there's nothing here for us, they will have to handle it themselves," he sent his thought to her. "Let's go back, Iva," said Geo, looking at the Hope figures swirling in front of him.

"Not yet," she whispered, turning to Geo. "Important things are happening on Hope. The Hopers unite into the great Hope Clan with a common purpose you discovered for them."

"Okay, but don't let it last too long. I miss the human form," added Geo, only to realize after a while that he might have made Iva upset by this statement. Iva didn't miss the Earth, and her stays there had always been associated with a danger to her life and health.

A smile lit up her face. "He worries about me," she thought as they went through the gate of the Hope moon.

"Come on, Iva, I can't wait to get my carnality," he directed his thought to her.

Iva opened the casket and they were back in the small house on the beach. The couch they landed on was the place they had moved from to Hope. The sight of the kitchen and the familiar furniture reminded him that here on Earth, applied different rules.

"I'm hungry," she said, shaping her voice into a whisper so exciting that Geo had no doubts what hunger she meant.

"Are you hungry for me?"

"For you too, but first I would like to eat something, but not burnt scrambled eggs," she added smiling.

In the distance, they heard the dog barking.

Geo looked worried. Seeing this, Iva quickly guessed his intentions.

"Alright, the food can wait," she said, getting up and, grabbing his hand, she dragged him up the stairs to the bedroom.

Saturated with earthly love and good food, which they ate in a cozy restaurant located near their house, they got into the car and went to visit Geo's father.

Their sense of time was typical of people on planet Earth. They already knew that two weeks had passed since their disappearance. Peter, however, felt younger, stronger and physically fit. "Is it the impact of travel to Hope?" he wondered.

Iva drove to Norbert's house confidently and calmly, and when they found themselves in Geo's father's cozy backyard, they knew that something bad had happened.

"You are sick?" He asked looking at his worried face.

"No, but I had a visit and your mother's grave was profaned shortly afterwards."

"Tell me," Geo asked.

"A week ago, two men and one woman came to see me. They pretended to be your friends, so I let them in. When they were sitting and telling me that you had been kidnapped by some unknown people, I almost believed them, and only after they mentioned your name, Iva," he turned his head towards her, looking at her with eyes expressing deep concern, "I understood that they were not earthlings, but some strangers from Hope. Nobody on Earth knew what your Hope name is except the three of us and your mother."

"It was, however, too late, because before that I told them where your mother's grave is, and after they had gone away, guided by some hunch, I went to the cemetery the next day. There, with horror, I saw the disturbed earth on HER grave. Two days later, having obtained permission, I dug up the grave. The eternity-box was open. The police is looking for these people. I recorded their entrance to the property with a camera. However, I'm not under a delusion, because I know that the police won't find them. What's happening? Maybe you can tell me what this is all about."

"About the casket," I replied without hesitation. Someone from Hope or whoever else wants to own it."

"Strange," Iva said. "Everyone from Hope has a casket, otherwise they wouldn't be able to transport themselves to the Earth. It has to be something else or someone else."

"And how it was with me? You said the Hopers wanted my casket when you were with me at my mother's grave for the first time."

"Back then it was about you and the fact that after your mother's death, the casket had no owner."

"I don't understand."

"I do. Then they could take your mom's box and use it. Now that you have it, no one can take it from you as long as you live. She is still with you, in fact in you."

"Yes, indeed and what happens to a casket when someone dies on Earth and there is no second Hoper to inherit it - just like in case of my mother."

"It was a special case, because every Hoper has their genti, and if they are both on Earth and die in one second, for example in a car accident, only then such a thing is possible, but for others it is a lifeless object of everyday use. After all, you know that it is assigned to one Hoper and only such a Hoper can benefit from it."

A flash of understanding lit my thoughts.

"Iva," I whispered in horror.

Her large pupils dilated more than usual.

"Impossible, no one has thought about it before," she sent me the signal of understanding. "Forgotten knowledge and skills, or deliberate actions by an outsider," she added in her already controlled voice.

"But who and from where?" we thought about it at the same time.

"Don't worry, dad, I have contact with my mother, such spiritual, so when I find out what's what, I'll let you know."

We said goodbye and left quickly.

Sitting in our house, we started discussions about why someone could care about the eternity-box and the remains of the Hoper there.

"They were just looking for a casket," said Iva confidently.

"Who was looking for?" I asked unnecessarily, knowing that Iva didn't know it anyway.

"Corridors. Someone used the corridors and wants to penetrate to Hope," Iva said it in a calm and very serious tone.

"It would mean an alien invasion of Earth."

"Not necessarily. There are Caps on Earth, but none of the Hopers knows where, just as no one knows from which place on Hope one can transport oneself to Earth. We know, and apart from us, Tora."

"Tora has her own casket and doesn't have to use any other way. It is probably someone unknown, or those who pose a threat to us.

We have to check if there is a possibility of getting to the Earth through the genti corridor. This could mean that the Earth has been visited by some foreign civilization, not necessarily peaceful towards us. Or alien afterglowers want to get to Hope. But why?" he thought intensely.

"Maybe they are some stray phantoms wandering through the corridors without memories, or they only have partial memories of Earth and the planet of the Three Suns. But where did they get the memories of both, you and your father from?"

Iva had no idea how close she was to discovering who the strange afterglowers were, so she decided that they would go to Earth through the genti corridor. Maybe they would find some information thread that would show them the way.

"Or maybe it was Hopers?" she added.

"Iva, it is certainly not them. I would sense it if it was one of the Hopers. Even the Green Dwarf and its knowledge don't give me any clue related to that."

"Is this a threat to Hope?" He pondered for a moment, looking at Iva.

"It can be a huge threat to our intangible world. We have no weapons or other means of defense against physical attack from outside. Our material people live on the moon and there are not enough of them."

Only now did a strong signal from Hope reach our genti.

"We received the signal from your genti. Investigate the matter on Earth. Tora has found a corridor coming out of Earth. Its cap is in an Aztec pyramid, but she doesn't know its exact location."

"We won't look for it, because it may take too long, we better transport ourselves to the Hope Moon, to the Hall of Tradition, and from there we will return to Earth without the casket."

"Will you be able to find this corridor if these symbols are not on our star map?"

"Now they are not there, but I know from the Green Dwarf that it is enough to modify the map image accordingly. They didn't know the temporal four-dimensional picture, so we have to search using a more primitive way, like that used by the inhabitants of the Three Suns centuries ago."

It took some time for them to return to the Hope Moon. They must have obliterated all traces behind them here on Earth. The detective and passion for writing crime fiction came back to Geo.

"We have to," he tried to convince Iva. "We should disappear from here as naturally as possible, announcing to all and sundry that we are going on a tourist trip to Hawaii," he added, lest she think that somewhere in space. Iva gave the impulse to Tora.

In the Hall of Tradition in which they found themselves there was already prepared a holographic image of the star map in the oldest version they could recreate. It was so incomprehensible to everyone that, staring at it, they couldn't even find their own planet.

But Geo knew perfectly well what was what. It reminded him of images from SF movies where future star wars heroes traveled through space.

"That blue dot in the corner of the map, somewhere on the fringes of the universe, is our planetary system," he explained to all the Hopers. After zooming in on the image, the familiar Sun and the third planet of the system appeared. The Blue planet.

It didn't take long for material people to visualize it and place its position in the time four-dimensional image of the star map.

"We haven't seen it before, because the existence of life in such a distant part of the universe wasn't taken into account by the local star map specialist."

"How is it possible that you use a casket to travel to Earth, and you don't know what part of the cosmos it is in?"

"It's simple," Tora told him. "The warping of space-time eliminates time and the ability to visualize everything that becomes curved in this space."

He didn't discuss it, he was a layman and knew nothing about it. Anyway, he suspected that they didn't know any more than him and used someone else's knowledge. Someone who had made the Hope Moon and the corridors and all that he was dealing with right now.

And the knowledge coming from the Genti Creators was passed on to them like an instruction 'for a monkey', in the form of drawings and pressing an appropriate button.

This time the thin thread from the Earth went straight to the planet of the Three Suns. The cap had symbols that Geo could easily decipher. Water and the green lungs of the Earth. All this in the chemical bonds of the atom.

"We will find this gate," said Iva.

"We'll go back to Earth through the corridor," added Geo.

"How?" the question came from the room.

"We have a way, but it is not available for other Hopers, only Iva and I can use such corridors," Geo lied. "We will let you know when we come across the trail of intruders."

Along the already known route, they went to the central point of the Hope Moon.

"There must be the corridor to Earth here," said Geo.

They were standing at the end of the corridor. In front of them there was a huge space with a low vault, dotted with a great number of corridors.

"Before, there weren't so many corridors here," Iva shared her observations with Geo. Indeed, there were definitely fewer of them.

"This is probably because the systems of planets, stars and their moons have common non-linear relationships into which our time is involved, so the appearance of this part of the moon that we see now depends on the present and past existing in the world in which we are or from which we came at the moment."

"Yeah, yeah," Geo muttered, looking intensely for the gate with the familiar symbols of water and oxygen.

"Search by blue or green," Iva told him.

They moved swiftly along the gates and corridors that concealed other invisible Caps. "Are they all inhabited?" Geo suspected. "Maybe not, but by following the rules of these corridors, we could probably live on each of the planets that the corridors lead to."

"And if this gate is not here, and it is somewhere in the passing place, how will we find it?" Iva asked.

"By using our awareness," he replied, thinking about what they had had to omit in looking for the corridor leading to the Earth.

"Old, it must be old and primitive," Iva fell into his thought process.

"Yes, you are right. Let's search again. Take my hand and concentrate on the old gate. Now," he added.

They instantly found themselves in one of the distant embranchements of the central point of the genti corridors. A blue cap with cascading water with white bubbles was visible in front of them, encouraging them to take advantage of the opportunity to get to the land of their ancestors.

"This is our land," said Geo.

"Your land for sure, but is it mine?" Iva replied impulsively.

They entered without fear, they knew where it would lead them, but they didn't know exactly where they would find themselves after crossing the inner wall of the second cap. As they stopped in front of the exit from the corridor, Geo ordered Iva to be extremely careful.

"We can encounter unknown intruders right away. They might have seized and secured their way back."

"You are right, but we have no choice," Iva replied.

"I'll go first, and after a while, you will follow me, alright?"

"Alright," she replied. She knew they were safe. Genti would have warned them which Geo kept forgetting about. She didn't undeceive him. "He worries about me," she said happily.

Geo went through the gate with his heart in his mouth. Darkness engulfed him. In this material body of his, he felt lost for a moment. "Damn, what am I supposed to light my way with now?" he thought, angry with himself. But he knew there was nothing he could do about it as he couldn't take a flashlight with him.

"Are you there?" He heard Iva's whisper.

"I am, but it's very dark here. Either it's night, and a starless one, or we are in a grotto."

"There will be light right away," Iva said, and Geo saw a bright circle of glow emanating from the open casket.

"Right, why didn't I think about it myself?" he said to Iva, looking around. "Something is wrong here. The air is as if different, more saturated with moisture. I wonder where we are. Do you have any associations?" he turned to Iva, who was sweeping with the light from the box the space around them.

"No, not yet, but it must be safe, although there is indeed something wrong."

"What?"

"The light of the box, as always, when we want to use its relay station, should open space to Hope. Now it doesn't, which means we can't get out of here with it. It's strange," she ended her dilatation, looking at the face of Geo, who tried unsuccessfully to pierce the darkness they found themselves in. "We keep going, finally we will come out of this darkness somewhere. Illuminating their path, they carefully moved ahead, bearing in mind that they were completely defenseless in their material bodies. A wide, endless walkway of hard basalt rock zigzagged to the right, and when they were back on the straight section of it, they saw a bright spot of light in the distance.

"It doesn't look like we're in the Aztec Pyramid of the Sun," Iva said.

"The exit is nearby," Geo blurted out.

"Yes, it's not far," confirmed Iva.

With each step, the bright spot grew larger and the space around them began to reveal its dark walls. The cave in which they were, was not as huge as they first had thought, and it was certainly inhabited, at least it had been earlier - they thought so when they found traces of a huge fire around which there were scattered white bones.

"What is this? Where are we?" Iva asked in a whisper.

"I don't know - it doesn't look like an old hearth to me. There are fresh traces of soot and smoke everywhere, only the host is missing." Geo was trying to hide his anxiety from Iva.

As they approached the exit, they were surprised by the sight that spread before them. A broad and high vault emerged from the slope of a small mountain, and beneath them there was a wide valley crossed by a pale thread of a lazy river.

"Look at these trees, I think it's the Amazon or some other South American forest," said Iva.

"Certainly not. There are no such trees on Earth, they are too big, and I don't remember any mountains in the middle of the Amazon," Geo denied.

"So where are we?"

"Certainly not in the non-existence but on some planet."

"But what? The signs on the Cap clearly indicated that this was the corridor leading to the Earth."

"To the Earth, yes, but whether ours. From the Green Dwarf, I have information about the time paradox created by the expansion of space during the formation of the universe. They claim that our solar system and that the Earth is a freak arose during the formation of this part of the galaxy. When our solar system, as a result of the expansion of the cosmos, reached its outskirts, space curved and a significant part of it was torn from our system, starting a separate evolution of forming into a twin system, with the difference that on the other side of the universe. So, two twin solar systems arose, each on the opposite side of the cosmos."

"We're going back," he decided, setting off on a return journey along the same corridor that had led them to this strange place. "There's nothing for us here, maybe another time we'll come back here to explore this planet."

"Okay, let's go back," Iva agreed.

An alarm went off at the Homoreproduks Base. "Someone has opened gate no. 2," signaled Repro X 567.

"None of our people, except some afterglowers who got lost in the genti corridors. But getting to the periphery of the universe can't be a coincidence. Send out a patrol and have it check the air around the gate."

The Secret Genti Center in their Corporate Building was so secret that no one except them knew that there was anything secret at all, several floors underground, covered with a beautifully landscaped lawn with charming alleys. The huge building with unusual architectural ornaments perfectly masked the hidden air inlets and the network of antennas enabling communication beyond the internal means used by the native inhabitants of this planet.

They were the guardians of the corridors. They guarded them not from humans, but from hostile Homo sapiens civilizations scattered throughout the cosmos. Only a small fraction of this species could threaten the local population, which was disarmingly for them seeking contact with an alien civilization.

Their history is typical of this species that had spread in the universe in such distant times that even they themselves didn't know who and from what planet had started this exodus.

Only the position of the Earth and its young age saved it from extinction. However, there were also such scholars among them who claimed that the Earth was the cradle of their civilization. The Earth, having come full circle in space-time, settled in this wasteland and yielded a crop of homo sapiens, which is the youngest representative of this species in the universe.

This was to be evidenced by corridors whose existence dated back to many millions of years earlier than life on Earth.

It is not, however, any evidence, because corridors could arise regardless of whether there was life here or not. For it to happen, only atmosphere was needed, so necessary for life on every planet on which Homoexpodus settled.

The planet could be a stop, an oasis, or a relay station for the civilization that created the corridors. Nobody knew and probably nobody would know the truth. Just as no one knew that corridor guards had lived here for thousands of years. But even They - Guardians of Genti didn't know every corridor that existed in the universe. It was a very small group of Guardians from a distant part of the galaxy, where life existed in a completely different time dimension. There, in order to survive several hundred thousand Earth years, they had to use the corridors of Genti, only this gave them the opportunity to survive. No evolution is permanent and you never know where it will end.

Their evolution ended quickly and abruptly. A huge star near their solar system began to grow rapidly changing all the gravitational fields of their system. It was then that they took advantage of the genti corridors and scattered throughout the universe. It was an exodus that lasted for many years. They were afraid because they didn't know what would happen to the corridors when the big bang happened. Therefore, some of them escaped as far as possible, using the Genti corridors, about which they only knew that they were there, but they didn't know where they would lead them.

Time was the greatest enemy of all Homo sapiens scattered around the universe. But not the time that separated them, and not the light-years measured here on this planet, because this obstacle had long been overcome. The obstacle was the time that existed in every moving planetary system. Because even when different civilizations were at the same time in their planetary systems, their time ran differently and their space-time couldn't be synchronized at the same moment, and when they wanted to check who inhabited the world they knew existed, they inevitably passed that planet being light years from it, which led to the fact that where they went, there was nothing that had been there when their time had been parallel. Seems incomprehensible and convoluted, but it was real checked and proven by those who dared to move through these corridors.

Their only familiar method of meeting different civilizations had been so far the warping of space-time by traveling in the corridors of genti.

Therefore, the same time and laws that governed it, was the best protection against surprises in the form of unwanted visitors of another species, because they also existed in that melting pot of the universe.

It was not easy to get two different civilizational Homo sapiens to meet at the same point in the cosmos. Even when both sides knew about the corridors and knew how to use them. The wise creator of these corridors set one condition for them. They must have achieved a degree of evolution that would allow them to travel through these corridors.

Therefore, the guards at the Homoreproduks base were not afraid that the Earthmen would take advantage of these corridors and knew that each opening of the Cap meant an encounter with the Homo sapiens species, but they didn't know how much they differed from them and what their intentions were.

The database at their disposal stored the samples of the air taken by Genti during the creation of the corridors. Each corridor leading to the planet had its own unique atmosphere composition. It was enough to take a sample to know what planet the newcomers were from. Until now, in the entire period of the existence of the base of one hundred and ten thousand Earth years, it hadn't happened that visitors from another planet didn't wait for them at the gate.

There were three such gates on Earth. Two on land and one at the bottom of the ocean. But now there was no one in front of the Cap of the genti corridor.

"Samples taken. The chamber was empty, no one was waiting for us. The newcomers went outside," reported the Repro X 567, sending data to the database from the reading of the air analyzer placed in front of the Cap.

"Come back, they are Hopeers," it heard after a moment the order of its commander.

Iva and Geo didn't realize that their entry into this Cap would raise the alarm on the planet. The corridor in which they found themselves after entering the next Cap surprised them. This was not what they expected. They didn't really know if it was their "Earth" or another planet.

Red old bricks, a high damp wall stood in front of them, blocking the way to the exit.

"I guess nobody has been here for ages," he said aloud. His words echoed in every nook and cranny of the room in which they found themselves. He liked to talk, and contemplating aloud gave him energy.

It was dark. Turning back together with the glow emanating from the cap, he saw a rock. Solid rock stretching from the bedrock all the way to the brick vault. "Someone walled it so that it was not visible. But the rock that conceals the Cap is millions of years old, and the brick wall, hundreds."

"Why?" He started to wonder aloud.

"Did the builders of this wall know the secret of the gate and that's why they masked it, did they do it out of fear because they didn't know what they were dealing with, or maybe they consciously did it to protect the cap?" Such thoughts swirled in them, causing a slight anxiety.

"How are we gonna get out of here? I think we have to go back and look for another corridor. There is no way out of here," Geo said as he surveyed the entire room with his box.

They were in some old dungeon with a brick wall on three sides, and above them a semicircular rock vault sealed off the entire room.

"No, this corridor can't be old. Look here," Iva replied and, turning to him, she took his hand just like a mother takes her child when she wants to guide it.

Opposite Iva, who was standing close to a not very large brick recess, there was something like a five-pointed star around which a sun was circling.

Only the strange black contour of the road that this brick spherical form of the sun traveled gave the lie to the essence of this drawing.

"This is our exit," Iva turned to Geo.

"Leading outside," she added.

"Am I supposed to hammer this wall?"

"No, you don't have to. There is surely another measure. But what?" She wondered aloud. Their materialized bodies were engulfed by a chill radiating from the clay soil beneath their feet.

"Look," said Iva. "I saw this drawing on our star map. This cannot be a coincidence."

Geo, lighting his surroundings with the box, began to feel the entire surface of the cavity. He sensed that there was a slight lump on each point of the star, not brick, but one smooth and cold like steel. He began to press down on those little protrusions. Each time he pressed, they heard something like a cog click, and after pressing the fifth, last protrusion, the Star was pushed outward.

"And what now?" He asked.

"Turn it," he heard Iva's suggestion.

He grasped the star with his fingers and spun it around its axis. He was surprised to find that it offered no resistance, and yet it could have been thousands of years old. There was a soft steel noise of the moving bolts and the niche jumped off the wall. He pushed it slowly until it opened its doors to them.

Bright sunlight fell into the room. Only now could they calmly look around the room in which they found themselves after passing from the corridor of the Hope Moon.

"It is a blind room specially adapted to our purpose," Iva noticed.

"It seems so, let's get out of here before someone notices the open niche." It wasn't easy, the whole area around that old outer wall was densely wooded.

In front of them, not far away, a second wall could be seen. This one, however, was tall with clear traces of repairs.

"It's a moat. Old moat, we are in some old building," said Geo, scanning the space around him.

Slowly, so as not to draw attention to themselves, they walked along the wall to the nearest bridge, whose wooden pillars pierced through the tall grass.

When they reached its wooden poles, they noticed two guards in their distinctive yellow vests.

"They're security guards, we're on Earth," Geo said, and began to climb the slope without fear. The wet morning grass made their shoes slip, and they had to use their hands to keep themselves from sliding all the way down.

"Where are you going? It is forbidden to walk there," said one of the guards.

"Sorry, my wife had to answer the call of nature," Geo began to explain.

"Yeah, yeah, now everyone says so," said the uniformed man and they calmly walked away towards the river.

"Where are we?" Iva asked.

"I have no idea, I don't know this place, at least that part of it, but we are definitely somewhere by the lake. Look, there is the water." After a few meters, a road appeared to them, and behind it a park with alleys and a large expanse of water.

They sat down on a small bench by the water and Iva, concerned about an unknown phenomenon asked him:

"You know, Geo, I don't understand how it's possible that the Cap is inside some structure. That it's even there. After all, it must have been formed hundreds of thousands of years ago, when this area was shaped differently. Its walling means that someone in recent times knew what this cap was for as well as knew the purpose of the corridors."

"Maybe yes, maybe no. The stone walls of the building are probably 600 years old and maybe those who bricked up this passage didn't know the purpose of this gate, and the one who built this corridor no longer exists, or the evolution transformed them into the shape of the Hope homo sapiens and they no longer need these corridors.

It may also be that the Hopeers know that corridors exist, but for them this is a very old form of travel and they no longer use it."

"Or maybe there is something that we don't know," added Iva, "and this is what we need to clarify, and quickly."

"But how?" Geo sighed.

"I don't know, I don't know yet, but I'll find out," she said and sent a help signal to the Clan Council. The answer came a little while later:

"Since using our Relay Station and the Time Caskets to travel to the Blue Planet, this form of travel has been limited by blocking the entrance from our Lunar Station to the Relay Station of the Genti corridors.

The entrance to the station at the level of our moon was blocked in the times of the great extinction by the Council of the Three Suns Planet, unaware that it leads to the genti corridors."

The signal was gone.

"I don't understand what they're talking about. After all, we got to the Relay Station," Geo turned to Iva, looking at her with the eyes of a student who is trying to understand what the teacher is saying to him.

"Not us, but you, and in a way that no one has ever figured out. Anyway, maybe someone tried, but couldn't succeed because didn't have the power you have." Iva smiled at him, embracing him tenderly.

"Essential question. Where are we?" Geo said it more to himself than to Iva.

Iva didn't know where they were, but she knew why the Genti corridor had led them there.

They walked across the bridge to the other side of the moat. From afar, Geo recognized with ease a well-known Fast Food restaurant's red advertising sign.

"Come on, let's go in there," he said to Iva, pointing to the Restaurant with his hand. "We will find out where we are and eat something." Iva rummaged in the box and took out a handful of banknotes.

"Are they right?" she asked Geo, pointing to them.

"I can't do that yet," he said. "How do you conjure up money?"

"It's simple - I send the thought to the box about what I need. Money, ATM cards, documents whatever I want, and I get them. However, it must be a precise thought so that there is no mistake and that you can use them safely here on Earth."

They went inside. Geo ordered two sets of food, a drink, and ice cream. He paid and they went to the table. Looking at the date of the bill, he said to Iva:

"A few days have passed since our last stay on Earth. We are not far from the airport."

He called, ordered two plane tickets and a taxi to the airport.

"Flight in two hours," he added. "There must be a way to find the afterglowers who visited my mother," he directed these words to Iva. He looked at her and said; "Sometimes it seems to me that we are here all the time, and our afterglow movement is a dream. I have two lives, one here and one there - which one is more important?" he wondered directing his awareness to Iva.

"Both are equally important, but the most important thing for us is time. It is it who defines our being, our striving for perfection. Over time, you will stop thinking about it," she added. "Now we need to find out what the visit in the cemetery means."

"Yes, you are right, as always," he said soothingly. Now he didn't want to dwell on the meaning of what he was doing. "Maybe later," he thought.

From the airport of the big city where they landed, they took a taxi to the cemetery.

"Mom, are you here? It's us, Geo and Iva."

The white form of the apparition quickly stood beside Geo.

"Geo," he heard his mother's voice in his head. "Two afterglowers were looking for the casket, unaware that with it they couldn't move to Hope. They are strangers, but peaceful ones. They got lost in the genti corridors, and as they explained to me, the only memories they had are of you, the Earth, the casket and Hope. They are not dangerous. They will stay here on the Blue Planet until you find them. Visit me again sometime."

His mother's genti was clearly weakening. Her phenomenal figure began to fade in the distance.

Iva hugged Geo. "Come on, let's go to your father. He needs to be told that everything has been cleared up so that he doesn't worry."

Chapter VIII

'Afterglow'

Both moons of Hope were forbidden zones. The first technical moon developed by their ancestors during the period of technical expansion was practically unavailable.

Who and when built, or actually created there, an energy source emitting genti, they didn't know. There were descriptions, some plans, but they regarded the technical side, told them what to do in order not to harm themselves when they were all material creatures. There was also a very detailed device manual. The problem was that there were hardly any devices of material origin, but a whole lot of biological dependence of one tissue on another. This system was made of living biological mass that filled the entire interior of the moon.

They didn't know anything about the genti nature. They didn't take part in its functioning, didn't supervise its action or carry out any work controlling its operation. They couldn't, they didn't have access to it. The entrance of any material being into the moon meant their annihilation by the field of consciousness that genti produced.

There were daredevils who got inside the moon in specially constructed suits, and it always ended with their death. They died due to the loss of their stem cells.

The rest of the moon was also a great unknown. If you looked at it from space, it seemed there was nothing there. The bare black surface absorbed whatever came across it. The light didn't seem to reach its cavernous surface. Bombarded with various gamma, infrared or radio waves, it didn't give any echoes, reflections or glare. It only reacted to the Hope mind, to their consciousness. Long time ago, even before the great extinction, waves similar to those generated by their consciousness were emitted for scientific purposes.

Without success. Each beam of such emission returned to them so multiplied that it destroyed all devices that produced it. Material Hopers in such a field of activity became vegetables without the possibility of contact with their surroundings. Therefore, now that the second moon was within its operating range, they must have worn special clothing to protect their consciousness. Their contemporary non-material figures felt exceptionally well there. This does not mean, however, that they acquired any special skills in this zone.

The official teaching was that the inhabitants of the Three Suns first settled the moon. Why? No one knew it.

The galactic 'Afterglow' was already waiting for its passengers, most of whom were several material technicians serving the Domes and other associated devices.

The artificial spaceport orbiting the moon was covered by a dome whose tall semicircular tunnel went from the Ordinary Dome to the orbiting spacecraft. Its path snaked around the strip buildings, some scaffolding whose intended use is unknown, and the command posts of this old spaceport. Here they split up. Brit and Rai headed towards the Afterglow, and Tybein and Seta went to the tunnel leading from the shuttle to the Hall of Tradition on the Technical Moon.

A small group of environmentalists studying the closed zones on Hope as well as three pilots greeted them coldly. There was no friendship between them. However, the mutual need for cooperation made their journey bearable.

The Afterglow - the lunar cargo and passenger vehicle, was a relic of their past. For a long time, nothing had been produced on Hope. All the technology had been transferred to the First Moon, where all construction, technical works and the acquisition of new technologies had been carried out for centuries. The remnants of the era of lofty ambitions of the Three Suns planet's former inhabitants had served them perfectly so far.

After the great extinction, many research stations, spacecraft, open-cast mines and other relics of that era remained, and ninety-odd percent of them were empty and unused by anyone.

A small orbital shuttle transported them aboard the Afterglow. They boarded from their mini-dome through a special portable corridor attached to the hatch of the spacecraft. They swam straight into a niche of peace and quiet where they waited for take-off. This part of the ship was meant exclusively for them. Only there could they safely survive the journey to the First Moon of Hope.

The start-up procedure went smoothly. The Afterglow nozzles, shooting gravity force, directed it into the Orbit leading to the First Moon of Genti.

The Captain's short official speech read: "Sit in place and stay out of our 'normal' activities."

But it was impossible, they had a plan and they wanted to put it into practice right after the start. Hijack the Afterglow and go to the forbidden moon. Was it possible? Could afterglowers pilot a spaceship?

Not all ships, but this one yes. At the time of the first personality transformations, spacecraft with a dual control system were built. The one in the 'Afterglow' had a system that was blocked, but in the event of a threat to the lives of material people or the 'Afterglow' itself, it automatically turned on, enabling emergency control of consciousness. And they were going to activate the consciousness control.

Not to be locked up under the ship's dome - that was their first task. The dome was not large, but it was sufficient for such a short journey. They only occupied half of it. The second part, hidden behind a specially secured entrance, concealed the entire duplicate system of life support for material Hopers as well as a synchronized, fully automatic control panel with the ability to steer the ship by afterglowers.

They moved alone through the corridor toward the other half of the dome, following the guidance given to them by the automatic awareness station. They themselves wouldn't have dared to navigate this corridor, relying only on their memories. They could end up going nowhere. Going out of the tunnel into non-existence, somewhere out there in the void of space from which no one had ever managed to return. There were a few cases of return, but only those afterglowers returned who wove the information thread behind them. However, there were only few such.

Rai was ready for emergency control of the Afterglow. When her genti detected the launch of the ship, she instructed Brit:

"We are taking off - stand by the blockade of the dome and, on my cue, turn on the emergency stream of energy."

Brit had practiced directing his consciousness before. It was not easy, but it was possible, so on the cue, the strong stream of energy blocked the automatic pilot. Not for long, but it was enough to switch the command console to the dome of the afterglowers.

The start-up procedure went smoothly but not everything went their way. A mistake was the temporary blocking of the Alpha automatic pilot. That small mistake they made led the ship into a curved space-time field used for intergalactic journeys. The great acceleration of the Afterglow after entering the field shook their consciousness.

The ship was accelerating steadily when, for unknown reasons, an alarm signal sounded on its board.

Alpha's voice dispassionately warned:

"Change of control. The intergalactic drive is on, we're entering the zone of space-time curvature. The crew immediately go to the rescue capsu..."

The voice fell silent, and severe turbulence began to shake the Afterglow. The uncontrolled traveling through the space-time corridor always ended with a passage into an unknown zone of the universe.

Disconnecting the Hydrorobots from controlling the Afterglow was not wise, it was downright dangerous. However, no one from the Senior Council, including Brit and Rai themselves, realized this. Having been taught to control consciousness, they didn't know that the old control system of this galactic ship didn't provide for such a possibility. Later alterations made to adjust it to the afterglower's voyage didn't involve controlling the ship with genti consciousness without the use of hydrorobots.

The vegetative season began for Brit and Raia, the Hope afterglowers. With no memories of the way back, they were stuck in the Afterglow dome waiting to be rescued.

After a dozen or so Hope years, the Afterglow was taken over by a ship of an alien civilization and landed on an unknown planet in an unknown galaxy.

Chapter IX

Artificial Moon

The few material hopers working on the Technical Moon gave orders to the hydrorobots on whose shoulders all the production for Hope rested.

Hydrorobots were the only automatons allowed to exist. After the discovery of Pol de Gar, the Great Council of Hope Clans decided to eliminate all other mechanical robots, foreseeing that they could be a serious source of trouble. Everyone knew that there would be few material hopers, and the afterglowers wouldn't be able to supervise or command all biomechanical robots. Of course, it didn't happen overnight, but gradually. Over a long period of time, the number of robots diminished in direct proportion to the arrival of afterglowers. Their role was taken over by the Hydrorobots.

Biological figures modeled after them, whose main source of intelligence was artificially grown brains. The rest of the body was cultivated in a specially created field brought from the planet of the Holy Substrate. In each field grew a different part of the body. Only those that were to be used for specific activities were cultivated.

DNA cells and stem cells of various creatures, animals, and not only of those inhabiting their planet, served as their building blocks.

A special biological zone designed and built custom hydrorobots.

In short, it was that a hydrorobot, which was to operate in an oxygen-free environment, was equipped with a system in which there was no breathing function. And a robot used to work in the water depths of seas and oceans, had a body structure that made it possible to stay at great depths.

They had two things in common - a drive that gave them energy and a biological engine that gave them strength. The artificial brain and the ability to dose its intelligence contributed to the development of hydrorobots. The brains were obtained from a randomly discovered planet where such a life form had been formed in the evolution of the Three Hope Suns lasting millions of decades.

As it usually happens, it was discovered by accident. In search of a planet capable of accommodating their dying population, the expedition crew found one of the planets in the Red Dwarf system, just beyond their Hope moon. They looked for the minerals they needed, not life forms. There was an abundance of oxygen on this planet.

There were biological brains living separately without shell and body. Huge cocoons growing out of a biological substrate, whose

DNA was 99.999% consistent with their own, indicated that they came from homo protozoa who had inhabited this planet using the genti corridor. They probably couldn't come back, so they started to adapt to life there. Unfortunately, it was not going evolutionarily forward, but back and, as scientists suspect, the degradation of their form created, in symbiosis with the biological substrate, a product that formed the central brain in an evolutionary frenzy.

And of its roots, grew out, because it couldn't be called a birth, living brains of varying degrees of intelligence. Who was the parasite there and who became its host, it was impossible to detect. The symbiosis was constant and profound. Imagine a homo protozoan - the first afterglower to land on this planet.

Who did it meet there? Beings similar to each other, but with a completely different system of life and birth. Different way of existence and values. The primordial people posed no threat to them as they were evolutionarily standing on a level well below theirs. However, their life forms were shaped by other values. There you didn't value your body, but your brain, which decided what bodie should have been assigned to it.

No body of the homo original inhabitant of this planet bore a creature like a parent.

The only form of reproducing a species was the substrate of this planet. In several hundred thousand such places, the substrates were biologically related to each other with underground and underwater roots.

Whenever any form of life on this planet expected an offspring, it went to one of those places. There it lay on this biological pulsating substrate in one of the many concave basins. Then a brown, soft and slightly moist discharge began to emerge through the pores at its bottom. Smoothly and steadily, it crawled all over the body. After completely tightly covering the lying body, it became stiff and motionless, forming the nucleus of a new life - such cocoon served as a womb for the development of a new life.

For a long time, their scientists were not able to determine what processes took place in such a cocoon. Their great number and variety as well as the constantly changing stage of development of such a cocoon meant that they saw only the effects of these changes.

After a certain time, different for each species, the cocoon fell apart, and a new being, never the same in the same place, appeared on the surface. There was no trace of the old specimen. Sometimes many new creatures arose from one cocoon. They were helpless brainless beings in their first phase of existence.

Such a form of birth could be considered strange, but not impossible, and only the fact that no one was equipped with a brain in the first phase of birth was considered by scientists an amazing phenomenon. The brain was born separately as a product or the transformation of their cells into a completely new organ modified by the Holy Substrate.

Only now was the connection of the brain cocoon with some body in another cocoon. This phase was called creeping consciousness by their scholars. The cocoon with the brain crawled - actually, it was being moved by its associated roots into a cocoon, which it found appropriate for its intelligence and size. The fusion of the two cocoons lasted two decades of the Hope moon and resulted in a ready-to-live individual.

It took a long time for their scientists to obtain the developed brains and direct them to cocoons, where they assembled previously prepared hydrobiological robots. Of course, in the early stages of the experiments, it was not possible to obtain the expected results from such connections, and it was only the implantation of certain DNA bonds obtained from the Holy Substrate into the hydrobiological robots that made the Sacred Substrate recognize them as a native species. Next, it was just a technical masterpiece in the form of obtaining a part of the substrate and transporting it to the Technical First Hope Moon to previously prepared scientific biological laboratories. There, the entire cultivation was under the supervision of Hope scientists. Several Hope centuries had passed before the serial production of brains accepting the birth of hydrobial robots was possible.

From then on, they replaced them in all their jobs, and although their bodies were as vulnerable to all dangers as they were, it was not a pity if one of them was annihilated, because it cannot be said here that it died, although in terms of intelligence, sensitivity or other features they were not inferior to those who created them.

Chapter X

The planet of butterflies

The search crew consisted of a few young Martians and two older experienced geneticists. They set off quickly, excited about their mission and curiosity of getting to know the New World. They walked quickly, bounded by the high ravine walls piling up to the right and left. The view was phenomenal for them. Unaccustomed to the greenery and richly decorated with various colors wings of great-butterflies, they didn't know whether they should have gone further or stood for a longer time to enjoy the green views they knew from viewing archival photos of their planet from its heyday.

After a few Martian hours, they finally saw the ravine widen its sides, revealing to them an enormous flat space, where in the distance you could see a high wall of greenery. The oldest Martian stopped the group with a wave of his hand. They were hungry, thirsty and were afraid of the enormous great-butterflies, which at the sight of them spread their huge wings showing symbols and signs incomprehensible to them.

Maho, their informal leader, headed towards the dense tracts of plants that attracted her eyes with their unusual colors. The humming singing of the flapping of butterfly wings attracted their attention, making them look at the cascade of colors and rapidly changing views covering the entire surface of the wings. These were the only creatures they had met on their way so far.

"There are no other animals here?" quietly, as if fearing that someone would hear him, asked Doh - the youngest participant of their expedition.

"There are some, but we don't see them," his older friend said shortly.

"It's a pity that these creatures don't make any sounds," said Maho. "There has to be some other way of communicating between them."

"Yes, but what?" said Kleo, who had been silent so far.

"I have no idea. Maybe they make noises inaudible to us, or they communicate through the views on their wings. I would like to know myself what these constantly changing motifs and colors on their wings mean."

Kleo, without any announcements, moved towards the steep slope of the ravine. He climbed the thicket of a limb overgrown with branches and walked towards the nearest great-butterfly.

"I have to see these views on its wings up close!" he shouted to them.

The great-butterfly was not frightened by his scream, but to his close presence it reacted with the wide spread of its butterfly arms and the display of colorful mosaic figures. When Kleo was about to go back, he was surprised to notice that these initially chaotic and shapeless colors began to form an orderly picture. First, he saw the blue speckled view of the field with flashing white dots. He didn't know what it exactly was. He didn't associate the stellar sky adorned with numerous stars with the sight of the great-butterfly wings. Their sky was red in the form of a rock vault. Admittedly, he had once seen the view of Mars, his home planet before the Great Change. He remembered the lessons in which they showed the world that was not accessible to them. They had never had the technology enabling space flights. "This is a sight I know," he thought, looking at the wings. "This flickering star, with a pale light illuminating the fifth planet of this system is probably the sun that warms its planet."

The great-butterfly, as if guessing his thoughts, flapped its wings a few times and stopped. This time, Kleo at once recognized Mars, their Mars, as he knew it. He froze, afraid to move, so as not to scare the sight away. Having took his eyes off the wings, he called out:

"We have contact! The great-butterfly is showing me our planet."

"It would be great," Naret muttered, irritated with the discovery of Kleo - so much he wanted to shine through something extraordinary to go down in the history of their new colonization discoveries.

They approached the butterfly carefully, so that it wouldn't fly away. They didn't yet understand that the great-butterfly was not afraid of them. It followed quite different criteria. It was genetically programmed to interact with the homo sapiens species, but only one of them. It didn't pass on the data stored in its memory to many individuals, but only to one who drank the white nectar from the common root of knowledge. It worked as a feedback loop. Drinking from one branch made them belong to this planet, to this ecosystem that was still unknown to them.

In the space-time in which they were now, all information had existed from the dawn of this world. Only the high knowledge and abilities of genetically modified creatures, which were great-butterflies, allowed them to capture elementary particles of knowledge floating in their planetary system, and to pass them on to those species of homo sapiens who were ready to read this knowledge. The little Martian was the first to come into contact with the great-butterfly and gain access to its knowledge but he didn't know how to take advantage of it.

All Martians were advanced enough to benefit from this knowledge. Yet their life in an enclosed space within Mars had blunted their ability to look more broadly at the possibility of telepathic communication, so sharpened and developed by great-butterflies.

When more Martian specimens were found nearby, the great-butterfly changed the color of its wings and quietly went back to preying. They missed the chance to quickly learn the laws that governed this planet.

"We can't see anything, you have hallucinated," the disappointed voices of the other participants of this expedition were heard.

"No, definitely not. I don't know why it can't be seen now," Kleo coughed up in a worried voice, looking at the great-butterfly with a pleading gaze, as if he had wanted to encourage it to repeat the transmission.

"We're going, we have to reach these green areas, maybe we can find water there. If there is water, we will probably find something to eat there," Maho gave the command to continue walking.

"Faster!" Kleo urged them, looking at the sky. "I think it will be getting dark." All his life he had seen only the red vault of the Martian corridors, but in some incomprehensible manner, the thought that night would begin soon rattled in him. A night that no one of them had seen before and that would always accompany them from now on. It was getting gray. The sun was setting behind the vault of the surrounding hills. As it grew darker there in the sky, below, beneath their feet, the vault started to be covered by the glow of green rays. The irregular lines looked like the roots of their artificially grown plants. With their shape and various thicknesses, they flowed in different directions, connecting with the branches of white-sap plants covering the walls of the ravine.

"These plants are one ecosystem," Tero noted. "They merge into one organism. This is how the plants grown in our fields took up water."

With each step they took, it got darker above them and greener below them. The great-butterflies on the sides of the ravine vanished from their sight. The walls of the hills parted in a gentle curve and lowered their height considerably. There was a valley in front of them, the end of which couldn't be seen, and beneath them, a series of green roots lit their way.

It was already completely dark when they noticed that every step of their feet on the ground produced a luminous impulse going forward, not in the straight direction, where they expected to find a green forest wall, but turning in a gentle curve to the left, into the unknown black depths of the night.

"Is it a trap? Does someone want us to go there?" he asked.

"Turn right," Tero commanded to Kleo, who was walking ahead with the belief that they were going in the right direction.

"Fine, as you like," he replied, and walked the other way. A light impulse that arose after a few steps of him surprised everyone. The bright green glow began to change its color to a harsh shade of purple light, simultaneously quickening the jumping rhythm. The farther they moved away from the originally chosen direction, the faster the color changed to the dark shade of purple.

"Stop, Kleo!" he shouted. "It must mean something, but what?" he asked in an anxious voice.

"It's a clue or a trap," said Lobos that had been silent so far. "We have to split up and go both ways, then we'll see who goes the right way."

"I'm not at all convinced that both ways are safe, each may be the last or the right one."

"It is a pity the worm is not with us - we would be safe," the youngest Martian complained.

"Here the worm would die instantly, it is not its environment and its rocky base."

"You're right, but we still don't know where to find water," Kleo worried.

"The water is where the forest is or near it. At least I think so. Anyway, here nothing is and will be the same or even similar to what we know from Mars, so it would be better if we quickly forgot about it and start getting to know the world in which we live. It is better than what awaited us on our planet anyway."

Mach didn't take part in this discussion because he noticed a certain relationship between what they said and the lights that appeared below them.

"The light responds to our thoughts - water, water, water," he quickly uttered the words while intensely thinking about what it looked like and what they needed it for.

Immediately in front of them, a carpet of bright blue light spread out from where they stood to the nearby clump of tall plants with soaring leaves, which glistened slightly in the dark horizon surrounding them.

"We're going there," he commanded, looking at the astonished faces of his companions.

They set off, treading on the green glow, and after a few Martian minutes, they stood in front of a gently gurgling stream.

"We have water, we need to inform the rest," said Kleo, bending down to draw water into a vessel he was holding, which he made from a wide, torn leaf by rolling it into a large cone. He picked up the leaf and carefully touched the water with the tip of his tongue. He tasted it, then, tilting the makeshift pot, he took a small sip.

"And?" Tero was curious what the liquid that looked like water tasted like. She knew, however, that a poisonous liquid could look the same.

"Try it yourself - it has a different taste, but I guess it's because I'm used to a different water. In our place, water has the aftertaste of iron. Here, I don't taste it," he said, and handed Tero the leaf with water.

She took the water in her mouth and, holding it for a moment, relished her crystal clearness. She knew the taste of such water. In her laboratory, she often purified water from their top springs and secretly sipped it - for experimental purposes, of course.

"How will we notify the rest of our discovery?" She asked.

"There's no such need, they already know," said Mach.

Indeed, a ribbon of white light flashed towards the gorge, disappearing in the distance.

"This is a hint on how to get here - but how does it work?" he wondered aloud. "I thought hard about water and how much we need it. The more I tried, the brighter the light shone beneath us," Mach shared his observations with them.

"So maybe now we will think about some kind of shelter, a warm and spacious one," Kleo joked.

"Okay, but we all have to think of the same thing."

"Specifically of what?" said Lobos, who had been silent until now.

"Of a large, safe and spacious cave full of warmth and comfort, one where we could all fit," Mach explained to him. "So, here we go," he added. They concentrated their thoughts and waited.

"It's pointless. It doesn't work like that," said Tero.

"So how?" he asked.

"I don't know, we have to try something else, but now we should come back, because how will they know there is water here? The light, if it reached them, won't tell them anything, it can only show them the way to the water."

"Go back with Lobos, we'll stay and try to find some shelter."

"It won't be possible for so many people," Kleo asked.

For some time, Geo had been thinking intensely about a refuge for all of them. He felt responsible for them to some extent. After all, this strange alien entrusted him with the fate of all of them, and this obliged him to search more intensely.

"How do you know what's here and what we can find? So far, we've come across some strange plants and something we know nothing about. Remember that we don't have any metal objects with us, which in my opinion means that this planet is some strange biological creation. And everything here is derived from its structure."

Kleo was not involved in this discussion. He thought hard about shelter. However, his ideas hovered around what he knew from Mars. Caves, clefts, pits or other products of various activities of nature that he knew had no reason to exist here, and his imagination and knowledge couldn't tell him anything about other forms and possibilities of shelter for so many people.

"What do we do?" Yroch, the oldest participant of the expedition, who had been silent so far, decided to use the customary right to a brief conference in order to determine the further course of action. He waited for Maho to let each of them present their opinion on the further way of conducting the expedition.

They gathered in a tight circle and each of them put their hands around the backs of those standing nearby. Each of them was entitled to one sentence. It was customary for the youngest to start.

"We're moving towards the purple impulses," Doh adopted a bold version of their group's past actions.

"We will split into two groups and each will go in a different direction," Kyteneg suggested, reasoning that the two search groups had a better chance of finding something to eat.

"Let's find shelter and wait for the new day." Kleo was more careful. She didn't want to expose anyone to an uncertain journey in the dark.

"We will wait for the new day before we continue our search," Yroch supported Kleo in a dispassionate voice.

"So, it's settled. We will wait the night out in the nearby bushes," Maho decided. They knew that now there was no other option but to do what Maho decided.

They decided to take refuge in the thicket of nearby bushes and wait for the new day. The place they reached was perfect for a shelter. At least they thought so when they saw tall green bushes, the ground of which was covered with short green leaves fallen from low-growing branches that formed a natural umbrella above it. Helping themselves with their hands, they brushed the branches away, creating a capacious space that could easily contain them. They covered the entrance with broken branches, disregarding the leaking white juice. They sat on the floor in a tight circle. They were neither cold nor hot, they just wanted to eat. They were hungry, but neither of them dared to drink white juice.

As they sat there, trying to sleep, a red ball loomed over the horizon. Its cold purple light was shone through the leaves, pouring into their makeshift shelter.

The impact of the sphere on the planet increased with the distance it traveled as it rose from the southern side of the Butterfly Planet. They didn't immediately notice what was causing the strange crackles and noises coming from the distant part of the clearing. Their first night on the Butterfly Planet was unlike anything they had experienced on Mars. The cold red sheen radiating from the low-hanging object made them fearful. They realized that its power was affecting their ground in a way that they didn't understand. The strange crackles and noises coming from the place where they were sitting and the luminous streaks seemed to be guided by a logic only known to them. At the same time, they watched the space in front of them attentively. They didn't notice any movement, there were no visible objects in their sight, and that calmed them down a little.

"We'll keep watch. It starts with Dah, then Yroch and Kyteneg, and ends with Kleo. Wake me up if something disturbs you," Maho ordered.

They were tired and stressed by the new situation, so they slept extremely hard when a shock woke them up. All the ground they were lying on quaked. Then they saw a phosphorescent light beneath their feet. Pulsating slowly, it faded into the surface on which they stood.

"Look," Dah exclaimed, excited at his discovery, "it's vanishing inside"

"So, should we dig pits?"

"No, just think and follow it inside."

"Think? What are you talking about?"

"I was awake, I was on guard, and I thought about the quakes on Mars, and then here the ground shook. I don't know how, but something tells me to do it. This is no accident," he announced in a firm voice.

"Then try it again to make us shake."

Doh tried but nothing shook them. It was extremely quiet so they lay down again trying to sleep.

Meanwhile, Tero and Maho set off back, following the traces left by the luminous roots.

Chapter XI

Planet of Souls

As the War Council was convening beneath the Domes of the Rebirth Nebula on Planet of Souls IV, an alien invasion began on the outskirts of their solar system. In the intergalactic space, an armada of spacecraft emerged, heading for their Planet of Souls V. All the domes on the Planet of Souls V supporting the life of the immaterial afterglowers were already empty, their inhabitants had already evacuated to the Planet of Consciousness under the largest Dome of their system. The planet of Consciousness, the cradle of their race, was the only planet that could resist the invaders. In its space, in the orbit of the first moon, a few war spaceships were stationed, which the Great Diviner in his original stage of surveillance of the Soul

System, out of caution, decided to keep for material individuals of their species.

Lodi - The armada commander remained calm.

"We will not attack the armada of foreign ships until we know who we are dealing with," he reported to the audience on the position of the War Council. "We have too few material souls who are qualified to conduct large-scale warfare. First, we will send our scouts whose task will be to take over one of the enemy ships. We have a technical advantage over them, but unfortunately not in numbers."

"How do you want to achieve this if their ships are huge space monsters that can alone destroy our planet. It was from inside them that combat units took off and destroyed our domes on the Planet V.

The manner and tactics of actions are decided by the Great Diviner, and it is he who gives orders to our commanders. All I can say is that the material supervisors of our planets are fully aware of the intentions of the invaders. The enemy destroys our domes, but leaves intact everything what is material. Our genti sends us information regarding the rationale for such action.

The Genti of the Soul System claims that the invaders may not know about the existence of the afterglowers. We are invisible to them, and they consider our Domes to be remnants of extinct races. They don't react to our Genti.

Evolutionarily, they are in the initial stage of development. The expansion of the cosmos that they started is to help them conquer a planet that will enable them to transfer their population to the planet to which they want to transport life from their native star, which in the mode of evolutionary transformation dies, threatening them. When sending our combat ships, we need to find a way to establish communication," he finished his lengthy speech, taking away from them all hope for a peaceful resolution of the conflict.

"How are we to let them know that they are destroying our lives if we are unable to reach their consciousness?" asked Kepud, the material commander of the flagship warship.

"Our Armada must make contact using all the technical possibilities at our disposal," answered Lodi. "We cannot allow a further escalation of hostilities," he explained.

"There was an uproar in the hall. There were heard shouts of discontent of material hawks eager to use their war skills.

"Their spaceships are poorly developed combat units, where primitive antimatter drives are used. They shouldn't be here at all. The speed they achieve shouldn't have allowed them to reach us. These are distances that exceed their life expectancy in several hundred generations. And that's the puzzle to be solved."

"For now, no one knows why they came here," Cub had to speak, he wouldn't have been himself if he hadn't shown that he had his opinion on this subject.

"Are there any questions?" Lodi added looking around, hoping that there would be no questions. He knew that they would do what the Great Diviner ordered them anyway. There were, however, questions, and specific ones.

"Can we destroy their ships without killing their crew?"

"We could, but that would mean that we would have to receive them on one of our planets, which, as you know, would be an interesting experience, but also a threat to all the afterglowers. I don't think I need to explain why."

"Of course not," Cub muttered to Nojuk, the first pilot of their flagship unit, standing next to him. "Everyone would start to steal their memories, which would bring chaos into our afterglow beings."

"Does it matter? After all, they would integrate with us, and they still wouldn't be able to get into our domes."

"They wouldn't, but we could get onto their planet with no problem. We couldn't create an umbrella that prevents travel on it, which would make our race outnumber them and this would lead to tensions and perhaps even war. After all, they are warriors and we are afterglowers with a small number of material souls. When all those willing began to materialize on such a planet, our afterglow form would lose its raison d'être."

"Let me not agree with you, rather it is them who would like to skip all the steps of evolution to get what we have now."

The consciousness asking for silence ran through the dome.

On the podium for the highest authorities entered - the representative of the Great Diviner, the Omni-planetary Emperor Lork I, who decided to personally open his soul with a strong message.

He began a conference of the leaders of the seven planets in the Rebirth Nebula.

"As you know, our planetary system was attacked by the unknown civilization. So far, we have not been able to defend our sister planet. It was taken over by the hostile army of creatures that we know nothing about. Their soldiers are homo planetoids. Our material scholars concluded that this species had only existed on the fringes of the universe where it had been sent by the evolution initiated by our Genti. But they came back and have an advantage over us in their material structures. With a cumulative attack, we will not be able to defend our planets against the hostile invaders without destroying the lives of the crew of these space ships. Let each of you gathered in the Dome of the representatives of all Rebirth Nebula's nations, join the stream of self and direct your genti to the Great Diviner."

"The Diviner is the material part of the Great Supervisor of one of their artificial moons, whose date of creation and creator are not known," thought Salta, a representative of the Protectors of the Rebirth Nebula family. "He's all we have. He is our entire past and future. He was built from our material DNA and contain all our knowledge that we had at the time. That cumulated knowledge in the Great Diviner is the only material thing in this planetary system, the only living tissue that is still young and resilient. A self-contained machine for making amazing calculations of the probabilities of future and present events. Our mainstay and sense of security, as well as defensive shield."

Only a few of the hydro robots derived from the Guardians of Genti knew where he was. Their planetary system with the Central Sun, several moons was the point in the universe from which each curving of space began.

The Planet of Souls was a mirror that reflected every light that came here, even from the farthest corner of the universe. It was the magic of the cosmos. Only here, according to the knowledge of the Great Diviner, all the Genti of the cosmos and their corridors were concentrated.

From here, black matter spread throughout the universe.

"I'm the beginning and the end of everything that existed and will exist," the Great Diviner told them when they asked about the meaning of his existence. That was what they were going to know now. In the face of the threat, all hope focused on his ability to foresee the future and his knowledge, thanks to which they could prevent the extermination of all their planets. The dome under which they were was shimmering with all the colors of the rainbow. All the thoughts addressed to the Great Diviner were intertwined into one message. Out of this cascade of various thoughts and wishes, the questions slowly formed:

'Who are the invaders? How to prevent a catastrophe and defeat enemies without destroying the lives of their crews?'

The Great Diviner replied to all the gathered people after a long moment:

"Geo is the next stage of evolution derived from a planetary system at the end of the universe. The Blue Planet is the cradle of our and your civilization. It has one sun and it is a third planet next to the Magellanic Nebula.

The Invaders is a species of homo raptus degenerated by the original version of genti. Their planet is dying, so they conquer and inhabit the planetary systems of immaterial beings derived from the homogeny of homo sapiens. Their warriors who move along the corridors of genti are all those who have lost their way in the universe and found themselves in non-existence. This is how they found our planetary system. They came on their space ships by means of the warping of space, gliding along its surface at the time of the nonlinear dependencies into which our space-time relays serving the genti corridors were engaged. You have little time and I have even less of it. In case of danger, I will self-destruct, which will destroy the entire planetary system. This is a security that my Creator has installed in me."

"How much time do we have?" asked Morg, Supreme Commander of the Soul Planet Defense.

"Hurry up. In case of danger, evacuate to the planet XNst 8934. I'm sending the coordinates of the corridor to all gathered."

There was a silence, all the audience froze with fear. It was a surprise they didn't expect to hear. The conference continued.

Now the cap was pulsating with blue tones due to messages from immaterial people, who once had been material astro historians, exploring the universe. They quickly found maps accumulated in the memory of their material history.

Two immaterial figures - Rapp and Appa, who had already had experience traveling through the corridors of Genti were selected to search for and establish contact with Geo and find the Blue Planet. The two inhabitants of the Fifth Planet of Souls had been one for hundreds of years.

"You will get support in reaching the corridors zone," they were assured by the Chief Guardian of Genti. "Move, we don't know if our and their time is synchronized with our Genti. We have guardians on all planets with non-material life. As soon as you enter the blue planet, the guards will find out about it. The Great Diviner has already bent the space, so go ahead and carry our cry for help with you." He opened his genti and sent them a signal:

"Now you have taken over all the knowledge of the genti corridors leading to the Blue Planet. Unfortunately, we cannot contact the guards who are there."

Rapp and Appa swiftly moved to the Great Cap Room on their second moon.

"Go," he encouraged them with a vision of the planet he had acquired from the Great Diviner.

He had the vision of the planet that existed in the memory of the Great Diviner, but he knew that it was different now, just as the time between them was different, or actually measured differently.

"Be careful," he chose his words carefully, not wanting to scare them.

"I don't know what you will find there now and what level of life there is on the Blue Planet," genti warned them.

Rapp and Appa entered the first corridor leading to the appropriate part of the corridor whose spatial curvature would direct them to a distant corner of the universe. Their genti could show them the direction, but not the exact way. They had to imagine this in such a way as not to send themselves to non-existence. Their knowledge concerned only the first part of the road leading to the great cluster of gates, out of which they had to choose the right one.

They didn't know, however, whether it was a direct corridor to the blue planet or whether they should have used the intergalactic relay station that could indicate them the right direction. But that's why it was they who were sent, because only they had returned from the Green Dwarf many hundred years earlier, when they had escaped boredom, looking for strong impressions for the next years of their immaterial existence.

The first corridor they penetrated through the Cap, which once had led them to the Green Dwarf, didn't differ much from their expectations, so they boldly imagined its exit, or actually a path to the wide intergalactic Relay Station, where there were caps leading to the next genti corridors with their incomprehensible symbols.

Appa from her material life had many cap symbols in her mind, but none of them concerned the shabby part of the cosmos that was their destination. The Green Dwarf, which they had reached hundreds of years earlier, wasn't a great attraction for them. Their lives under the same domes differed too much from what they were used to. The green homoafterglowers no longer had memories of their material existence from the time before discovering their genti and the possibility of further existence in the changed form. Now, for hundreds of thousands of years, they had been interested only in the lives of others, watching all forms of life in the cosmos, not only those of the Homo sapiens species, but also those furthest from them. The greatest entertainment in their long Green Globe life were bets.

Bets on everything, and the highest price of losing was the complete loss of consciousness and memory of what had been. The stakes were small and large, and they concerned the transfer of recollections stuck in memory. First, such small, insignificant memories of travels to other worlds changed owners. Then, as they became addicted to gambling, they put all their memories at stake.

Those who were lucky could get memories of hundreds of their fellows over the course of thousands of years, and then their afterglow life was rich and interesting.

Woe to anyone who fell into a gambling addiction and, having no luck, got rid of all memories. They were becoming a poor afterglowers devoid of pleasure in their long life. It ended almost always the same. In order to get new memories, they set off in search of other forms of life, moving along the corridors of genti to distant corridors unknown to anyone, where the spatial curvature had been initiated by the Great Builder of Genti so much earlier that no one remembered what the symbols on the Caps meant and where they led.

The most dangerous were the blind corridors leading to the planets where time was out of sync with their own and life on that planet was over or hostile to them. The lower forms of evolution posed little threat to them. Possessing knowledge beyond that of the indigenous people, they blended into their culture, drawing from it everything that could have any value for them.

Many of them fell into nothingness, into a void, of which there was no way out, and remained there until the end of their afterglow existence. In those who were lucky and ended up on a planet where any form of life existed, there was a need to spread faith in their afterglow life. It wasn't easy, however, because they were invisible to any material life form.

The mechanism of the Cap gates was brilliant and timeless. Whenever they went through the gate of a Cap in some unknown world, it was the Cap that decided what form of life they should have chosen where they landed.

When they encountered the friendly forms of afterglowers living under the protective umbrellas of the Domes, their own form of existence didn't change.

When there were no such Domes on the planet, they assumed their material form, which was equal to threats in the event that their form was different from those encountered on the planet.

The afterglowers from the Rebirth Nebula in such extreme cases had a way to change their form into a glow invisible to the general population of this planet. When Genti Guardians existed on a given planet, the situation was comfortable because they could always return to a more friendly corridor. Appa and Rapp were not gamblers, but curious afterglowers eager for new memories. Now, however, their striving to discover everything unknown was to save the Rebirth Nebula with Planets of Souls from destruction, and them themselves from forced emigration to another planet.

It would have seemed that it shouldn't have mattered for the afterglowers under which Dome they were, but it wasn't so. Traveling to another planet had always been associated with the loss of some memories. Those memories that concerned them and their lives on the planet when they had still been in material form. They got rid of old memories in favor of new ones they acquired from the indigenous peoples of the planets. The trade of memories was voluntary and there was no duress or theft. Now the Green Dwarf closed his Caps to them, fearing for his planet. They knew perfectly well what threat could pose the release of any afterglower that came to them from the Rebirth Nebula, seeking refuge and peace. Appa and Rapp knew that they could reach the Green Dwarf, but they wouldn't have been released from it, so they had to decide for themselves which Cap to use to reach the Blue Planet.

Dozens of caps rotated in the holographic image, whirling around the central point of the Distribution Station. A large map of the cosmos, spread out like a thin slice of ham, was divided into pieces leading to unknown corners of space. For them, standing in this central point, the presented fragments of the cosmos looked like a huge pizza cut into a dozen triangular pieces, and each of them was growing from a dot symbolizing the cap to a wide semicircle, the end of which was the edge of the universe. This is how genti corridors worked, bending space in such a way that the time and space of a given part of the cosmos were divided into such small pieces that it was possible to reach every star and every planet in this curved particle of the universe.

"But which piece of this world leads to the Blue Planet?" they wondered, looking at this spinning picture.

"What do we do?" Rapp flashed the thought to his companion.

"We are looking for the Cap closest to what the Great Diviner told us," Appa replied.

But there was no such cap. All the symbols on caps were unknown to them. They didn't know what complicated mathematical formulas or graphics and pictograms of various colors and shapes meant.

As they thought about it, communicating their observations, they received a strong signal warning them of the impending danger. They knew what such a signal meant.

Already before, during one of their wanderings through the genti corridors, they had received such a warning. This time, they didn't wait, but quickly jumped into the nearest cap. The bright red cap full of incomprehensible symbols was a temporary protection for them. They swirled around it, not wanting to go further down the genti corridor, as they didn't know where it would have led them.

"Who could it be?" Appa flashed the thought.

"I think that someone from the unknown race of afterglowers, one of those who fell into non-existence and are now wandering through the corridors of genti, looking for their home planet," Rapp shared his insight.

"Such an afterglower wouldn't be a threat to us."

"You know the Genti principle. Travel along the corridor of two different races of homo afterglowers poses a threat to everyone. On such a journey, we may end up where they go, or they may end up where we go.

For both races, this may be their last journey down the genti corridor. You know that not all afterglowers are friendly towards each other and can materialize and pose a deadly threat to the original races inhabiting the planet to which are heading. Especially when it is not protected by Genti Guardians."

"We're not waiting, we're going back to the station," Rapp decided. Having penetrated the Cap, they found themselves again in the center of the Distribution Station.

It was not a good move. They immediately sensed the presence of alien afterglowers. Their pale glow signaled that they were not of the same race or species. Two individuals immediately tried to take over their consciousness and steal their memories.

Unable to cope with their power, Rapp and Appa burst into the nearest cap and, immediately surrendering to its vortices, set off to an unknown world. They knew, however, that the aliens followed them. Each time the corridor was a long straight stretch, they could sense the faint signal from their genti. Having reached the exit cap, they immediately went through its gate. The planet they found themselves on immediately materialized their afterglow form.

"Where are we?" they asked themselves, looking at their material bodies. They hadn't seen such a sight of themselves since their had come to the Green Dwarf.

On the planet in its secondary stage of development, they had received a signal from the dormant Guardian Genti. The indigenous inhabitant of one of the planets of the HD188753 system outthrusted half of his figure from the water depths of the swirling vortex next to the rocky part of the hill, where the Cap gate which they had just penetrated was located.

"Their planet orbits one of the three stars in the Cygnus constellation and is inhabited by the Homo-aquatic race. Three-quarters of the planet consists of water with a temperature that varies depending on the distance from the sun it revolves around," the guard recited the learned formula.

They already knew that they had been recognized by the genti security system and considered friendly individuals to this planet. Nothing threatened them from his side but it didn't guarantee safety as they could be threatened by homo water people.

Looking at him, Appa and Rapp realized that the inhabitants of this planet were little similar to their race. The only common shape was their head, which is nothing extraordinary, because almost all homo sapiens species living in the universe, and in a stage of development similar to them, had an oblong head shape with a highly pointed skull cut off from the front part, where the communication centers and eyes were located. The rest was always a different appearance depending on the degree of evolution that a given homo race had undergone in its development from a homo protozoa to an afterglower.

The guard unfolded a protective umbrella over them, covering the rock gates where his permanent base was located. They knew that they had now become invisible to the inhabitants of this planet.

A great three-dimensional image of this part of the constellation greeted them at the very entrance. They were in a section for all travelers who knew how to use genti corridors. Here, in a separate room, there was a Genti Station, containing information on each species of Homo afterglowers that arose from the DNA of those who had built the genti corridors.

"Your place is also on this map," he flashed a molecular formula and a part of the cosmos with the Rebirth Nebula appeared before their eyes. Then, at a crazy pace, the path they had traveled was shown to them. The real path without the curvature of space-time was so distant that it was unreal. It led to a part of the cosmos completely unknown to them.

"How far, or otherwise," Rapp corrected himself, turning to the Genti Guardian, "show me the corridor leading to the Blue Planet."

After a while, the Rebirth Nebula was replaced by the solar system of the Blue Planet marked as a small point on the outskirts of the Universe. The grid showing the distances showed them the number 149.

"That's 149 light years away," Appa remarked.

The image changed its structure to a four-dimensional hologram. According to the superstring theory, this world existed in the eighth spatial dimension. In that part of the universe in its four-dimensional world where the Blue Planet existed, there were laws that defined three spatial dimensions and one-time dimension. Now they were shown the area of the planet on which they found themselves, with the entrance to the two Caps and two separate corridors leading to their destinations marked. Both corridors didn't lead directly to it.

"Could it be difficult to do?" Rapp asked the guard.

"I have no such information," he replied. "The entrance to the first corridor is under the grotto vault at Keaton's Holy Place, four hundred meters below the surface of the Sea of Justice."

The name meant nothing to them, neither did the place, but the Guardian showed them what they had to face in order to get to the first corridor leading to the Relay Station.

"Two afterglowers have entered the Cap from the planet Hope," the Guard told them, and he went to the meeting.

It was his automatic duty, and he wasn't concerned with the animosities and clashes that could arise between the two races in direct encounter. The silhouettes of the afterglowers from Hope were ideally suited to those of inhabitants of the Blue Planet.

They, being from the Rebirth Nebula, were so different in appearance and body structure that they couldn't have materialized unnoticed on the planet they were heading for.

The protective umbrella opened and two Hopers entered the room.

Rapp and Appa immediately recognized that they were the afterglowers they had met in the corridor.

"How did you get here?" asked Rapp.

"Following the thread that you dragged behind you," one of these beings replied.

"I'm Tybein from the planet Hope. And this is Seta," she indicated her companion with her hand.

"I'm Appa," she said, and was surprised to find that these two Hopers had crept into her consciousness.

"You're looking for Geo from the Blue Planet too," said Rapp. "Why?"

The question went unanswered, but all four realized that they had the same goal, but is it common?

There was no time to figure out what and why, for the Guard immediately directed them towards the exit.

Chapter XII

Fish Planet

A roboguardian went first. Its silhouette didn't differ from that of representatives of the species inhabiting this planet, which couldn't be said about the afterglowers accompanying it. While it was not a problem for the guard to plunge into the depths of the surrounding sea, for them it had to create a protective barrier allowing them to stay in this water deep.

A specially prepared vehicle was used for this. Built from the aquatic structures of the coral, it resembled a large creeping water lizard more than the living tissue of retro building material, which here in the water depths of their seas was used to make everything that could be artificially created for their needs. This universal material was based on copied DNA of a certain species of Plastela, an organism that lived in the depths of the Canon of Eternal Darkness, at the outlets of underwater hot geysers.

Such organism had the remarkable ability to regenerate its cells by rebuilding itself into any shape that could be modeled with simple hand movements. Therefore, the most respected caste of inhabitants of every level of the depths were those who, like earthly sculptors, were able to model something that could serve them as a shelter, vehicle, a place to rest or some fantastic building. This structure was like living clay, and in their vehicle, it was modeled so that it resembled their oblong fastest fish, with a huge tail devoid of the rough scales of these creatures.

Without thinking long, they entered its interior. At the controls of this fish-water taxi sat an intergalactic pilot - a zero-class robot specifically geared to driving such a vehicle. Its hydrobiological silhouette was dominated by limbs, or rather their substitutes, because its feet so popular in all varieties of homoafterglowers derived from the original homo hydro branch were replaced by wide fins.

"I hope we won't have to use these suits," said Appa, looking at the row of greenish suits hanging in a long row, which looked like the diving suits they had used in the past.

Their material lives were full of various activities designed to prepare them for the journey through the genti corridors. And one of the most important ones was acquiring the ability to temporarily stay under water. Water was the largest part of the area on all planets that they could encounter on their journeys to worlds unknown to them.

"They're not suits," the pilot said. "It is a biosynthetic skin that imitates the appearance of Hydro inhabitants. When you put them on, you will get the appearance of an inhabitant of this planet. It also allows you to breathe underwater. However, it is not perfect, and hydro warriors can recognize that there is another species of a Homo afterglower underneath it. However, they can only see it when they come close to it at a distance of several water pressures, so very close."

The pilot started the water transportation and they quickly descended, heading towards the grotto. Swimming at a considerable distance from the enormous ocean domes, they gazed at the familiar sight of their kin.

"They haven't moved on to the next stage of development yet and haven't discovered the law of Pol de Gar," said Rapp in surprise.

"And it will probably never happen, because the environment in which they live is not conducive to learning about the laws governing this universe. And they don't realize that their Creator has spread our species to the countless planets of our Universe and perhaps to all other worlds parallel to us," Tybein replied looking with appreciation at the surrounding water landscapes.

Tybein, who had the most memories from the history of the cosmos, decided to share them.

"They may know more about matters inaccessible to us," she said, looking at the bright dome of the great city over which they were just sailing. "Their environment is a great unknown for us, and although life arose in water, and then inhabited the land, here we are dealing with life that has returned to this water."

A series of vehicles similar to their water taxi left and entered the city through a dozen circular tunnels linking the intermediate stations to a great platform towering over the dome. This connector was both a landing place and a runway for thousands of water vehicles plying between the cities of this piece of ocean they traversed.

"Interesting buildings," said Appa. "They use natural material to rear them. They have everything in abundance here." This idyllic conversation was interrupted by the strong voice of the pilot.

"Put on the suits, we have an audit."

Above their heads, appeared a large vehicle with a round transparent dome protruding over its flat body, in which three hydro water people sat.

Small red bubbles began to form around their vehicle. They slowly surrounded them with a tight cordon that made movement impossible. The pilot turned off the drive and succumbed to the movement of red bubbles, which turned out to be small creatures that could clump together around any object in a way that in the case of a living creature ended in its death, because they sucked all the water from its surroundings so that, paradoxically, it died due to the lack of the possibility of taking oxygen from the water. It choked like a fish thrown onto their hard ground. The red bubbles were a cooperative species and intelligent enough to be guided thanks to taming, so they were used to control all water vehicles. Due to their spherical structure and herd behavior, these creatures, sticking together, formed the fastest way of moving known in their world. Gregariously, they took water from the environment and, throwing it behind them, formed an almost rocket propulsion, beating all other creatures. Nobody and nothing escaped them, they were able to move so quickly in the aquatic environment. However, they also had their limitations, which was the depth. The deeper they moved, the slower was their swimming.

"It's a warning signal," the pilot's calm voice explained them the meaning of this phenomenon. "We have to stop and submit to the inspection," he continued.

The four of them quickly put on the greenish suits that instantly made them look like hydro water people. Looking at each other, they released a long-forgotten laugh.

"It can bring us closer to each other. It is always so, that common danger unites," Appa thought, looking at the, perhaps not a recent former enemy, but Hopers reluctant towards them. Their vehicle was motionless, waiting for a robot in the shape of a spinning seahorse, which, having detached from the hull, was approaching their entrance lock.

"This creature is the Identification Inspector," the pilot explained. "It examines water molecules by taking them from a body. Don't worry," he continued to explain, "the suits will give it prepared samples, the identification of which should show your hydro ancestry."

"Should - it's not enough, we need to be sure we're not in danger," Tybein said anxiously.

"My job is to bring you to the Canton Cap," the pilot explained in a flat voice.

"Just alive," Seta added with fear in her voice.

"Go to the control capsule," the pilot ordered. In front of them, the upper part of the vehicle opened, above which you could see a transparent dome. Such a miniature version of the underwater domes that they had just viewed.

The control dome room they entered closed noiselessly and immediately began to fill with water, and they were amazed to see that the wetsuits they had put on allowed them to breathe oxygen taken from the water. They waited calmly for the inspection. The water inspector swam in and immediately got closer to Appa. She didn't even notice when one of its tentacles stuck the sharp point into her. Its antennae claws attached to its leg immediately analyzed the fluid it pulled from Appa. Then, one by one, it stuck the pin in the same place on the suit of all the others, who were watching its swift actions with anxiety. He didn't ask, didn't send any other messages, didn't touch them or look at them closely. Here, the most important value was the fluid identifying their water bodies that had developed in their organisms over hundreds of thousands of years. It was their personal pattern that set them apart from other living individuals on this planet. There were many species derived from the common line of life, and some of them were their original forms, whom evolution grudged acquiring an intelligence equal to their's, but didn't differentiate their appearance, so their guiding principle for the preservation of the species was to prevent other life forms from mixing with different aquatic races. There was no food competition here, and didn't function the pyramid - the bigger would eat the smaller one, but there was a struggle to preserve the species, in the world where everyone could have offspring. This evolutionary error, or a blessing of nature as some of them have claimed, made it possible to survive in an environment where there was no competition. This factor was, on the one hand, a boon to them, and on the other hand, it contributed to a regression in development. For while life on the hard surface of their planet was a constant struggle for survival, when they adapted to life in the waters of their seas and oceans, it was idyllic. This was due to the easy and trouble-free availability of food. Their underwater crops of various plants rich in everything necessary for life as well as various species of living creatures that, using these fields, provided them with meat and other nutritious juices, made entire populations rest on their laurels and not being interested in science or research of those aquatic areas to which they didn't have access. But this doesn't mean that from these great depths other living creatures didn't enter their world. They were creatures that sowed fear and panic in their orderly lives. Many such attacks thinned their population, forcing them to take defensive actions, and therefore for two generations different reconnaissance systems had been created. It began to be realized that the attackers were not their native species, but unknown individuals. However, it was not possible to establish where they came from, and a few scholars they had, had such dissenting opinions that it was impossible to say which of them was right.

Their Water Council was inclined to assume that these were the remnants of the former inhabitants of the hard surfaces of their planet. However, not everyone agreed with this and pointed to the distant part of space, which was never in the field of their interest, suspecting that since they were thinking beings, perhaps intelligence had been also developed there, and not one so peacefully oriented to everything that lives like them. The inspection, as soon as it began, ended just as quickly and their vehicle moved further, and the red bubbles preventing them from swimming, instantly disappeared inside the guards' vehicle.

When they moved away from the inhabited water zones, the pilot turned on the plasma engine and at breakneck speed, they set off into the gorge where the Cap was located.

"Now nobody and nothing can stop us," said the pilot.

"Will they notice our movement?" Appa asked anxiously.

"Yes, of course. They have long realized that the sounds and swirling of water that our engines are making are not a natural phenomenon in their world. They sense our movement from great distances, but they are unable to do anything, they don't have the appropriate technique or raw materials to build something that goes beyond their consciousness. For them, all that perhaps lives outside of their aquatic world is abstract. However, they know that from time to time someone from outside penetrates into their world. They used to take us for creatures that came from the depths. Now they know we are from the outside. For them, the cosmos and the universe are something they sometimes look at, but they don't know what and whom it is for."

It seemed that this joint journey would somehow bring both species of afterglowers together. They already had the entire evolutionary path behind them, as a result of which they achieved the highest degree that a homo protozoan could achieve.

"Now, like the inhabitants of this planet, we are returning to our roots, to our cradle, and to ask one of us for help," Appa thought, not realizing that the two afterglowers from the planet of the Three Suns had crept into her consciousness and read her thoughts.

"They're also looking for Geo." Tybein passed on her remark to Seta.

"But for a purpose other than our's," she said.

"So, what, but they are in danger that can move through the corridors also to us."

"Yes, you are right, we need to consult our Council," she ended this instant exchange of thoughts.

The road they traveled was a complete surprise and a great blessing for them. They acquired valuable memories that they would be able to use for years. Though their afterglow mind registered little now, their afterglow consciousness recorded everything within genti's action reach. Only later, in their asylum, which looked different for each of them, would they get to all the information obtained during the entire escapade. They would be able to know the details of everything that they missed due to the speed of information flow, of changing views, sounds and smells. So it was worth the risk and traveling the genti corridors. It gave meaning to their later afterglow life.

"But what about those who failed?" Appa thought. They fell into oblivion. When she thought about it, her whole body shuddered, which wasn't slipped by other afterglowers. Immediately an attack on her consciousness began.

"They want to get to my memories," she noted, and quickly closed the path to her consciousness. After a while, however, she couldn't stand it and said to the others:

"We can cooperate, and not attack our memories. Are you open to exchanging memories about Geo?"

"Why Geo?" she said, looking suspiciously at Rapp. "What do you want from him and how do you know about him? How did you get the memories of him? After all, your planet is a planet of afterglow souls, and Geo is an Earthman hundreds of thousands of years below you."

"I don't really agree with that," Tybein interjected. "The paradox of time is that it doesn't pass at an equal pace everywhere. Taking into account my memories from the time when I was material, I would like to point out to you that the evolution on the Blue Planet made a circle and returned to itself at a different time, which would mean that life on it had run in one direction, but when the era of homo protozoa ended, there was a cosmic catastrophe there and life died out all over the planet. The cataclysm, however, didn't manage to destroy the Cap and the genti corridors, so our Creator sowed life there for the second time, and its fruit is homo sapiens."

This idyllic journey was interrupted by a sudden shock. The vehicle was decelerating, and from outside there was coming noise like scrubbing of the steel hull on a surface harder than water. The pilot turned off the engine and began to go to the surface. When he turned on the external lighting, they saw a huge rock grotto, the upper ceiling of which was lost in the darkness.

"It is so high that light cannot penetrate this darkness," noted Seta, who was the first to realize that they were in the underwater cave.

"Here we are," the pilot's dry voice cut in on their exchange of thoughts. "Not far away, there is an entrance to the genti corridors. You have little time. Hurry up, the chase is near, and the second part of the grotto is inhabited by water residents of the race that centuries ago began the evolution of the return to hard lands. It will take them thousands of years more, but now they may be dangerous to you. They can live in water and on land. They fight everything and everyone who is different from them, and you differ a lot. Our suits will not help here, and it is not part of our program to eliminate the threat. We can only protect you by hiding you in our vehicle. Unfortunately, it is impossible to swim further, so you are now on your own."

Saying this, he handed them the only weapon he had, long sharp spears ending at the base with a small container in which a large electromagnetic charge was stored, paralyzing all living things.

"Before entering the Cap, twist the handle firmly - you will initiate a self-destructing charge that will prevent the spears from getting into the wrong legs," the guard told them and quickly disappeared in the water taxi. After a while they were alone.

"We're moving," said Appa, unconsciously taking command of the rest of the afterglowers.

The spear blade emitted a narrow beam of light that let them go on. There was no indication that anyone or anything was threatening them. They had been walking for quite a long time, carefully treading on the wet, hard rocky ground. They were already close to the Cap, whose vibrating structure emitted three symbols of the sun and golden rays directed towards the unknown symbolism of the cosmos.

"This is our way to the Blue Planet," Rapp said not too loudly, fascinated by the sight of the Cap.

Then the genti warning reached them - the same for all afterglowers. So expressive and unambiguous that they immediately stopped and aimed the beam of their spear lights at a single point. Though their own appearance differed from that of the arrivals who had blocked their way, they could easily see that they derived from the same line of homo sapiens. Large erect figures with an elongated slender head and luminous oblong eyes, whose body was flat and skin shiny and smooth, stood in front of them, holding a primitive weapon in their upper legs. Their membranous fingers held some strange animal, the flat head of which, armed with a narrow-elongated snout, was directed towards them.

"What is it for?" Seta asked with the thought.

"For attack and defense," passed on the knowledge Rapp, most familiar with various forms of primitive weapons. He received this information from his genti. "It is a water arbok - it spits venom over long distances. When it hits, its venom eats up any matter," he added with obvious fear in his message.

Appa directed her beam of light at one of the newcomers, who was distinguished by its figure and followed their movements with an expressive eyesight.

It was evident that it was their leader, an individual on a different evolutionary stage than the rest of its fellows.

"It is a hybrid of one of the afterglowers - some species have crossed here. Perhaps one of those who ended up here by accident," Rapp flashed his thought.

"Don't use your spears. We stand at a safe distance. We will try to communicate," Appa told them. She took a step forward, and as the other three continued to illuminate the newcomers, she directed the beam of her spear under the hybrid's feet, put her leg to the place important to each afterglowers, to her heart and, striving for peace, she sent to him a telepathic thought of peace and good intentions.

"Who are you?" she asked.

She and the others were very surprised when they got the answer.

"Inhabitants of the grotto," they all heard. "And you?"

"Inhabitants of the sky," answered Appa. "We live in the stars there, and our way home is through this Cap."

The hybrid looked briefly at the place Appa was thinking about. A smile lit his face. He waved his leg and the creatures disappeared from the membranous hands of his people. Then they all fell to the rock floor and froze. Only the hybrid, having bowed slightly in their direction, straightened his figure again.

"Why are you so different from each other?" She asked.

"We come from different stars, but we were all one once. I knew I would see you someday. The roe of my roe assured us that its roe had come through this sacred place to us long ago."

"Where did it come from?" Tybein asked, unable to contain her curiosity. After all, she had been once a prehistorian.

"From a milk roe," he replied after a brief moment of reflection. "There was its shoal. It showed our ancestors the place of its birth."

"We live there too," Appa tried to get more information by involving the hybrid in her confessions.

"I don't know anything more. We have signs in this grotto, left by our Roe. Unfortunately, we don't understand what they mean. Perhaps you can tell us what sacred signs our Roe left us."

Telepathy was a primitive form of communication of the afterglowers, which served them even at a time when they couldn't get rid of their material bodies. However, it never vanished from them, because it was the basis for that time's penetration of consciousness through the way of genti.

Appa turned to the others.

"Maybe we will go see these signs?"

"You know the law of genti - you don't interfere with the lives of other forms of homo," protested Tybein from the Planet of the Three Suns.

"We'll see where he came from and why he crossed with the local life form, and maybe their planet needs help," Rapp noted.

"I doubt, we'd better give up searching for new memories, it might be too dangerous for us, and besides, we don't have time."

"You don't, but we don't have to hurry, so here we'll split up."

Appa looked at the heavy form of the Hoper, who was willing to give way to them in search of Geo. "Or maybe he wants to use us to find the Earthman," she thought for a moment. "No, probably no, after all, they are already in the correct corridor of Genti and will get onto their own planet themselves.

I don't know what to think about it, how do you think?" Appa conveyed her doubts.

"I think they are driven by the urge to get memories. After all, it's not their planet that is endangered, so they don't have to hurry," she added, "apparently Geo is of less value to them."

Tybein easily penetrated the protective layer of the inhabitants of the Planet of Souls. Their system of communication and protection against unwanted access to their consciousness was not an obstacle for her. She didn't know why it was like that, maybe as she suspected, they didn't deal with the takeover of hostile memories, so this protective shield was too weak for her genti specializing in memory stealing from the Hopers. She didn't, however, show that she knew their thoughts. Why go looking for Geo and risk landing somewhere on an unknown planet again. They will find him, and then I will find them," she speculated, looking at the hybrid waiting for them. Curiosity about what she would see there prevailed, so she said to Appa:

"Go and look for Geo on the Blue Planet, just remember, he is the same hybrid as this one, the only difference is that he has tremendous power. His genti is capable of sending you into oblivion and even annihilating your consciousness."

Appa approached the hybrid without fear.

"It is our weapon," she sent him telepathic information about its operation. "Let it help you in the further evolutionary development of your shoal. When your shoal, after many spawning seasons, reaches a degree of development equal to our's, the cap through which your roe came to you, will be open to you."

The hybrid timidly extended his leg to get the spear, then bowed low and sent something like a thank you to Appa, adding at the end:

"I'm Nifled."

He turned and left.

"What you have done is forbidden," Rapp rebuked her.

"But it will help them shape their own identity," she growled angry at her for the admonishment.

Rapp set the spear's mechanism to self-destruct, then threw it into a deep rock crevice.

Without fear, Rapp and Appa approached the Cap and went individually through its gate. They didn't see the Hybrid and all the rest of the warriors watching them. They treated the Cap as a place that killed everyone and everything that dared to enter through its gate. They hadn't known that only one who reached the evolutionary rank of the afterglower could enter there with impunity, but now they learned that one day it would be possible for them. Following their memories, Tybein and Seta made their way quickly down the genti corridor to the next Relay Station, the same from which Geo and Iva had set off to Earth.

The rest of them went further with Nifled and his people. They walked one by one, creating a narrow lane of figures meandering on the rocky path leading them between the walls of the grotto. The path they followed, ascended sharply, and the few chambers and corridors separating them became more spacious. Suddenly they saw quite clearly a bright point of white light high above.

"This is our spawning ground," said Nifled. "We live there."

The next corridor they entered was fully illuminated by a strong stream of diffused light, the color of which made Tybein wonder.

"It's artificial light," she flashed her mind to Seta.

"Indeed, where did it come from?" she wondered for a moment. Immediately afterwards, she noticed a large wall, the color of which clearly differed from that they had seen so far.

"It reminds me of the shell of our spacecraft," she remarked in a puzzled tone.

They didn't, however, have time for further deliberations, because from inside this structure, came a group of figures very similar to Nifled. It was, however, evident that they were as if from another population, slightly different one from their leader's.

The shouts and screams they gave at their sight, made them both point their spear blades at them, as if fearing for their safety.

"You are in no danger," Nifled reassured them.

With one decisive gesture, he caused everyone to fall to their knees and touch their forelocks before the unknown individuals. Then, as if nothing had happened, they got up and walked ahead of them into this strange corridor.

The closer they got to the entrance, the more real it seemed to them that they were dealing with the Genti Guards' station. The local inhabitants, or at least those with whom they became acquainted, didn't seem to have the intelligence and technical capabilities to build such a huge structure. Entering the building's interior immediately made them realize that they were inside an artificial corridor illuminated by huge oblong light generators. The semi-circular walls surrounding them, were ribbed with various devices unknown to them. And the special gates through which they passed reminded them of the hermetic bulkheads that were on their spaceships.

Seta walked over to a small basin on the left side of the partition leading to another corridor and pressed one of the buttons.

"It doesn't work," he sent the thought to Tybein.

Only when he thought that maybe their intended use was more complex and that another way should have been used to get inside, the button glowed blue.

"They can be controlled by consciousness," he told her proudly.

As they managed to notice, the duplicate buttons were controlled by consciousness, but all other types of mechanical switches, bolts, buttons, indicators or devices within their range didn't respond to their commands.

"I'll try to give some command," she told Seta. "I have some associations," she added, looking at the unknown to her forms of construction of these devices, but correctly reasoning that since they served the Genti Guards, they should have responded to their commands.

"Just make it safe," Seta warned her.

She looked around trying to define the thought so as to reach the automaton controlling this room. Tybein directed her awareness to the lighting control console. It seemed to her that it would be the safest, so she imagined the desktop responsible for controlling the light of the part in which they were.

"Dim the lights," she commanded.

To his surprise and horror of the natives, the lights in the corridor dimmed.

Nifled looked in their direction in surprise.

"Who did it?" Frightened by this unexpected phenomenon, he knelt down on one of the legs.

"I did it," Tybein replied.

"How?"

"I gave the order."

"Can you talk to the Great Spawning ground?"

"I don't know what the Great Spawning ground is."

"No one has entered there yet," Nifled muttered, angry that someone didn't know such an obvious thing. "Follow me, I will lead you out of here, and you will see what the Great Spawning ground is."

"Lead on," Seta replied to him.

They walked along the corridors, passing through various rooms that the natives had adapted to their daily needs, and although none of them had memories that could tell them what they were dealing with, all the afterglowers were guided by the common thought.

"The natives are a species related to them; they are homo sapiens evolved in the conditions of aquatic existence." They set off, curious about what Nifled was going to show them.

However, not all of the tribe members walked on with them. The children, women, and the non-warrior rest of the tribal community stayed inside.

The last platform of the huge hall leading beyond the facility of the great base was ended with a gate and a wide landing, the end of which was based on indigenous green vegetation. The sight they saw took their breath away. In front of them there was a great valley filled with lush greenery, among which a wide river meandered, disappearing somewhere at the foot of low mountains, whose peaks were covered with a white wrapper. The sight reminded them of the memories that everyone on their planet had passed on to each other for generations.

"This is what the Planet of the Three Suns looked like once," Tybein said in a voice filled with emotion.

They began to descend a steep platform.

"Don't go there now. It's dangerous," Nifled tried to stop them from going outside. The afterglowers didn't listen to him and, screaming joyfully, scattered around the area. Seeing that his warnings were ineffective, he sent several of his warriors to protect them.

"By the glory of our suns!" screamed Seta, who, turning back, saw the familiar sight.

"It's an artificial structure," Tybein whispered, staring in amazement at the great wall of the first section of the base from which they had just left.

There was a huge word 'Hope' above the exit. The stout silhouette of a transport shuttle had had to dig the local ground with its hull, making a wide indentation in it. Only now did they notice that they were standing in the gap that the ship had made before it had been slowed down by the grotto which it had hit with its left side. The plucked part of this piece of the hull lay in the near distance, frightening with torn pieces of plating. The force of the impact was so great that the entire hull of the ship was thrown from the rock breach and froze motionless, raising its plasma drive nozzles high upwards as if calling for help. Nobody and nothing would help it here, it will never soar into space, and its engines will never thunder again at the time of take-off.

They knew that the large round cylinders standing nearby, based on cushioned supports, had come from their planet, but they didn't know how they had gotten there and how it was possible that they had traveled such a great distance. They had sent their ships into space during the era of the great extinction, which would mean that for tens of thousands of Hope years the base prepared for their arrival had served as a shelter for the local inhabitants.

"When did the Hopers build the base here?" Seta asked looking at a series of rooms for future colonizers of this planet. She knew they had been built by automatons, but she wasn't sure if any group of Hopers had gotten there after that. The period of the great extinction manifested itself in various displacement actions. Occasionally, spacecraft were hijacked. There were also many cases of stowaways flying with the robots, who thought it was their only chance to survive. "Did any of the Hopers come here alive?" She wondered, looking at the cylinder in the center of the base.

"I don't think any of the Hopers were here during its construction. If it were so, they would welcome us with joy," Seta was of a different opinion.

"They might not have lived to our times, but they could have left a trace of their stay by crossing with the natives, and I think Nifled may be an example of this," Tybein had her opinion on this subject.

They stared at the base and didn't notice four local creatures sneaking up on them. In appearance, they resembled the natives they had met earlier. Their bodies were covered with tiny scales, and the slightly pointed head had an elongated face melting into a mouth full of sharp fangs. It was evident that they were natives who moved with equal ease in water and on land. The great oblong bodies were armed with long legs ended with sharp claws, with the help of which they hunted everything that emitted heat. They besieged the hopers without having a feeling that they were not their daily food providers, but beings able to defend themselves.

The two of them closest to Seta rapidly attacked. The first of the creatures got her, sticking the sharp claws of its front legs into her body. Seta felt pain piercing her entire body. Out of the corner of her eye, she saw the other monster.

"Be careful!" she, however, managed to shout to Tybein standing two steps away.

Hearing the painful exclamation of Seta, she immediately directed the spear blade there and, seeing the attacker, pressed the trigger. The blue lightning flawlessly hit the monster, which, paralyzed by the plasma charge, fell on the green stems.

"To me!" She shouted to the rest of the warriors.

The natives efficiently closed ranks, directing their little creatures towards the monsters preparing to attack. They immediately struck their attackers with venom. The spears of Tybein and Seta sowed their destructive power, hitting them again and again. Nifled with his warriors threw deadly charges trying to hit the leader named Lydokork - a muddy representative of a not very intelligent faction of the Homo water people.

"Attack!" there was a sharp scream of the largest monster. He didn't understand why its warriors fell dead to the ground and gave no sign of life.

Lydokork stood a little to the side, waiting for the first meal of the day. They had had food trouble for a long time. Their hunting territory had shrunk both in water and on land. Therefore, now they decided to attack the hydro people from the rock crevice. They knew that to get inside, they had to defeat Nifled and only then would they have been able to get to the spawn inside. Obtaining their Spawning would have provided them with food for a very long time. Tybein, seeing that there were more attackers coming, and Seta was injured, ordered a retreat. She knew it would be easier for them to defend themselves in the corridor.

"We're going back inside," she sent everyone the very clear message.

The entire group started to retreat to the center of the base in tight formation. Walking up the platform that connected the corridor with the hard ground was a dangerous moment for them. They couldn't all fit on it at once, so having created a lane, they surrounded the entrance platform, first letting in the wounded warriors.

Shocking with their loads the Lydokorks who were attacking them fiercely and efficiently, they evacuated all the natives inside. The last to board the ship were Tybein and Nifled. Several monsters followed them, trying to climb onto the metal surface of the platform. However, it was an impassable obstacle for them. The Genti Guards platform had been programmed to distinguish between species of homo sapiens and other species of crawling, flying and jumping creatures. It created an electromagnetic field around itself called the field of consciousness that could differentiate between species belonging to homo sapiens and afterglowers.

When an individual of a different species or of a lower degree of evolution wanted to board the ship, they were immediately recognized by sensors. Then the ion protection from the launchers hidden beneath its surface shocked them with paralyzing charges. They fired at anything defined by the computer as a threat to the ship and crew.

Tybein didn't know that she, the ship's crew and all the robots had biochemical identifiers implanted that were intended for anyone who wanted to get on board. It was an automatic and painless procedure, introduced unknowingly for anyone born on Hope.

"Why does the base consider hybrids as crew members?" Tybein wondered as the hybrids safely entered the ship.

"Seriously injured Seta must receive immediate help," Nifled offered his services, or rather the services of his Rotkod, who helped all sick roe on their spawning ground.

"They were Lydokorks," Nifled explained later. "They live on the outskirts of the water zone of the land called Great Vovors. They can adapt their appearance to the environment around them. Now they are at war with us."

Tybein and Seta didn't listen to what he had to say, but exchanged their afterglow thoughts.

"How to open the door to the inside of the ship? There is biogenetic regeneration of the bodies," Tybein wondered.

"I know what to do. First, we need to find the capsule control room. Hope has been set to obey the afterglowers' commands and don't respond to the mechanical impulses of controlling its devices. They have been blocked. The control cabin is somewhere inside the ship.

"Give an afterglow command to the autopilot to open the locking mechanisms. You've already done it with the light in the corridors," he added, looking at his torn arm. "I need the recovery capsule. Only it can heal me."

Nifled couldn't keep up with the reading of their afterglow thoughts. He wasn't genti, he didn't have the needed skills.

"I'm not in the afterglow being. Genti is telling me to go to the rescue capsule and issue orders from there. Only there are the right conditions for such an action." The afterglow builders predicted a partial variant of destroying the ship and controlling its mechanisms from the escape capsule.

"Nifled, do you know where the escape capsules are?" Seta asked.

"I don't know what you're talking about," he replied telepathically with more ease.

"I know," replied the young hybrid clinging to his leg.

"Who is this?" Seta asked, astonished, looking at the young being similar to Nifled.

"My tadpole from the mother's roe. She is the ruler of all creatures of the Great Spawning ground."

"So young?" Tybein blurted out.

"She has the power, only she has returned from the Great Gate."

"It wasn't difficult," the Tadpole replied.

They didn't notice that the Tadpole communicated with them using the afterglow awareness. "Lead on," Tybein asked.

The Tadpole walked confidently straight into the side corridor. When they reached its end, they saw a closed partition in front of them. Beside it, there were a number of different defunct devices.

Only one small open recess sparkled with a pale blue light. The Tadpole stood on her membranous toes and, without hesitation, put her little hand inside it. All three received the message she sent deep into this sensor.

"Open up," they got the thought from her awareness.

They had no time to wonder how this was possible, but the latches of the gates slid open noiselessly before them. They entered the first segment of this great spaceship without fear. They immediately knew they were in the right place.

The young hybrid led them without hesitation, walking through the corridors and opening in the same way all the doors to the individual rooms intended for the crew of this base. It was evident that he knew the layout of the rooms very well, but he didn't know what they were for. But they knew, and most memories had Tybein, who in her youth had been a pilot of a spacecraft that admittedly had surpassed Hope in its technique, but some systems and devices hadn't been so different.

Finally, the Tadpole led them to a room next to the afterglow dome from where they could see an open door leading to the control panel of all the devices in the base.

This time, Tybein took the initiative. Holding the Tadpole by her leg, she entered the Central Command Post. She looked at the indicators of various devices, glowing with colorful lights. Without hesitating, she walked over to the screen and sent an impulse:

"Restore command for the material people," then put her hand to the blue glowing recess on the control panel. In an instant, all the lights flashed and a laser beam of blue light fired from the depths of the control panel, and an image of a virtual Hoper appeared in the center of the room. They heard the metallic voice of an automatic pilot.

"I'm Beta - the automatic commander of Hope. Welcome to the Hopers' Base on the Fish Planet."

"Turn on all mechanisms. Full readiness to accept the new crew. Activate the robots," Tybein continued to issue commands.

"Systems on, all teams fully operational," the autopilot's impassive voice sounded in the room.

"Lead to the recovery room," she cut her off, "we have an injured man, quickly," she demanded in a firm, confident tone. She wasn't sure if this biogenetic robot made of their DNA would listen to someone who wasn't a regular on the base's crew.

It obeyed, because a small biorobot broke away from the wall and, flashing light, rolled towards the exit. They quickly followed it.

"I hope we save her," the Tadpole expressed her concern to them.

The recovery room was close. Two robots who took care of the sick members of the crew walked over to them. They quickly and efficiently placed the wounded man in a capsule filled with a jelly-like substance and the process of renewing damaged tissues and organs began.

The rest stood at a considerable distance, separated by a transparent hermetic wall beyond which no foreign bacteria, microbes, let alone other forms of life could pass. Here, no material form was allowed to enter, it would have been too dangerous for the wounded man lying on a biological table who was subjected to fully automatic processes of repairing his bodily shell.

"There's nothing here for us, we'll wait for a little longer before he joins us. We have to take care of our new homo water people," said Tybein, assuming the role of commander of this small group of thrill-seekers.

"As you can see, fate didn't spare us new memories, but now our goal is to ensure safety and help in the development of the community of future afterglowers, represented by the young Tadpole," she said to the gathered, looking at them with questioning eyes, as if searching for confirmation in them that they were receiving her message.

"You're right, but it won't be easy. This planet has such different life forms that it will be difficult to predict which one will dominate the rest and become the prime species on this planet," she received the message from Seta.

"I managed to look carefully at them and I believe they are the closest relatives of our common single-celled ancestor. Our scientists have known for a long time that these unicellular microbes assimilated bacteria more than two billion years ago and thus gave rise to cells whose organelles are wrapped in cell membranes, which is a common feature of all intelligent creatures of the homoafterglowers species.

This is why we need to help our young leader, although it seems to me that she can use the genti corridors without hindrance, but she doesn't because she has no knowledge that it is possible for her."

"How did it happen that she has such possibilities?" the tone full of amazement testified to the fact that she had not yet gotten used to this thought and hadn't glozed over it.

"We are about to find out from whom she acquired the ability to use our genti," Tybein replied, sure of her gut.

"The curvature of space associated with the temporal entanglement of the quanta is the cause of this evolutionary leap," Seth put in her insight. Lying on the recovery table, she hadn't lost awareness, but just the possibility of movement. In her material life, she had been a quantum physicist studying the evolutionary jumps of elementary particles and their effects on changing their evolutionary partner at any cosmic distance.

"Although, as I can see, not everything went as it should, as the young hybrid is more similar to the homo water people than to her afterglow roe."

"You will have a lot of memories when you answer the question why this happened, and now we go to their holy place," Tybein ended this silent exchange of views. She looked at the Tadpole every now and then, and was more and more sure that she must have had some unknown ability to acquire genti knowledge. "We'll probably learn more about it there," she ended the discussion.

"Beta, how many Guardians do you have on board?" She asked.

"Seven," Beta replied.

"Three are coming with us, they are to protect us. Program them to neutralize anyone who attacks us or the natives," she ordered Beta.

Three hydro guards emerged from down the corridor. Each of them had a plasma ejector of paralyzing gas. They were virtually indestructible and made an excellent defensive arsenal. When they left the base, they were surrounded by several Nifled warriors armed with creatures.

"They come with us; they will protect us as we fight our way through the lands of our kinsmen. They don't accept any strangers in their territory," Nifled told them.

"Who are kinsmen?" Tybein asked.

"A long time ago, at the time when all races were united and their members made spawn together, a group of homo water people arouse, that didn't tolerate other types of hydro water people. Its roe was stained by an 'unknown person' who came from an 'unknown place' and began to threaten our roe. We call them Loina - they are very similar to us, but they can hover above the watery space of their spawning ground. They don't oviposit and therefore need a vector for their spawn.

They kidnap anyone who cannot defend themselves against them. They have one weakness; they don't have any weapons. Their areas are the water world and rock chasms, where they feel safe. They hunt only when the sun is over our spawning ground."

They walked through the rock grotto until they got to other side of the hill. The sight they saw, coming out of the rock chasm, astonished them profoundly. They were convinced that the planet didn't have large flat spaces, and here there was a flat valley in front of them, behind which a sheet of water gleamed, crinkled with a slight gust of wind with a strange fishy aftertaste, which reached them due to the breeze blowing from the water side.

"These are their spawning grounds?" Tybein asked.

"Yes, they live in the slope above us, in the upper rock clefts, which they constantly widen, throwing out rock debris, which is why we have such a rubble under us."

Nifled's warriors standing nearby looked up intently, searching for Loina.

"We need to get away from the water quickly. Loina doesn't move away from the rocks, so the farther from the water, the safer.

We're going! Quickly!" the Tadpole shouted in their direction and ran out into the empty space, heading towards the strange object protruding from the plants surrounding it. "There is a Sacred Hybrid site!" she managed to scream to them and ran madly in that direction.

"She looks funny when she runs," thought Tybein, looking at a huge cluster of plants several hundred paces away, with strange twisted shapes, among which shone effuse flowers of various colors.

Several warriors with creatures in their legs followed the hybrid. She felt what the hybrid felt. She was not afraid for her; she knew that where she ran it was safe for her and all the others who accompanied her. So, she didn't run, and let the Tadpole and the rest of them walk away from them. When they were halfway, a luminous figure with large white membranous wings soared from the water near the shore and hovered for a moment. It was evident that he or she was following their group. After a while, without attacking anyone, the figure disappeared under the water.

"They're about to attack." Nifled stopped a group of his warriors with one move of his spear. They knew what to do in such a situation. They quickly closed ranks to form a circle. They stretched their legs with creatures above their heads and froze in anticipation of the attack. They didn't have to wait long, as a dozen or so Loins flew out of the water and, gliding, headed towards them.

"They obviously need a new spawn," Tybein said, stepping out of the circle. One of the Guardians of Hope moved with her towards the attackers. He stood a few steps from the circle formed by the natives and shot up a stream of energy.

The blue cap of the protective field spilled over them, creating a wide semicircular surface surrounding all individuals below it. The thin protective film of the plasma vibrated and glowed in a variety of bright colors.

"This is a warning sign for any intelligent homo sapiens," she thought.

But not for the Loin, who attacked with the sun behind them and didn't manage to see the protective umbrella that stretched beneath them. The first few who fell on its surface bounced off it as if from some armor and, sliding on its oval surface, fell outside its boundaries. They lay motionless, and their outspread wings unknowingly folded on their backs. The ones flying behind them, seeing what happened, tried to change the flight path. They weren't able to do it. They couldn't flap their membranous wings fast enough to soar in time. They were flying in the gusts of rising wind, and for a little correction of flight they used membranous fins stretched between their legs. They masterfully changed the horizontal flight path, gliding over the plasma protection. Then, like vultures, they circled over their would-be victim, wondering why their kin lay there with no signs of life.

"Go on, I'll take a look at these creatures," Tybein sent the signal to them.

The entire group continued on, and the Guard moved his protective umbrella over them so that they were always within its reach. Tybein and the other guard separated from them and walked over to the winged creature lying nearby. "They would look like me, if not for the membranes on the back," she said, looking at the wings growing out of Loin's body. "Whole body without an armored scale," she continued, looking closely at the lying figure. "The legs are almost the same, and those grasping fingers."

"Wake him up," she ordered the Guard.

He put his steel gripper against Loin's body and injected antidote into it. Loina opened his eyes as if they were a steel gate in the base corridor. He looked with his round blue pupils at the would-be victims standing above him.

"Who are you?" She asked telepathically.

At first, Loina seemed unable to answer. He looked at the figure standing above him and made no sign that he understood what was being sent to him.

After a while, Tybein received a strong telepathic message.

"I'm Fallen."

"Why are you attacking us?"

"We have no new spawn, and we will die without them."

"What do you do with beings like us when you catch them?"

"We oviposit in them."

"And then?"

"When the sun sets three times behind the great moons, we give them to the Great Spawn. They are there until a new Loina is formed in them. Then they are free, but then they don't want to return to their spawning ground."

"Why?"

"Our spawn is like the sun that gives them warmth and shelter."

"Well, maybe it is really so," she thought.

"Who are you?" Loina asked.

"We are from the sky. You can't oviposit in us. Fly away and pass it on to everyone.

Let it fly away," he ordered the Guard.

"It was not that simple, however. Loina must have taken to the air, but he could only do so when he was in the water or by jumping down a slope. He could also swim under water, where he picked up a speed that allowed him to take off from the crest of the wave and immediately be carried away by gusts of wind. Gliding, he moved up through the air. He was not able to flap these wings so quickly, so as to take off without a gust of wind, so he guided the flight, steering his legs, turning them towards the chosen target.

The Guardian turned on his plasma drive and, taking the Fallen in his arms, he rose up. He flew him without fear to the first chasm on the slope of a rocky cliff. He placed him gently on the edge of the water surface and flew away. Only then did the other Loinas lurking in the nooks and crannies of the chasm dare to peer at the top of their spawn, watching the strange creature retreat in streams of orange flames.

The Tadpole and the natives accompanying her reached the place where the Holy Spawn was. Around him, there were tall plants, which with their sharp peaks, obscured the view of the little spaceship. On its shiny hull, there was a slightly worn inscription - Ollopa 51.

"When did they get here?" She was surprised. "The ship is not wrecked and has not crashed, so what could have happened?" she wondered. "Make contact," she instructed the Guardians.

Two of them moved quickly forward. Going round the rock fragments scattered all around the ship, they quickly approached its hull. From their side, the ship showed its powerful propulsion nozzles. The guards were not far away when two plasma laser shots were fired from hiding. Both struck by its enormous charge, they slumped to the flat ground directly under its right engine.

Instantly a strong protective field opened around them, embracing the guards and the entire group headed towards the ship.

"Identification," she shouted to the third guard of Hope. A strong identification impulse was sent towards the ship, understandable to any civilization on the homoafterglow level.

The two guards moved forward in the direction from where the shots had been fired at them. They didn't shoot, but for defense, they surrounded themselves with a protective field. Their sensors detected two hydro robots hiding behind a rock ledge next to a lowered stairs leading into the ship's interior.

"This is Ollopa 51, a transport passenger ship," they picked up the strong afterglow signal. "The Holy Spawn Guardians prevent access to anyone who is not roe from our spawning ground," the Tadpole told them. She walked over to Tybein.

"I have to mark you, then you will be safe. Give me a leg," saying it, she stretched her leg out towards her.

Surprised, she unknowingly extended her hand. She felt a strong prick and immediately gained access to the hydro robots.

Without waiting for the Tadpole to mark the others, she used the safety procedure and sent a signal disabling aggression in all robots within its scope. It was a risky move, as the signal cut off from the base the robots which had the same safeguards.

Now they climbed the steps into the ship unhindered.

"Who are they defending?" Nifled asked.

"The dome," Tybein replied.

She knew that only in defense of the dome, could robots be so aggressive.

"Dome?" Nifled was surprised. He had no memories, so he couldn't know the past.

The Tadpole, without concern led everyone to her familiar place. Tybein knew that their identification didn't allow her to open the rooms on the ship. It turned out, however, that these laws didn't apply to her. She opened the individual compartments leading to the Holy Place.

"How do you know all this?" Tybein, curious, turned to the hybrid.

"From my roe. It passes on her awareness to me and tells me what to do."

Inside the ship, in a great room, the wall of the Dome blocked their way. A stream of a strong electron beam was coming from its upper base, disappearing into a circular device attached to the ceiling of the room.

"There are the afterglowers here," Tybein communicated her insights to Seta, "but I can't understand them.

Who are they?" she thought for a moment before getting the flash.

"Tell your spawn that we are from the sky," she asked the Tadpole.

"They know," she answered her.

"So, let them reach our consciousness, otherwise we won't be able to help them."

"They can't, they don't have memories."

"Who are they?"

"They don't know."

"Where did they come from?"

"From the sky." The Tadpole willingly acted as an intermediary in this telepathic exchange of thoughts.

Tybein thought intensely how she could help the afterglowers locked in the dome. She roughly knew what might have happened.

"Lead to the ship's command console," she asked the Tadpole.

She knew the Tadpole didn't know the way; it would be the afterglowers in the dome that would guide her to her destination.

After a few moments, they were at the large command post. In the seats, they saw the four bodies of this ship's crew.

"They're pilots," she said, looking at the patches on their suits. "They didn't survive the passage through curved spacetime," she guessed the cause of their death.

"Show me the flight history," she directed the request to the ship's Central Computer. She knew that since the Guardians had carried out her earlier instructions, the ship's computer, which also acted as an automatic pilot, would listen to anyone who was an afterglower.

In the front part of the transparent screen simulating the view that stretched in front of the ship's nose, the figure of a virtual pilot appeared, who introduced itself in a dispassionate voice.

"I'm Tamotua - the automatic pilot on the Afterglow, the passenger and cargo ship from the planet Hope.

As it spoke, the image on the screen showed them an area of space with the planet of the Three Suns marked on it. A bright spot broke off from one of its moons. The path it traveled to the second moon was suddenly changed. The image flickered and a black void of space appeared.

"What happened?" she asked.

"Command of the ship was taken over."

"By who?"

"Passengers from the afterglowers' dome disabled the material crew's ability to steer the ship."

"What happened next?"

"They fell into a curved space opened by other afterglowers traveling through the genti corridors," the pilot said and fell silent.

"Keep talking," she demanded.

The Tadpole wasn't interested in the pilot's story, so she slipped away to her spawn.

"No information was written further until it enters the galaxy."

The screen flashed again, showing cosmic space dotted with stars as well as the course of the Glow to the Second Moon of Hope plotted by the material pilot. However, not everything went as planned. They didn't predict the trajectory that crossed the space-time corridor. They fell into oblivion. The afterglowers protected by the dome, survived the emergency landing."

"Tamotua - where are we?" said Gonda, the 3rd mechanic who regained consciousness after exiting the space-time corridor.

"The planet on which I accidentally landed meets the living conditions for Hopers."

"What about the crew?"

"Only the third mechanic survived, all passengers are dead. The third engineer took command of the ship. He cut off the links to the emergency controls in the dome."

"Any damage?"

"None."

"Why don't we go back," Gonda asked the question.

The afterglowers took control of the ship," he heard the reply of the automatic pilot. "I can't unlock the flight system."

Gonda didn't feel responsible for the deaths of crew members. He knew it was the fault of the afterglowers.

A moment's pause and Tamotu's calm voice directed to the afterglowers' dome was heard again: "Gonda, the third mechanic is informing you that he is disabling communication with me. You're supposed to use genti. The return of the Ship to the Three Suns is postponed until further notice."

The visor flashed and went out. From that moment on, they plunged into the afterglow existence, and although they had no remorse because they had no such memories, they knew that it was they who had contributed to the death of the crew. The only penalty was the inability to regenerate cells, which was not unusual for them. They couldn't take a journey to the Blue Planet, so the end of their existence was approaching quickly. However, not as quickly as the end of Gonda's life, who, for reasons unknown to them, didn't want to return to Hope. This was the case for many Hope years until coming into contact with the Tadpole - the first hybrid to possess the Hope genes."

A moment of pause and the screen darkened, only the rapidly flashing clock, swallowing the following years at breakneck speed, made them aware of the flow of time. The clock stopped and the screen in front of the ship showed a basin surrounded by small hills, the shores of which were doused by the waters of a great sea.

"I tracked down an identification signal from the Hoper's base, so I decided to land where any form of homo sapiens life exists," explained Tamotua. Then you could see the ship safely landing on a flat land full of greenery and tall bushes, the flowery color of which seemed friendly to everything that surrounded it. Near the ship, there was lush vegetation speckled with enormous flowered trees growing out of its base, the double branches of which soared into the sky, but each of them in a different direction, so that the plant could continuously draw life-giving heat from the two suns that appeared alternately in the sky.

"How much time has passed since landing?"

"Fifty Hope years," replied Tamotua.

"Show the first arrival of the natives," she gave the order. She knew that there was no point in showing the afterglowers because they were invisible to any form of image and sound recording.

The screen flickered and a native who was running appeared. Every now and then the figure turned around, looking at Lydokork who was chasing her.

"She has no chance, he's about to catch up with her," the Tadpole put in her comment.

Then the native saw the ship. He went that way and ran up the lowered stairs. "Close the entrance hatch," you could hear from the rescue capsule.

"Who let him in?" Tybein asked.

"The afterglowers - they have disabled the protective system," Tamotua explained.

The native stood in the center of the chamber. She was a young savage - a native inhabitant of a nearby spawning ground. Standing, she gasped and stared in horror at the equipment there.

She was in a fully automated biological treatment plant chamber. Detectors and automatic analyzers checked whether she posed a threat to the crew and the ship.

"All indicators are normal," said the voice of the computer pilot from the screen.

"Guard, lead the native to the biological recovery booth," the same voice commanded the last Guard. But she didn't want to go anywhere. She was standing scared and would have loved to go back outside to her world. It didn't matter to her that Lydokorks were waiting for her there, at least she knew them, and everything she saw here was unknown to her and filled her with fear.

The guard sprayed a small dose of enslaving gas in front of the native and lightly pushed her towards the corridor. Now she walked passively wherever he led her.

"Turn on the protective field," the command was heard.

It was the voice of Gond, the only surviving material crew pilot who had been in the rescue capsule while traversing curved spacetime. He was the only one who had managed to take refuge there before the ship had fallen into the space-time vortex.

"Direct attack on the ship," Tamotua's voice sounded. "I'm closing access to the ship."

The huge hatch of the entrance closed noiselessly and energy charges fired from the cannons. Lydokorks, struck by the strong impulse, fell to the rocky ground.

However, not all of them. A protective umbrella stretched over the fallen ones. A few Lydokorks who were out of range of the field tried to approach the lying ones. The slightly bluish wall they came across, which looked like a bubble from a hot spring near their spawning ground, was an effective barrier that they couldn't break through. Everyone who touched this bubble was struck by an energy impulse that didn't kill, but caused a temporary paralysis of the muscles. They quickly realized that what was visible behind it was steering this strange big bubble. The dome faded when they walked away from it. However, when after some time they tried to approach the ship again, a blue lightning flew out of it and the bubble again protected access to the place where their breakfast had disappeared.

The screen froze as if waiting for further commands.

"The rest can be conjectured, but we will check how he died," Tybein loudly expressed her thoughts. "Show the end of the pilot's life," she added.

The screen showed an old Hoper lying in the recovery room. He was clearly weak and decrepit. Here, on the ship, he couldn't turn his life into the afterglow existence, so at 156, he died. The native, the only companion of his life on this Fish Planet, gave his body where all from her spawning ground for centuries had ended their lives. He fell from a great cliff into the depths of water which were their eternal resting place.

"Show me how the Hoper and the native crossed," she gave the order.

"I don't have a recorded moment of the intersection of the native and the second pilot. The data has been deleted."

"Then show the birth of the first hybrid."

The screen showed the recovery room. It was seen how was born the first hybrid, a crossbreed, a descendant of their race and a native of this planet. Her mother was lying in a jelly-like basin, holding with her legs the little hybrid Tadpole, Gond's daughter.

Then the image on the screen sped up to show the little native walking away to her shoal in her mother's embrace.

"It's the Tadpole, only she has a body like us. Show me the results of her DNA test," she demanded.

'99.9999% match with our DNA' - the result of the test made right after her birth was displayed.

"That 0.0001% difference can be of colossal importance to our species," Tybein said in a dispassionate voice.

"What do you mean?" Seta couldn't resist to ask, as Tybein's biological diversions were incomprehensible for her.

"She may not have offspring from someone of her shoal. She needs to find her roe for an evolutionary breakthrough in this shoal. As you know, everyone here can have spawn with any other person, but I don't think that with her.

It's time to get to know our afterglowers," she said. "We have a problem with them, not with the Tadpole."

They all asked themselves the same question - how to transport the afterglowers to the nearest Cap, through which they could return to their planet?

The Tadpole knew that it wasn't possible. She knew how to save all those she had not seen but with whom she had been communicating from birth.

"I know how," with the strong, decisive message she attracted attention.

Before it passed away, my roe told me that only I can save the Holy Spawning."

"How?" Tybein asked.

"I am to fly with them to heaven to the Great Spawning ground of my spawn."

"Is it possible?" Tybein asked the automatic pilot.

"For her and the afterglowers in the Dome, yes. For you, it's not."

"Why none of us can go to the planet of the Three Suns?"

"In your material existence, you wouldn't survive the flight. In order for the flight to be successful, you must program the launch into a curved space, which can only be opened when you enter the Cap."

"Why will the hybrid survive the flight?"

"She will enter the hibernetic capsule."

"How many capsules are there?"

"Five but only one operational. Remaining capsules couldn't be repaired."

"One," surprised Tybein looked suspiciously at Tamotua. However, she had no grounds to doubt what the automatic pilot was saying. She sat down at the desk and entered the data into the central computer.

"Will you fly?" she turned to the Tadpole. "Only you can decide about it," she added. She looked at her as at an equal Hoper, not a hybrid from another planet.

"I will fly - my other half is waiting for me there," she conveyed it through the message as if she had been a Hoper from birth.

"Who is the other half?" Tybein couldn't hide her surprise.

"I don't know, but my roe told me that he would find me when I return to the Spawning ground in my shoal."

"You have time until the second sun sets to say goodbye to your spawn. Hurry up. At the same time, you must take off, and we must go through the Cap in Keaton's Canyon."

"I know," she replied.

"How do you know what I'm talking about?" She looked at the hybrid, not believing that she really knew what she meant.

"From the other half of my roe. I'm aware of his awareness. It is weak, but tells me to fly to his heaven."

For Geo, staying on the First Moon was not a problem, but it was burdensome, so he returned with Iva to their Paradise Island whenever they could.

"Why not go to Earth to our house?" he asked Iva each time.

"Geo, you know that it's dangerous for me, but if you want, we'll move there."

"Just for a moment, for a few days, you won't feel that time at all - you know how little time my father has left."

"Go, I will wait for you on our yacht," she agreed to his request in a sad voice full of resignation. When the casket carried him to the small house by the beach, and when he opened the door, he was immediately seized with a strong sense of emptiness, such emptiness that engulfs anyone who has to leave a beloved person. Then as soon as possible, he tried to visit his father, go to the cemetery to talk to his mother, visit friends, as well as absorb the Earth's air and saturate his body with warm rays of the sun touching his face, rays that were completely different from those there in the far universe, where each sun had a different dimension and color, completely unlike the one that had accompanied him from the moment of his birth.

How is it possible that a few years had passed here on Earth, and there, in the universe time flowing in a different dimension, had caused that he hadn't aged like all people on Earth? It was an obstacle that couldn't be explained to all those acquaintances who had not yet passed away, and it was this relentless passage of time that made his stays on Earth less and less frequent. One more foray into distant galaxies might have caused that he would have had nobody to return to.

He tried to figure out a theory of time that even Albert Einstein couldn't handle. Where he was, the star systems and planets, revolving around their suns, followed a different path and were subject to different laws, and although the speed of light seemed to be the same everywhere, he found that this was not always the case. There were areas of the cosmos where light didn't spread at all, so it had no added value, but even on the contrary, it could have a negative value which would have meant that you could travel back into the past. Such a negative value was the jump with Iva through the genti corridor to the other Earth, but he was not sure if it was really the second Earth and not the first one on which he lived now. In that time area, time took him back into the past.

"No, I can't figure it out myself, so why analyze something that I have no influence on?" he thought as he sipped his coffee and looked at his father who wandered in his small garden, picking up early vegetables for him. It was spring and the first rays of the sun awakened the vegetation, making him melancholy towards the surrounding reality.

A strong genti message interrupted Geo's thoughts.

Immediately after that, Iva sent him the image - an impulse of wanting to be with him. The vivid sight of her memories of the Paradise Island was to remind him how much she loved and missed him.

"Dad, I have to go back to Hope. Important things are happening there that will affect our planet."

"I know, I know, you have to save the world. Your mother always said that when she wanted to visit Hope, just don't forget that you are human," he reminded him of such an obvious thing with a smile on his lips. "Come with Iva as soon as you deal with this new task - I'm already old and I would like to manage to see your children," he joked with a very serious face. It was a signal to Geo that he didn't have as much time as they did.

Geo could go back now. He had dealt with all the matters that had bothered him during his stay on Hope. The impressions of the stay on the Paradise Island were not enough for him, so he came back and bought this little house next to the beach. He wanted to keep it for himself and Iva.

"Tom, I'm going away again for a long time," he said to a neighbor who lived nearby. "Here are the keys, please see if everything is okay every so often. And here's the alarm code. If something important happens, call my father. Unfortunately, I can't give you, my number. In Africa, where I will be, there is no way to answer the phone," he lied smoothly, looking at his neighbor's kind face.

"Okay, Peter, don't worry, I'll take care of everything. I will take care of your new acquisition. I wonder why you bought such an old house." He was surprised. "You probably need solitude to write about these journeys. I have read all your books. I like the most the one about these women from the African bush. It is very quiet here except for the summer season," he babbled, glad to be able to talk to someone.

"When I come back, I will give you the newest one with a dedication, but now I have to come back, the taxi is waiting. I left the car in the garage, I will not take it to Africa," he joked.

"Let you do well there," he replied, and walked heavily towards his house.

Geo entered the living room, opened the casket, and right after found himself in the Hall of Tradition. Iva threw herself into his arms, and Tora sent him a kind smile.

"What's up?" he greeted those present with the typical earthly phrase. "Our cargo ship, which got missing on the way from Hope to the moon, returns after many Hope years with an alien representative of some civilization. It is not known why, but the alien has the awareness of an afterglower even though she is a native. Her messages are amazing. She can communicate with us and has tremendous ability to absorb our knowledge."

At this point Geo thought about the knowledge the representative of the Green Dwarf had passed on to him.

"As our scientists assume, the alien is a hybrid born of a father, a material Hoper - a mechanic from the Ollop 51 ship, and some native. We don't understand everything. She gives us her memories quite chaotically. By our standards, she is a female hybrid. The Tadpole, as they call her, saved Seta by opening a recovery room. However, the main reason for summoning you is the envoys from the Rebirth Nebula. They came from the primal part of the universe to meet you. How do they know about you at the other end of the cosmos, we don't know. They only want to talk to you. They are the afterglowers ahead of us in evolution by many hundreds of thousands of Hope years."

"Look at the star map," Tora interrupted her. "I will show you where their planetary system is." In the upper left corner of the great four-dimensional map of the cosmos, a pulsating white dot glowed. "The Rebirth Nebula with five Soul Planets. The five afterglower-inhabited planets in the caps of our genti corridor bear symbols of the atomic compounds of the neuron of afterglowers in their original stage. We don't know yet where the cap leading to their system is. However, taking into account the path they traveled to us, they must have been very determined in their quest to find our planet."

When she finished her sentence, their computer rolled the picture, showing the universe as a great trombone trumpet. A white star shone on its outskirts - it was their Hope. Then a thin white line flew out of it, which, writhing spirally on the surface of the trumpet, headed for the central red point of the map, symbolizing the beginning of the universe as the epicenter of the Big Bang. Next to this focal point, shone a second pulsating star - "this is their star system with the Soul Planets," Tora explained.

When the two points came together, the space became curved. It was like a great trombone trumpet that twisted like glow DNA, and its upper surfaces were connected by a short line linking the two worlds.

"We can't show the genti corridors on this map yet. The lines connecting the two worlds are computer animation, but that's how the genti corridors work," said the chief specialist on the genti corridors research team.

Chapter XIII

The Hybrid

The Tadpole without hesitation undertook the risky journey on Ollop 51 to Hope - the Planet of the Three Suns, although Tybein didn't give her great chances to survive this journey.

The great acceleration during the gravitational turbulence as well as a jump into the spacetime shortcut was so dangerous that the chances of survival were minimal. As the Tadpole made its way through the ripples of space-time, they were already waiting for this lost spaceship and, navigating through the genti's corridors, they arrived faster than the ship with the Tadpole on board.

"Why is this old ship so important?" the commander of the moon's space base asked. "After all, there are no Hopers on it."

"There is a hybrid on it. The child of a native and a Hoper who survived the ship's journey to the Fish Planet," Seta explained calmly. "So you are wrong in saying that none of our people is there, because she has 99.99% of a Hoper's genes, so she is one of us."

The Great Hope Council decided to let the Tadpole into their world. All scholars were curious to see what looked like the hybrid which was a proof that an evolutionary leap was possible. It also confirmed the theory that a child of an afterglower and a native of the Fish Planet could be born. They were amazed at the report of the robot supervising the flight. "The Tadpole can efficiently use the genti consciousness and navigate through the genti corridors," was the short message from the ship.

They were even more surprised by her ability to adapt to the different conditions in outer space. She wasn't afraid of great overloads, high acceleration or the possibility of taking oxygen from the water. In more recent times, in an aquatic environment separated by high hills from other water bodies, there was less and less room for their species living in the depths of the water, where faint rays of light didn't allow for the production of sufficient food for all.

When evolution forced them to leave their birthplace and adapt to life on land, her species already possessed the skills that all the inhabitants of the blue planet lacked, and then there was a slow expansion into the open space of solid land. It took them tens of thousands of years to adapt to the double way of breathing, and twice as much to acquire the ability to obtain food outside the aquatic environment.

The breakthrough was the landing of the research ship "Hope" and the construction of the Base by robots, for future colonizers.

They realized that they were not the only inhabitants in the surrounding reality and that somewhere high among the stars, there were other beings. Admittedly, they didn't look like them, but they were indestructible, strong and well organized. They were amazed that they didn't kill when under attack, didn't seek contact with them or interfere with their lives. This lesson of otherness lasted so long that it enabled them to learn by imitation, and later, when, for reasons unknown to them, strange visitors left them and returned to the sky, they could use some of their things left on their planet.

Although they didn't know how to open these strange buildings standing next to their spawn, they learned to use all the other machines and devices. They had observed them using the apparatuses for a long time. When they had realized that it had been safe to move around and be among them, having a great motivation to imitate and an innate tendency to live in a group, they had learned, like the newcomers, to apply a leadership hierarchy, not one of strength, but of intelligence. The more curious and courageous of them imposed their will on the rest slowly but constantly gaining knowledge and skills, finding out that a thrown stone can kill someone, and a sharpened rod can be an effective weapon. They realized that the things left by the newcomers could be used to fight the enemies of their spawning ground.

The most useful skill for their community was to master the skill of using fire. The first fire was started by the newcomers burning the vegetation surrounding their base. Many died then without escaping, and watching the flames rapidly approaching them. The little creatures living in these grassy areas died with them. Their food after the passage of the flames became more palatable and useful for consumption. No one remembered how and who had started the fire first after the visitors left their Fish Planet, but it was then that they established the sacred custom of guarding the eternal fire, which was the beginning of each fire set up for their needs. They were no longer afraid of the cold and the taste of raw food and didn't worry about scaring off their enemies. If they hadn't gotten out of the water, they would have never known a fire that didn't exist in their natural environment. They would have never ventured into distant forests and looked for food there, and they would have still drawn all their basic needs from water. They would have used a live species of a kind of crustacean that was friendly to them, which had lived with them for centuries in a water symbiosis and served them as a lethal weapon, terrible in its consequences.

The message they received from the Tadpole when she found herself in the sphere of influence of their genti aroused considerable surprise among the council members. The strangest thing for them was the Tadpole's questions about her other half.

"Is my other half waiting for me?" this was the first message they received from a distant galaxy as soon as they made contact with the ship.

"You don't have the other half. Your genti is not on our moon," was their reply.

"I have, my spawn from your spawning ground assured me that my other half would be waiting for me here."

At the back of the room, a soft, velvety female voice interrupted them, announcing:

"The ship Ollopa 51 moored to the lunar base."

The picture changed to show the moment the ship joined the transport base airlock. After a short while, the face of the hybrid appeared on the screen and her voice was heard.

"I am the Tadpole from the Fish Planet. Hello everyone from the Spawning ground of my spawn," a woman's voice sounded. "Alpha, your computer taught me the Hope way of communication," she added after a moment of silence, as if wondering whether to reveal the destination at once.

"Is my other half here?" she repeated the question. "I flew to the Great Spawning ground to meet the other half of my roe. Roe from the Big Spawning ground assured me that I would meet her here," she flashed awareness to Geo.

"It is impossible that she had her other half on Hope. She is not an afterglower but a hybrid," an impulse from Iva reached him.

"I'm a hybrid too," replied Geo.

"You are different."

"Why?"

"Your mother was a Hoper."

"Her father too."

"But your mother was a female embryogenetic, so she could interfere with your conception."

Geo didn't manage to answer because the message from the Tadpole burst into his consciousness:

"You're talking about me without me. Are you a hybrid too, Geo?" she asked.

"How is it possible that you penetrate into our consciousness?" Iva retorted.

"I don't know, Alpha couldn't answer that question. It doesn't have any information on this in its memory. But when someone thinks about me, I know it and I pick up their memories. I wanted to know the Great Spawning ground of my spawn. We have a lot in common," she added before she disappeared inside the capsule that transported her to the Hope Hall of Tradition.

The message faded out and the Tadpole's face appeared on the screen.

"I'm flying to you," she managed to say before taking off.

"This is fascinating," muttered Geo. "I would probably not be able to pilot this capsule myself."

Everyone in the room was waiting for the Tadpole. Her behavior amazed them. Each of the material Hopers wondered how it was possible for the Fish Planet hybrid to jump from the primitive era to their modern world in such a short time.

The Elder of the Hope family turned to the assembled:

"We decided that Geo, as a Hoper and Earthling, would represent both planets in the meeting with the first representative of the Fish Planet. He is most predisposed to this role as a hybrid."

"Thank you for the honor. I think that the representative of the Fish Planet is perfectly able to communicate with all the Hopers," Geo answered them, knowing what they had no idea about.

Geo, thanking them for this honor, didn't reveal that the Tadpole had reached his consciousness much earlier. It had been at the lunar relay station when together with Iva and Tora he had walked along the stream of self into its interior.

"I'm just like you," he had received the strange message. "I am alone, I will come to you. Wait for me."

He hadn't been very familiar with the use of genti consciousness at the time, so he had thought it had been the message from some afterglower lost in the non-existence of the universe.

"Where are you? Who are you?" he had sent the return impulse to know who had wanted to contact him. He hadn't gotten any reply then, so he had quickly forgotten about the message. Now, while waiting for her arrival, he associated the two messages and knew it was the message from the Tadpole.

"I'm Geo, I received your message and I'm waiting for you, I am like you," he sent the message to her. Surprised, Iva turned her head to Geo.

"What message are you thinking about?" Iva managed to pass on the questions to him when the Tadpole appeared in the entrance. She walked steadily and decisively. She was headed straight for Geo, who stood at the center of the Hall in front of the great podium with the representatives of the Family of Hopers gathered there. It seemed that she was interested only in Geo.

"How does she know I'm Geo?" He thought, surprised.

"From the genti of the Great Spawning ground," she replied in a flash. "Go to the second state of consciousness," she asked him.

"How?"

"You know how. Concentrate on your power. The second level of awareness is the instant transmission of consciousness, inaccessible to others," she added.

Then an enlightenment struck him. Of course, he had already used this form of communication. He had turned it on when he had wanted no one, not even Iva, to reach his consciousness. He realized that the Tadpole was just like him from another planet. He flashed the thought at her:

"I'm with you."

He watched her calmly and confidently walk along the lane of material Hopers who parted before her to form a narrow corridor. She looked almost like him, except her skin glistened in the glow of lights directed at her with some mysterious glow shimmering with different colors of the rainbow.

There was a smile on her face. It was evident that she was happy. Slightly bulging blue eyes with black halos and yellow pupils looked intently at Geo standing in front of her.

Tora took a step forward and held both hands out in front of her. The Tadpole replied with the same gesture, but she turned her legs to Geo. The movement made her long blue hair sway slightly, giving the impression of unruly strands playing with each other.

Geo looked at the little legs stretched out towards him. They didn't look like his hands. They were slenderer and more flexible. Each leg had two joints and could bend to both sides. The slender, supple, five-fingered hands were narrow, and the long fingers tipped with blue triangular translucent nails showed through, revealing tiny veins. Between the fingers, the pink membranes connected all five fingers.

Geo took a step forward without fear and heartily embraced her hands. She thanked him the same way. Her grip was extremely strong for her physique.

"Welcome to Hope," he said aloud. He approached her face as if in earthly greeting, he had wanted to kiss her cheek.

"You are beautiful," he whispered into her flat ear closely adjacent to her slender head.

He couldn't restrain himself from his earthly habits. He didn't count on understanding his words by her, but rather on hearing a hint of admiration in his voice. They communicated in a second level of consciousness, inaccessible to anyone in this room.

"You are different from my spawn, but you are the same as the spawn of the Great Spawning ground," she sent the message to him, making a happy, high-pitched sound.

Geo got roused from his astonishment and admiration caused by the sight of her.

"Strange," he thought. "I think I've heard a sound like that before. When was it?" he tried to remember.

"We welcome the first representative of the Fish Planet. We are glad that you reached us safe and sound. Thank you for helping our Hopers and saving our castaway," he turned to the Tadpole, looking at her with curiosity.

Iva translated his words to all material inhabitants of Hope gathered in the Hall of Tradition. The Tadpole turned to the material Hopers in the hall and spoke in a Hope-like manner while sending messages to the afterglowers all over the planet.

Iva fell silent, surprised.

"By a strange twist of fate, two different civilizations came to you at the same time," the Tadpole spoke in a strong voice. "Because my roe from the Great Spawning ground taught me that there is no coincidence, I believe these events were guided by the genti of your planet. I don't know the reason that made us meet here and now, but I do know that the genti was guided by premises important to all of us." She was silent for a moment.

"Geo, do you feel what I feel?" she sent him the question.

"I'm getting a message saying we are to be transported together to the Rebirth Nebula.

"Dear Council! My countrymen - the Tadpole and I have received a call for help. Strong and clear. The system of Planets of Consciousness in the Rebirth Nebula needs our help. We ourselves need this help. The threat that occurred there may threaten also our hope and terrestrial planet.

The System of the Planets of Consciousness with the Planets of Souls has been free from violence and material existence for many hundreds of thousands of years. The laws that prevail there don't allow to kill and use violence against anyone, even at the cost of own existence.

Homo expansers broke into their planetary system and want to invasively and forcibly take over their five Soul Planets. The afterglowers left the first Soul Planet and took refuge in their largest dome on the fifth planet.

The material inhabitants of the five planets are degenerate due to the passage of time, and most of them are half-homo sapiens and half-robot androids. There are few of them and they cannot fight the invaders. They have implanted anti-aggression safeguards."

Geo, Iva, and Tora, along with the Tadpole, stood in front of the Big Screen in the Hall of Tradition and searched the Star map for an area of space where the Great Diviner believed the alien planetary system was to be located.

Tora quickly made contact with a Green Dwarf afterglower, who, like her, dragged an informational thread when she made her way through the corridors of genti to the Planet of Souls. "We'll get there following your traces. I will help you and together we will go to help. Send me all your memories of your journey," she asked. "I will take you to the Blue Planet, you will have memories for hundreds of years, and maybe you will like it and want to visit us more often," she tempted her with the new possibilities. But Appa didn't need to be convinced. She found Geo, and that was the most important thing.

Geo could sense the presence of representatives from the distant Rebirth Nebula. He was material, and the two beings identifying themselves as Appa and Rapp, communicated directly with him using the second channel of consciousness. Even Iva couldn't do that.

"We found a cap at the Relay Station leading to your moon," he received their signal. "This is the way to the Green Dwarf. We know the further way. The Great Diviner asks for help. Will you help us and our planets?" Appa asked directly.

"Yes, but I have to take the Tadpole with me, she is the key connecting our worlds. By acting together, we have a better chance of winning."

Surprised, Iva looked at Geo. The needle of jealousy reached her heart. "What is he up to? How did he get news about which I don't know?" she was amazed.

Geo received her full of amazement message and opened his awareness to her. She felt that she was the most important person for him, that he loved her and wanted to protect her, therefore he didn't take her with him. It was she and only she who was his other half and therefore he left her on Hope.

"Come back soon. I love you," she sent him the loving message.

"I'll be back as soon as possible," he replied, sending her a radiant smile and memories of their crazy moments spent in the small house next to the beach.

A conference on the alien invasion of the Planet of Souls was taking place under the largest dome of the Afterglowers' Assembly. Geo decided to go to help without hesitation.

"Iva, understand," he explained to his other half. "It would be better if I made this trip alone. You can't take part in this war, it's too much of a risk. We don't know who we're dealing with. You will transport yourself with Tora to the moon and look for the Cap leading to the Soul Planet System. I know it is there and you will find it. You will wait in the Hall of Tradition until I contact you. Anything can happen, even that we lose this war and we have to evacuate from there, then I'll send you a warning. You will have time to prepare for defense."

"Geo, I'm scared," she said, afraid. Her voice was soft but calm.

Geo sensed something else in it, besides fear for him, there was a hint of jealousy.

"You are only half a Hoper, and you have not yet attained the rank of an afterglower. You may not be skilled enough to engage in combat with the unknown race of invaders."

"That's why I will go with the Tadpole. She will support me. In these areas, she has remarkable skills that we lack."

He smiled at Iva. She didn't have to tell him that, she knew his thoughts perfectly well, and she knew that he believed the opposite. Precisely because he was not a full afterglower, he had an advantage over whoever was it. And the fact that the invaders was the homo expans species, gave him an advantage over them. However, deep down in their souls, they both knew it was about the Tadpole. It was she who caused anxiety in Iva. Although she was a hybrid and was far from an afterglower, she could have aroused some interest in Geo in her person. According the beauty criterion Iva used, the Tadpole should not have aroused the interest of the Hopers, but Geo was only half a Hoper, and the Hopers knew no other race, except for theirs and the race of Earthlings which, however, weren't so different from them. She knew that Earthlings had a very different approach to the beauty of a female body, and the Tadpole, despite some differences in the external features of a female body, also didn't differ that much from the other women of the Blue Planet, and that bothered her.

She also had something that no one on the planet Hope had. This could be exciting for Geo and dangerous for their relationship. She sighed heavily. She had known from the beginning that Tadpole was someone special. Extremely intelligent, wise, quickly assimilating the knowledge of others, she aroused the admiration of all those with whom she dealt. Even Geo was amazed at her adoptability.

She looked at this young representative of the Fish Planet, her blue delicate skin smooth as silk caught the eye.

She stood half naked in front of them. Her figure, devoid of a hint of shame, beamed with the charm natural for her world, through which shone the rays of the distant sun, which, painting on her skin all the shades of the rainbow falling into the water, aroused the admiration of all those who couldn't compete with her with the color of their bodies. Each of the viewers saw a different play of colors, because the angle of light refraction on her skin changed depending on the angle of view. In her natural environment, the color effect of her figure resulted from belonging to a specific subgroup, and the deeper was the place the group of her species occupied in the water world, the less pronounced was the effect.

Chapter XIV

Strangers

"We must attack the next planet as soon as possible!" Kaldyb screamed into the three-dimensional visor linking him to all the ships of his navy.

He paced nervously around his command post that occupied the entire front of his galactic cruiser. A dozen galactic cruisers in their war armada monitored everything within a few light-years. The great electrokinetic catchers of stellar particles showed planets, moons orbiting them, and all the stellar scrap. Everything that consisted of matter couldn't escape their attention. Microscopic fragments flying only in the direction known to them were caught in advance. Those that threatened to collide with the ship were destroyed with an anti-gravity cannon.

They didn't only see what they were most interested in - the war fleet of the System of Consciousness Planets. They knew that such a fleet existed, they just didn't know where it was. An entire armada of his fleet hid behind the moon of the last planet of the Consciousness System.

Dozens of tals back - units of the Libed time - when their sun began to swell rapidly, they realized that if they hadn't escaped from it, no one would have survived its outburst. And then a miracle happened. Aliens came to their planet. The fact that the two aliens in their material shells ended up on their planet is pure coincidence. They claimed that they got to it thanks to some corridors in which they got lost. These corridors were to be connected with other planets. They had their Gate of Wonders, but they never associated it with any corridors scattered throughout the universe. Two Kytilops - that was what the aliens called themselves, shuffled all their knowledge of the laws governing the universe.

Giving them knowledge for which they would have had to work for thousands of tals, they built galactic ships that were to enable them to settle planets somewhere out there in space and thus save those who had decided on this journey.

They sent out reconnaissance ships with the decision that they would either inhabit a planet or get missing somewhere in the universe. The optimistic version assumed that they would settle on a planet on the outskirts of their star system and return for the rest of the Libeds. However, this didn't happen.

The ten tals of waiting for the good news from the scout ships looking for a planet to move to, passed quickly, and with them passed the hope of finding such a planet.

When news came to President Araiw that aliens had landed on their planet, he treated it as an unusual case of fate.

The meeting of all Libed ambassadors began in great secret from all the visors of their individual factions of their clans. This was because of the need to keep the arrival of the two aliens from outer space secret. Although in fact, they didn't come directly from the sky, but got to them by passing through one of the caps in the Wonders Gate. The Libeds knew two such gates. The third cap they knew nothing about and through which they came was located in their old mine of meteorites, the remains of which were discovered by searching for minerals important to them. The properties of the shards of cosmic matter allowed them to create a propulsion for their spacecraft. However, the greatest value of the residue of the asteroid that had hit their planet millions of tals before was its use for the civil development of the Libeds.

The tiny bits of this matter served as the propulsion of their vehicles moving through their overpopulated clusters. They warmed, glowed, and energized their Libedorobots. Their entire civilization was based on the properties of these meteorites. They used them to drive their engines using antimatter.

Their scholars were very surprised when the Kytilops assured them that their greatest achievement was an antiquated propulsion system, and compared it to the fledgling evolution of homo sapiens.

"Only representatives like us, descended from the common ancestor of the homo protozoa, can travel the corridors of genti after attaining the existence of the afterglowers.

Your Gates of Wonders are corridors for the communication of various species of Homo sapiens, which are a species spread throughout the cosmos."

"What level would we need to reach to be able to use this form of travel?" Cosmobiologist Selim stood up and turned to the newcomers with great indignation in his voice. "Are we supposed to believe your stories just because you look a little different from us? Maybe you have your spaceship hidden somewhere here and you're telling us nonsense, fearing we won't let you fly away. The DNA tests performed have confirmed that you are indeed a different species than us. You look different, you think differently, but this is not proof that you went through the Weird Gate. Nobody and nothing broke through the Gates of Wonders, although we tried everything. So, it is doubtful that you came to us this way."

Cerdem from the planet Kytilop rose from behind the big seat and addressed the audience in a strong voice: "If you had the right level of evolution, I wouldn't have to speak to you through the biorobot, each of you would know what I mean. The voice communication is used in our place, but only by the material inhabitants of Kytilop. When their life comes to an end, they become afterglowers and then we use consciousness to communicate with each other, which is common to all the afterglowers of the universe. In the afterglow existence, we have no body, we are immaterial consciousness."

"What does that mean, how is that possible?" were heard the doubtful voices of the gathered Libeds.

"The invention of Pol de Gar allowed the use of space-time curvature and travel in genti corridors. This is the higher form of evolution that you haven't gotten to yet. Only an afterglower can open the cap. There is also good news, every homo sapiens can travel along such a corridor and for you it is a chance to survive - we are your chance," he added.

There was such such a buzz and noise in the room that the Chairman ordered silence and went on to ask questions himself.

"Does that mean we can all move down the corridors of, as you call it, genti?" One of the newcomers interrupted him.

"But where?"

"I don't know," he replied and, before he could elaborate on that, there were shouts again, this time menacing and hostile ones.

"They want to deceive us, maybe they need our bodies, they will turn us into slaves, and maybe we will be their food," was heard from the hall.

Kytilop raised his both hands up and screamed:

"Silence, silence, I am able to prove to all of you that we are telling the truth."

"How?" the chairman asked doubtfully.

"I will go through your Gate of Wonders with representatives chosen by you, and we will come back, and they will be able to tell what they have seen."

"Where are you going to take them?"

"I already told you that I don't know. The cap through which we will go leads to some planet that makes life possible for all homo sapiens, unfortunately I don't know what planet it is. Its symbols that define where it leads are incomprehensible to us. Know however, that each such journey in the corridors of space-time is fraught with a certain risk," Cedrem impatiently wondered for a moment whether it was right thing to do, to reveal to them his origin and the secrets of the corridors.

"What?" The chairman interrupted him.

"From where we find ourselves, we may not be released. We can also be captured, imprisoned or killed." In the room you could hear again the murmur of disputes between the ambassadors about the credibility of these words. The bustle was interrupted by the chairman who, without consulting other members of the Council, announced:

"For the sake of a future rescue expedition, I'm ordering an end to the gathering. You will be notified of the results through the direct visors. Thank you all."

It signified the end of the meeting, so they started to leave the Debating Chamber.

Cerdem, although reluctantly revealed to them the secrets of space-time corridors, he had a purpose in it. Both he and Nyterk had no memories of returning to their planet. They had wandered the corridors for so long that they had lost the possibility of returning, and then they stumbled upon energy, pure energy with memories - Delmek that Geo had thrown into oblivion. They took over his memories of the Blue Planet, casket, Hope and Geo. It was a chance to travel to the Planet Hope. They just needed to get to the Blue Planet and find the casket. Then go through the cap.

The two Kytilops were held in a secret base housing their headquarters for intergalactic ships seeking a habitable planet. It was an endeavor that seemed doomed to fail in advance due to the distance to travel before reaching the two planets likely to be suitable for their Exodus.

So, they desperately and at dizzying pace worked on hibernation methods to make this journey possible. The hibernation time of the Libed to date, allowing them to survive, was several hundred light years, which was not a problem for their propulsion. The problem was that they couldn't find such a planet at this distance. The closest planet XR 14 U199 in the constellation Orion was 1,500 light-years away, and no Libed was able to survive such a journey.

The newcomers lived in a special part of the secret pavilion, where 206 tals before their arrival, there had been a small spacecraft intercepted by their war cruiser, whose mission was to explore a little-known part of their star system. Strange anomalies were discovered behind one of the stars.

There, cruiser Torg discovered a neutron star that their scientists suspected was responsible for producing these anomalies. Using its gravitational forces, they returned to Libeda along a route coinciding with their sun. No one had ever flown along such a trajectory, but they chose such a path to be able to explore this part of the cosmos. Halfway, their visors discovered a small object. When they were about to pass it at a safe distance, the instruments noted the existence of strange energy.

The course was changed. Decreasing their speed was no mean feat. The idea was not to lose the object in the visor and get close enough to it so that its surface could be examined. Already from a short distance, it was noticed with surprise that it was not a meteorite but an object of regular shape. When they got closer, they saw that it was a spaceship of an alien civilization.

"Suspend the operation," commanded Captain Dor. "Summon all commanders to a conference. Send a signal to Libeda - a non-libeda spacecraft within our visors.

Lieutenant Nell, send two reconnaissance Libedorobots to check all possible visors of this ship. Don't go beyond the range of our protective field - appoint the best pilots for the task. Check the energy sources. Report on everything."

There was great commotion on the cruiser. The news spread like wildfire that there had been an encounter with the ship from an alien civilization.

Such a thing had never been produced on Libeda. They were surprised to see the lack of nozzles of the anti-gravity drive. This ship had nothing to compare with any spacecraft built on Libida. The foreign object didn't respond to any signals, it didn't change course, and its propulsion system didn't work.

"There is nothing we can do, we will not enter it," said Lieutenant Mach.

"We can take it on our transport," the First Pilot made the proposal.

"I don't know if it's safe," the bioenergy specialist objected to them.

"There are no signs of life in it."

"You can't be sure of that, there may be life in an unknown form. We don't know what we are dealing with," the bioenergy specialist continued to try to discourage them from this idea.

Meanwhile, the order came from Libeda: a top-secret operation.

"Take the alien ship on the transport board. Use the third degree of danger. Surround the ship with the quarantine field. Don't try to open its access hatches. Come back to Libeda at full speed."

"We won't do anything. We'll surround it with our protective field and in this state, we'll bring it to Libeda," Captain Dor said dryly.

"We are to take it - this is an order, so prepare to haul the object onto our board," the commander ordered.

It was not a very difficult operation. Their cargo ships were also picked up by them from the orbit of their moon from which they obtained resources. For a giant like Torg, which could accommodate several dozen of such objects on board, it was a bit more difficult operation due to the inability to cooperate with the ship.

"Does the Captain do the right thing, taking aliens aboard?" Were heard the voices of those crew members who were more aware of the dangers that alien life could bring upon them. The only argument in favor of continuing the operation was the fact that the ship showed no signs of activity. Its engines didn't work, it didn't respond to any signals or emit anything that could pose any threat to them. The only puzzling fact was its small energy source, which their sensors registered.

When they found themselves on Libeda's orbit, a transport shuttle was waiting for them, capable of transporting the alien ship to their secret base.

Since then, despite many different attempts, it hadn't been possible to establish any contact with the ship. Its hull was covered with a strange structure that resisted any attempt to study it. It didn't reflect any light, it also absorbed all forms of bombardment of its surface with various radiation types, and it was impossible to even scratch its hull by any means of drilling, blasting or striking it with small charges from antimatter cannons. After many years of research, the ship was placed in the remote training ground of a secret base, where a handful of the most determined scientists continued their research. The only thing that was constant in it was the low energy read by their devices. They quickly concluded that it was the life energy known on Libeda, but they had never managed to generate enough of it to emit a beam as strong as on the foreign ship.

The hope that the newcomers poured in them allowed them to be optimistic about the future.

"But is what they say true?" Wondered Gzom, their greatest scientist. "Apart from words and appearance, they have nothing else to confirm their words. And that's not enough to quit all research and concentrate on trying to save our population using their method. I don't quite understand why we are to let them go through our Gate of Wonders and take off with our entire Armada at the same time. To entrust to their words our whole future world. In the depths of his mind, he believed that only this course of action could save them from extermination, but he felt that the aliens had a purpose in this. "But what?" He wondered.

The meeting in the briefing room for the commanders of their armada of the war was stormy. The army took care of the newcomers and focused on developing a method that would allow their idea to be implemented.

"Only the strong Armada fleet is able to save our population and take everyone to the planet XR 14 U199. In defense of our ships, we are able to destroy any hostile civilization. Our antimatter cannons can easily annihilate the entire planet with every civilization that lives there."

"And then what? When you destroy the planet, where will you land?" the chairman asked derisively.

He was from a different faction and had always disrespected Kaldyb. His buffoon speeches, however, reached a large part of the Libeds and gave him strong support in the Council of Ambassadors.

At the beginning of his military career, Kaldyb had become famous for destroying most of the living organisms on the small planet Dag where their robots had discovered the evolution of the great monsters of the Dag family.

He decided that they were a threat to the Libeds and with a small load of antimatter, he tore the planetoid passing nearby into many smaller pieces. The blast changed its trajectory and several larger debris consisting mostly of iridium hit the planet.

The explosion created a large crater with a diameter of several hundred Libed meters, and the force of the impact changed its functioning.

Volcanoes erupted and the entire planet was covered with a layer of gas, obscuring the sun. It caused a cooling of the lower layers of the atmosphere, as a result of which there was a global breakdown of the environment, leading to the extinction of most species of animals and vegetation on the planet.

Nobody cared about the fate of the planet where there were no intelligent creatures, not supposing that in their lifetime this planet could be their new home. Did they regret intervening where they might have moved now if they hadn't destroyed the planet's atmosphere for the next few thousand tals? Maybe it would have been so, but only Kaldyb and the handful of military people who had allowed experimental use of the latest weapon knew about it.

When many tals later, Libedorobots, who were looking for a new place to live, came across the planet Dag, they sent a dry message from it:

"It is not habitable. Volcanic eruption and no clean atmosphere." They didn't even land to see what its surface looked like.

The breakthrough came when alien representatives of another civilization appeared on their planet. It was then that scientists from a secret base decided to lead the Kytilops to the alien ship.

At the back of a small old repair hall, on a special platform, there was the space ship of the alien representatives of the unknown part of space.

There was a commotion among the Kytilops when they approached the hall.

"We feel genti," they sent the signal to each other. It was weak, but the feeling of it increased with each passing moment.

Before entering the hall, the Main Technician stated with a certain amount of pride:

"In this hall there is a ship of an alien civilization. Unfortunately, for many tals we have been unable to make contact with it as well as board it, so we don't know who it belongs to ..."

"It's afterglowers' ship," Cerdem interrupted him. "We feel genti. Turn off your protective field. You are safe."

"How do you know whose ship it is?"

"I don't know whose, but we know what type it is. Only afterglowers' ships can emit genti. When you turn off the protective field, genti signal will be stronger and we will make contact with those who are there."

"How is it possible that someone is there? So many tals have passed that no one can be alive there." The Base Technician was looking at them with a great dose of surprise. He shook his head disapprovingly, thinking that the aliens were talking nonsense.

"Afterglowers can and if they are there, we will find out about it." A quick consultation and permission were received from the Supreme Commander of the Base to disable the protective field. It wasn't something extraordinary, they had already turned the field off, otherwise it would have been impossible to make any attempts to come into contact with the ship.

Everyone stopped in front of the ship. You could feel the tension that prevailed among the Libeds. Two alien civilizations tried to communicate with each other on the planet of the third civilization.

"Won't it cause us trouble?" the Commander-in-Chief was asked by their Base Commander who immediately appeared next to them, not wanting to miss such an attempt.

"I think not. If they had hostile intentions towards us, we would already know about it."

"They may have against each other - we don't know who we are dealing with," doubted the Base Technician. "We don't, but I think they do. See how confidently they behave," retorted the Supreme Commander of the Base.

Indeed, the Kytilopes freely approached the ship as much as the protective field allowed them.

"Turn off the field. I'll open the hatch to the ship," Cerdem said it as casually as if it had been about some ordinary door. They had tried for so many years and hadn't achieved anything, and this strange alien wanted to open the hatch with his bare hands.

"The field has been disabled," sounded the voice of the automatic Force Field Guard.

The Kytilopes' awareness signal swam to the ship.

"We are from the planet Kytilop. Open the hatch."

The hull of the ship lightened, and after a while they saw the top layer of its hull drain into one of the small openings in the upper part, just above the pilot house. It was as if the thin layer covering the hull of the ship had been sucked in, revealing the real shell of the spacecraft. Only now did they see their visor turned towards them. Its protective layers slowly parted, revealing a pale blue light.

There was a clang of metal. The two halves of the door opened in their upper layer and began to fall, forming a steel platform, the top of which rested on the ground on which they were standing.

Two hydro robots appeared in the doorway, and there could be heard a long, whistling sound.

"Turn on the messenger," he gave the command. "Identification," he requested.

The holographic face of a woman appeared in front of the audience.

Her face was like that of the libeds.

Alpha - the main pilot of the "Glow" ship from the planet Hope in the Crane system.

The image vanished and a stellar map of their home planetary system appeared with Hope flashing in the distance. Then the great turbulence and the "Glow" found themselves in the Crane System, which on the screen turned into a bright star from which a blue dot, symbolizing the ship, broke away. As it flew towards the Milky Way, it fell into a concentrated belt of dark matter. Sudden speed reduction and change of direction. The picture changed again to reveal the four dead bodies of the crew placed in the hybernetic cabin. They hadn't survived the abrupt deceleration and the enormous force of gravity.

Then the room was unexpectedly shown in which the outline of a small dome was visible. The image flickered and Alpha's computer face appeared again.

"Ship control impossible. Autopilot system blocked by the afterglowers. Another life form took over the ship," Kytilop explained calmly.

"The afterglow beings within this dome have no memories of how they found themselves alone in the void of space. They lost their memories during a long stay inside this dome. But I assure you that they are there and we can communicate with them, that the afterglowers from the Hopers' ship "Glow" knows a way to reach the stars to which all of Libeda inhabitants could move.

As they tell us, there is a System of Planets of Consciousness in the Rebirth Nebula, which is outside the Libeds' galaxy within a few million units of Libed's light-speed time," Ksut, the informal leader of all afterglowers explained to them.

Nobody believed them until at the Great Meeting of all representatives of their planets, they stated that they knew a way to reach the stars to which all Libeda residents could move.

"How is it possible to achieve a goal that is at an unimaginable distance from us? We don't have the hibernation technique that could enable Libeds to survive such a journey," objected their greatest astrophysicist, Yrdam.

"The proof that it's possible, are we ourselves. We came here from an equally distant part of space," explained Xut, their leader with the most memories. "Admittedly, we came to you by accident, but it doesn't matter. We know where and how you can transport your ships with colonizers."

"How can you be sure of what you are saying if you don't know yourselves how you got here?"

"It is true that we didn't know where we would end up traveling through the corridors of genti," Cerdem spoke in a calm and confident voice, hoping that the automatic communicator correctly translated his words. "But your Gate of Wonders is the gate through which we came to you. We know for sure that it will lead us to one of the homo sapiens planets. As you know, it can't move your navy, but it can transport the entire population of the Libeda. But first, you must fly there and prepare the planet to receive all of you."

"Since our entire population will not fit on our galactic ships, how will we transport those left and how many tals will it take?" asked President Araiw, looking at Cerdem.

"We don't have much time," he said, thereby showing everyone that he agreed with the arguments of the strangers - after all, they had opened the ship of the alien civilization. What they had said about the apparitions earlier was also confirmed. "Anyway, we have no choice, staying here is a certain doom," he thundered in a thick voice, trying to persuade those unconvinced from the opportunists' faction.

"What shall we do?" Now he turned directly to Cerdem.

"Prepare all your galactic ships capable of covering such a distance. Load them with as many Libeds as possible and with everything that is important to you in this new journey. For the mission to be successful, all of your ships have to take off simultaneously when we open the Wonders Gate. The synchronization is crucial for the success of your mission. Ships must fall into space-time, which we will open for you at the Wonders Gate."

There was a discussion lasting several long tals. Finally, the Libed Supreme Council approved a rescue plan for libeds presented by the aliens. Preparations for the settlement mission began. The order and instructions that Kaldyb received before departing infuriated him. He was held back only by the fear that the other Armada commanders would have revolted if he had tried take over the leadership on Libeda by force.

They realized that without their knowledge, they would not find a second planet to which they would be able to transport the inhabitants of Libeda.

Kaldyb was furious that he had to listen to stupid apparitions he couldn't even see. He tolerated them only because the advice they gave him might have led him to the Nebula of Rebirth.

The apparitions made it clear to them that the planets in this system were populated by the homo sapiens species and, as they assumed, being higher than them in terms of evolutionary development. But they knew nothing more.

None of the apparitions had any memories of this star system. They didn't know what civilization inhabited it or what the inhabitants of the planet they wanted to colonize looked like.

There was one more thing that made him reckon with them. He completely didn't know how to return from this part of the cosmos. He worried about it, although he didn't have to come back right away, because the task entrusted to him by the Libed Planet Council consisted in populating the Planets of the Consciousness System with the colonizers he would take with him on board his ships and only then returning for the rest of the inhabitants. Only this discouraged him from taking any radical steps.

One of the conditions to which all the military crews of the navy had to agree was to leave their families on Libeda. In this way, the command wanted to give itself the chance that they would return for them. The core of their war armada were the crews of galactic ships. Along with them, they sent the greater part of their passenger fleet adapted to such an extreme flight. The rest of the inhabitants must have believed that the ships would come back for them.

The entire armada of Libeds waited in orbit for the take-off signal. Commander Kaldyb, in command of the Armada, paced nervously around the command post.

"Bearings, have they given you bearings for the Star Map?" he asked First Pilot again and again.

"I report that there are no bearings of the Rebirth Nebula. We have bearings for the space-time corridor of our Wonders Gate," he replied stoically.

The First Pilot of Nitup, their flagship had practiced maneuvers with Ceder many times and knew what to do. They discussed every detail of the take-off. His role was to synchronize their flagship with all other ships of the Armada so that they passed safely into space-time. The rest would be done by the automatic pilot of Nitup and the apparitions in the dome of the 'Glow' stuck in their hold.

"The Glow is a kind of guarantor of the safety and success of our mission," this is what the Council thought when agreeing to the mission.

"ATTENTION! ..." The Base Commander's voice sounded across all the ships. "Strangers at the Wonders Gate. We are counting down microtals to the take-off, starting at 10. The take-off in 4 ... 3 ... 2 ... 1," the calm voice of the Base Commander counted down the time left to the take-off. All the antimatter engines were running smoothly.

"Let's go!" Commander Kaldyb's voice raised due to excitement initiated the take-off procedure.

For the first dozen or so tals they flew to the space-time corridor. When all the craft entered the corridor, the apparitions from the Glow took control of their ships.

Two afterglowers from the planet Kytilop, following the recollections stored in the memory of Dalmek, moved towards the corridor leading to the Blue Planet.

"The Cap has been breached ..." sounded the Genti's Guard metallic voice. The sent hydro robot found the two materialized afterglowers by the Cap. He quickly took an air sample and analyzed it immediately.

"The afterglowers from the planet Kytilop," the Guard's dispassionate voice reported the data to the Genti Station Center. He wasn't interested in the rest. The afterglowers from Kytilop didn't threaten the Blue Planet, and although they differed slightly from its indigenous people, they could mask their different appearance.

"Lead to the Center," Agura commanded.

Cerdem and Agura turned off the field of consciousness and followed the robot.

Genti's Second Central Station on the Blue Planet wasn't the first station they landed on while traveling through the genti corridors. However, this Station surprised them with its construction. Deep, perfectly masked from the increasingly intelligent inhabitants of this planet, who had the technique of detecting, spying, photographing everything on the ground by satellites placed in orbit, it was covered with a genti protective umbrella. Several hundred meters under the oldest structures on earth, they had existed there for hundreds of thousands of years.

Cerdem and Arua, having obtained documents, money and appropriate clothes, left the station as two tourists returning from the trip. They headed straight to the nearest airport. They had a long way to go to the town where Geo's father lived.

Chapter XV

The Rebirth Nebula

The journey to the Rebirth Nebula, Geo and the Tadpole made without any problems. They returned, following the information thread left in the corridors of genti by an unknown wanderer who had had to visit the Planet of the Three Suns much earlier.

"The Great Diviner, in his unfathomable wisdom, foresaw the existence of the information thread with which it was possible to communicate with our system.

Genti is extremely strong here. We don't know why this is happening, but it has to do with your Second Moon," the Tadpole explained to them.

"How does she know about this?" everyone gathered in the Memorial Hall of the Soul Planets wondered. Everyone except Geo. He was the only one who realized that the Tadpole was a unique hybrid with remarkable ability to learn quickly.

The representative of the Great Diviner led them to the Central Command Post, where all the significant material commanders of their navy had gathered. The huge hall under the dome on their largest planet was a great spherical edifice containing five small domes that allowed all representatives of their five planets to participate in the deliberations. From upper central points of the domes, white streams of plasma energy shot upward, merging into a single source of genti. As Geo and the Tadpole entered, a small platform flew towards them from an invisible part of the dome. The lectern glittering with a blue light, with a series of incomprehensible symbols encouraged them to come in. The platform, or rather the flying podium, silently lifted them up, heading for the opposite wall, where on a much larger and shinier platform sat the most eminent commanders representing all five planets. Borein, Commander of the Defense of the Soul Planets, stood up to greet them.

"The Great Diviner, for reasons unknown to us, believes that only you, Geo, representative of the Blue Planet, can reach the consciousness of the aliens and stop them from hostile actions. As we can see, you came to us with the representative of the Fish Planet. You are the first representatives from such a distant civilization to reach us. We welcome you."

"Except for the foreign invaders," the Tadpole sent the message to Geo in the second degree of consciousness, checking if it was readable for Borein.

"It's not," said Geo. "At least for these material andreorobots."

Geo got up, bowed according to the earthly custom, and spread his hands in a truly theatrical gesture.

"We welcome all inhabitants of the System of the Consciousness Planets. We came to you at the request of the Great Diviner and representatives of your civilization. We will do everything we can to help you." He paused and looked around.

The andreorobots, biorobots and a dozen or so biological homo sapiens sat in amazement and looked at each other.

They knew Geo was speaking, but they understood nothing. His speech didn't reach them. He looked at the Tadpole. She smiled at him.

"You speak your native language. They pick up nothing. Repeat with awareness."

Geo repeated in the Hope way and immediately saw the hosts' faces lit up with the satisfaction that Geo was one of them and they didn't have to use such an archaic way of communication as spoken language.

"I'm a hybrid - an Earthman from the Solar System, from the Blue Planet, and the accompanying Tadpole is a hybrid from the Fish Planet, from Andromeda. As he spoke, a blue stream rose up from the top of the Debating Chamber and instantly created a large picture of the stellar map of the universe, showing the audience the systems with their planets mentioned by Geo.

"Maybe they'll show where their enemies came from," he sent the impulse to the Tadpole.

"They don't know, they have no contact with them," she replied.

"How do you know?" he asked unnecessarily, because he immediately understood that she was absorbing their knowledge directly from their consciousness.

"Yes, you are right," she replied to him. "Perhaps this is the reason for which the Great Diviner thinks that we can help you and ourselves."

Then she turned to the Grand Assembly, bowed respectfully and, pointing to the holographic screen, she requested:

"Please present the situation."

At these words Kepud stood up and pressed a button on his lectern. The star map changed the view, showing the Planets of Consciousness. The five planets orbiting their central sun and the three moons presented a realistic picture of this part of the sky. Each of the planets was covered with the afterglowers' domes. Starting with the first planet farthest from the sun, the image was rapidly approaching its surface, revealing great expanses of green earth, water oceans and seas, and high mountains with snow-capped peaks. What was astonishing in this sight, were several great circular areas with a barren surface on which nothing grew. There were no visible technical structures resembling cities or other clusters indicative of inhabitation or other civilization signs of expansion of some living creatures.

"This is what our planets look like when invaders look at them," Kepud commented on the view.

The image changed color, showing the planet in an ionizing magnetic light. Among the real nature, in places of barren soil, appeared white domes and streams of plasma energy connecting them with one of the moons.

"The invaders with their entire military fleet are revolving around our fifth planet. One of their scout ships crashed on its surface. We took the data from its computer. It was piloted by robots. Our analysts say that the aliens found our System uninhabited and habitable. They know about the technical moon and detect our genti's stream of consciousness feeding all planets. However, they don't know what it is for." He sat down, resigned and tired of the speech. His memories of the afterglower from the time of using this method of communication were a very distant relic of the past. Between themselves, they used direct conscious telepathic means of communication unavailable to other afteglowers.

The Tadpole stood up and lifted her right leg with spread toes. The membrane was barely visible, and not even Geo paid any attention to it. He didn't know that there were additional receptors in the membranes connecting all of the fingers in the four limbs to pick up the streams of consciousness. To the great surprise of all those gathered, she turned to them in the telepathic consciousness way, as if she had been an indigenous inhabitant of this system.

"Please, allow me to read the information on the computer of their reconnaissance vessel."

"It is a huge material encoded in several hundred bioDNAs of capacity. It took us many revolutions of the fifth planet to recreate it," said the Chief Biogeneticist of their technical moon. The Tadpole, however, couldn't be misled.

"Accumulate everything into one impulse and display it on this screen. It will take as long as it takes to pass the information on to all the inhabitants of Hope."

All those present looked at each other in disbelief, wondering if this strange being from the era of the first homo protozoa overestimated its capabilities - such an association passed through all the inhabitants of the Planets of the Consciousness System.

"No one on our planets can absorb such a big amount of material in such a short time," said Kepud with a hint of disbelief.

"I just mastered your way of communicating," she replied to them. "So don't judge anyone by appearance and place of birth. My roe from the Great Spawning ground taught me that anything in the universe is possible. I'm waiting for the message."

"Carry out," the Chief Biogeneticist ordered.

"You're as smart as you are beautiful," Geo sent the compliment to her. He was surprised to see that her silky skin began to pulsate with shades of blue. "You have more of homo sapiens than I thought," he added, looking at her eyes glittering from satisfaction.

She turned to him and with a gentle, feminine move, she placed her little leg on his hand and squeezed it lightly. He felt a slight chill. He realized that her body temperature was slightly lower than his.

"I'd love to warm you," the thought broke out of him.

"My spawning will be soon. I invite you to my roe," he received the message from her.

He refrained from exchanging his thoughts further as the screen showed the wrecked alien ship and their bio-robot leaning over their central computer system. A moment of pause and rapidly changing information files appeared on the screen in the Debating Chamber. After a while, the screen dimmed and then burst into a dark fragment of the sky, showing the silhouette of their largest flagship warship.

A telepathic silence overcame the Debating Chamber. Everyone fell silent closing their consciousness. They were waiting for the Tadpole to speak.

They didn't have to wait long. The Tadpole got up and placed her legs on the platform's control panel. She turned it slightly to face the representatives of the Five Soul Planets.

"I took control of your visor to show you what is most important to you and all other civilizations that may be threatened by aliens," she began very freely her message to everyone present.

Geo was surprised to see that she was sending him the same message in his mother tongue at the same time.

"It is phenomenal, when did she learn it?" he wondered. "I have the powerful ally - it's good that not the enemy," the reflection came suddenly to him.

"It is not true what your biogenetics say, that foreign invaders don't know about the existence of domes on your planets. They see them, but they don't understand their intended use. They are at a stage of evolutionary development that prevents them from comprehending life after life. On their largest flagship cruiser "Nitup" they hide a transport ship that has crashed in a distant part of space. By coincidence, another group of afterglowers traveling through the corridors of genti ended up on their planet. Having made the aliens aware of their location, they informed them that their planet was going to be destroyed. In order to save themselves, they had to convince them to leave their home planet in search of another place where they could all move.

They led to a great exploratory expansion of a new place to live. They were taken with their ship aboard Nitup, a flagship cruiser of Lebida - that's what their planet is called," she added. "Intended for intergalactic flights."

Using the information gathered, she pointed to a dozen or so transport ships on the star map. "There are several hundred thousand colonizers there, which in hibernation are waiting for a new opportunity to live. Their planet doesn't exist anymore, so it's up to you whether we destroy them or give them a chance for a new life."

There was a commotion in the Debating Chamber. Their material inhabitants couldn't imagine that they could annihilate the civilization with common homo sapiens roots.

"What is the way out of the situation?" Kepud asked.

The Tadpole looked at Geo.

"I know Geo can infiltrate the cruiser Nitup and try to negotiate with their commander. We will show them your strength and peaceful intentions, but it is only up to you what steps we take. You can accept them, or try to force them to leave the Consciousness System, which in practice means war," she calmly informed everyone about the way of carrying out the task entrusted to them. "We must hurry, they can attack the next planet at any moment."

Now Geo got up. He knew what could be done.

"I know how to get on their ship, and I think the chances of avoiding war are great. There is something else I would like you to know. The cause of the troubles is the different stage of your and their world civilization development. I also know that the general rule of all afterglowers is not to influence the development of other worlds. However, I'm counting on you to depart from this rule in such special circumstances." He sat down at the Tadpole and wondered if, with such a great difference in evolutionary development, the afterglowers from the Consciousness System would want to make any contact at all. It was like talking to Stone Age homo sapiens.

"What can they give us without endangering us?" Kepud asked the Tadpole.

"Peace," she replied.

Heavily, as if weighed down by the received messages, the Chief Biogeneticist spoke:

"The representative of the Great Diviner will convey your message to him and he will make a decision. Until then, you will be our guests. We will call you when we know the answer. You will be accompanied by Azjeg, who will lead you to specially prepared guest rooms." After he said it slowly, everyone began to leave the Hall. Geo and the Tadpole on the same platform moved to a separate part of the planet for their material inhabitants. Geo was surprised by the form of the rooms they entered.

"These rooms have been created especially for you. The model was very old records from our archival memory containers, encoded on our technical moon," Azjeg announced to them looking pleased at their delighted glances.

Geo was delighted, but the Tadpole was shaken by mixed feelings. She came from another world, from the water civilization which, evolutionarily, had barely crept onto solid land. She knew there could be artificial structures. She didn't suppose, however, that those that met their imaginations coded in consciousness. Her chamber had a large water reservoir. The Tadpole supposed it must be artificial, although on this planet, the concept artificial didn't exist, here everything you dreamed about came true in such an obvious way that it was unreal, at least for them. She was very pleased to be able to take advantage of the water bath. When she immersed herself in a body of water, she immediately understood that it had no end in either distance or depth. It got bigger in the way she wanted. And although she didn't have to go back to the water, now that she was approaching the slightly undulating water, her roe was delighted that she would be able to take advantage of the sea, and not only to relax and rest.

"I wonder what the hosts came up with for Geo," she went onto the outside terrace and from there to his room. She found him without a top garment.

"This is how you look without the scale?" she joked, going inside.

She walked over to him and gently touched his muscular chest. She ran her fingers up and down, then embraced him and began rubbing his shoulders.

"It's a pity that I don't have roe now," she said in a voice to him, knowing how much he liked this way of communication.

She moved away from him and unfastened her long tunic, the edge of which barely covered her breasts. She slipped long, thin straps off her shoulders in one move and stood naked in front of him.

"I'd rather be with you like that, and not wearing those artificial scales," she told him without shame.

Geo froze, struck by her beautiful body and the strange halo emanating from her. And although she differed from her earthly counterparts in the color of her skin, the smell and glow coming from her excited him.

"What do you emit when you're naked?" he asked, curious about her sexuality.

He walked over, took her hands and wondered if he could pull her to him. He knew nothing about the sexual habits of the inhabitants of the Fish Planet.

"It's the ethereal secretion of my genitals," she replied, surprised that she didn't know such obvious things. "As my spawning is approaching, the glands are starting to emit a special smell - a decoy for the roe from my spawning ground. Come on, let's go swimming. I have a lot of water," she smiled at her own joke.

Chapter XVI

Great Diviner

For the next few revolutions of the planet around the sun, the Tadpole didn't have time for Geo. Invited by scientists to the Universe Research Center on their artificial moon, she worked very intensively, arousing the admiration of the biogeneticists. Thanks to her absorption of knowledge and drawing conclusions from the learned lessons, she quickly gained recognition for her and the civilization she represented. During this time, Geo was busy exploring their naval fleet and learning about the techniques that the inhabitants of the Consciousness System had at their disposal. Their level allowed the destruction of the invaders in one attack without any harm to the attackers.

"Why do they refrain from killing, risking even destroying their home planet?" he wondered, not understanding their respect for everything that lived.

He figured out and knew how to implement the Tadpole's plan. He considered transporting himself to the flagship alien cruiser possible, so when the Great Diviner called a meeting in the Council Chamber, he was ready for action. The message of the Great Diviner was brief, and the orders were understandable to all.

"Geo would transport himself to Nitup and give the invaders an ultimatum. We will give them the fifth planet on condition that they neutralize all their warships and aggressive weapons as well as completely disarm with respect for the laws of all planets in our Consciousness System.

In return, we will help them develop the fifth planet and help the colonizers to orient themselves to life on it. We will show a picture of the explosion of their sun and the destruction of their world. They have no reason to come back, no one survived. Their civilization only exists on their transport ships. The refusal means turning back all of their ships to where they came from. Their chances of surviving such a journey are zero."

He fell silent pointing to the big picture, which showed a dozen or so war cruisers of the Consciousness System. They located crosswise in the orbit of the fifth planet. Their range of operation covered the entire armada of the enemy. They themselves were invisible to them, which didn't mean that the enemy was neutralized.

"We are not sure if they don't have a weapon that can penetrate our protective field, then the aliens would be able to destroy all the domes on our fifth planet."

"Geo, will you transport yourself to their flagship cruiser?" asked the Great Diviner, addressing him directly, which was an incredible honor for them.

Geo, who analyzed the whole situation with the Tadpole, replied without hesitation:

"I'm able to try."

Mindful of earlier discussions with the Tadpole, he was of the opinion that one of their war cruisers should have been destroyed and then the terms of their surrender negotiated.

"It is impossible," she argued. "Their afterglow beings long ago cast out aggression and violence, and their guiding principle is - don't kill. Let others live as they want."

"I know you are right, but aliens have different criteria, and I know that in order to save their civilization, they will not hesitate to attack with all their might. I have to, however, respect their wishes and come up with something else. I was hoping the afterglowers would show me how to act. Their Great Diviner is some kind of galactic neurocomputer who knows what to do, but doesn't know how to do it.

"Use the power you have and make your way to their ship, and then to the dome of the afterglowers. Reach out to their consciousness and convince the aliens together that all five planets in the Consciousness System are inhabited planets with a different being. Tell them the conditions and persuade them to accept them. Your civilization and theirs are evolutionarily similar, and although the aliens are ahead of you, you have similar criteria and values. I don't have your power, but I have knowledge. I will support and protect you."

"You are the revelation and salvation for our worlds. You are very important to me and I know I can count on you. On you, I pin my hopes for the success of my mission. However, if I don't come back, take care of my father there, on Earth, on my Blue Planet. He has no one but me. I know that with Iva's help you will be able to transport yourself to the Earth and convey my words to him."

"I promise," she said, "but it won't be necessary, you will introduce me to your spawning ground yourself."

Hugged, or rather rubbed by the Tadpole, he set off into the genti corridors.

"This is a farewell of the two beings close to each other, and it was irrelevant that each of us come from the two different planets," he thought a moment later, as he transported himself to the artificial moon, to their Relay Station, which resembled the one from the trip to the Hope technical moon. It couldn't be a coincidence that the two stations were so similar to each other even though they were separated by unimaginable distances from the universe. He knew that in the memory of the hope moon, where the knowledge had been stored since the formation of their worlds, there was no record of who and when created the artificial moon with its genti energy and corridors to other worlds. He only knew that each of them functioned and fulfilled the roles assigned to them by an unknown person.

Without fear, he went through the Cap into the technical moon, and just like on the Hope moon, he immediately noticed the 'light of life' - a beacon leading him to his destination. He moved towards it, knowing that he was awaited and would be led to the genti stream, with the use of which, he would be able to transport himself to the afterglowers' ship inside Nitup. The corridors through which he traveled were confusingly similar to those he had moved along with Iva and Tora.

"I'm inside their technical moon. This is living tissue. I miss you," he sent the message to Iva. He knew that since there were genti corridors that could be used to travel from there to the planet of the Three Suns, his message would reach Iva.

He hadn't forgotten about the Tadpole.

The Great Diviner is the brain of the moon, its heart and the source of the genti energy. He controls this intricate living tissue of someone or something, created in very ancient times, or regenerating like a phoenix from the ashes when a homo sapiens civilization manages to reach the level allowing to use the genti corridors.

"Who was the creator of the world, where did he come from and where is he now?" he sent this question to the Tadpole. He knew she would diagnose his questions faster and more accurately.

Moving towards the lighthouse, he felt a greater surge of energy and power with every moment. The closer he got to the bright point luring him into his embrace, the more he became convinced that he was guided by some force that watched over him. Finally, he stopped in front of the Cap which had no symbols, patterns or pictograms.

Its surface shone with the black symbolism of the cosmos and waved slightly rippling its surface like the surface of a lake when a gust of wind crapes its water. When he took a step forward, the surface brightened and became transparent. Behind it he could see a fragment of the sky, the ship of the afterglowers, and the dome in it.

"Go, I will bend the space," he heard the polyphony. Not a metallic artificial robot voice, but a soft, gentle one with a great deal of kindness.

"Who are you?" He dared to ask.

"Genti - the creator of everything that Homo sapiens needs to move in the universe. Go, it's time for you to go."

Geo entered the Cap without hesitation. He knew what his consciousness had to imagine in order to reach the goal. The spiral tunnel of the corridor carried him through curved spacetime to the place where the war fleet of invaders was stationed in the orbit of the fifth planet.

At the same time, to his horror, he noticed that at the end of the corridor there was a hole, a black hole sucking in material objects that found themselves in its gravitational force of attraction. He felt himself being pulled in. Some force at first gently, and then more and more violently influenced his afterglow existence.

"So, this is the end of the genti corridors," he thought. He felt like a power capacitor charged to the limit of its abilities. He began to resist, and his consciousness searched for an escape from the force of the black hole absorbing everything that was in the orbit of its gravitational field. Planets, stars, and entire galactic systems that found themselves in its gravitational field were lost in its interior.

He saw it clearly, and although it happened billions of years earlier, he knew it was a warning showing him that the genti corridors could also be annihilated by the forces of the universe. He realized that he had to act immediately if he didn't want to end up in the black hole's nothingness. Now he knew there was no return from this nothingness for anything or anyone. He also knew that on the other side of the black hole there was a world different from what he knew.

Nothingness is a black hole, a curse of the universe and its blessing at the same time, something ends so that something can begin. He remembered the cemetery and Dalmek, and believed in the power of his consciousness. He concentrated it into one bright ball and threw himself to the side of the corridor. To no avail, he only bounced off its spiral surface and began to move faster and faster towards the black hole. In the distance, he saw the nebula with stars and stardust which, spinning around its axis, headed for the center of the black hole. He was afraid he couldn't do it, and that fear made him furious. He focused again, squeezed his awareness, forming a sphere and jumped to the side. Having broken through the genti corridor, he felt like a cosmonaut after stepping out into the void. Darkness engulfed him. Stars were shining all around, and a cosmic vortex was raging in front of him. The long, shiny, spirally twisted genti corridor got thinner until it shone with a white thread of plasma electrons drawn into the distant point of the black hole, it vanished in the distance.

Geo's consciousness seemed to regain concentration, and focus on the computer thread that was heading towards the dome of the afterglowers. One flash of awareness and he materialized right next to the genti electron stream feeding the dome of the afterglowers' ship that was stuck in the depths of one of Nitup holds.

"I'm Geo from the Blue Planet," he sent the signal to its interior. "Who are you and where are you from?"

"We are from the Planet of the Three Suns. Our ship has crashed. All the material afterglowers died. We need help - memories where we can transport our consciousness."

Your Ship and the dome are on the flagship alien cruiser in the Planetary System of Consciousness. Wait, help will come." Geo was in control of the situation by receiving the messages of the afterglow consciousness. He sensed that they were not sending him the whole truth.

"Alpha - open the platform," he gave the voice command.

The automatic pilot answered him in a soft female voice from the four-dimensional hologram that loomed in front of him.

"Ship's drive damaged. The module command teams are operational. Normal vital signs.

At the same time, the huge bolts of the entrance gate noiselessly moved and a descent platform emerged from the bottom and softly fell onto the hangar deck. Geo stood at the entrance.

A strong acoustic signal sounded beside him. He realized that his presence had been detected. The transport hangar where the afterglowers' ship was located, was swarming with aliens. Now he could see them closely. They looked like earthlings. At least their faces, which resembled the angels of his church. Long, pale gold hair fell over a strange material hiding the whole body. This cover performed a function unknown to him. It was like the armor of the ancient knights that distinguished them from the androids who were their bodyguards. The robots could be recognized by their weapon, long slender pikes, which they held in their metal three-finger steel tongs. At the end of each pike, glowed faint red plasma light.

It was mistakenly assumed that he was one of those who were in the dome and for some reason unknown to them escaped outside.

"Relax, Geo. I'm close to you, on Commander Kepud's cruiser. I have taken control of their armada's command system," he heard the Tadpole's calm message. He sensed a hint of pride in it. "I covered the entire afterglowers' ship with the protective field. The aliens can't defeat it. Start negotiating," she added. "I will process your words into their way of communicating."

"Amazing," he thought. Then he calmly got onto their board. Seeing the robots running towards him and wanting to surround him, he extended his hand towards them. He focused and sent a strong impulse of genti energy in their direction. Four rows of robots were blown to the far wall. The others opened fire, pointing their energy pikes at him. Magnetic missiles flew out of their tips and bounced off his protective field, without making any impression on him.

Geo raised his other hand and spread his both hands in front of him in a gesture of earthly greeting.

"I come in peace. I'm an envoy of the Planetary System you entered without permission. I want to speak to your commander. Take me to him." He looked at the robots lying still. The strong impulse sent by Geo destroyed their movement and communication systems. They become useless scrap metal. From the back of the androids came two material members of Nitup crew who looked very much like Hopers. They approached Geo carefully.

"We are from the planet Libeda. We have a peaceful intention," added one of them.

"Do you know of the afterglowers in the dome of this ship?" he asked.

"Yes, we couldn't get its systems running, it's not our technique. They are from a different civilization," he added quickly, as if fearing that this strange afterglower would consider them enemies.

Seeing that among the crew of the cruiser, a shuffle of robots trying to surround him with a protective cordon began, he moved forward.

"I have an important message to convey to your commander."

"Come with us, we'll take you to our commander," he heard the Tadpole's voice translating their strange way of communication.

It was as if they had communicated using facial expressions and the almost imperceptible movements of their hands and fingers. Plus grunts and puffs.

"Damn, my dog looks at me like that, guessing what I mean."

"Beginnings of telepathy, but they can't yet communicate their thoughts directly," the Tadpole said.

The aliens, unable to reach his consciousness, were very concerned. They felt that some force was penetrating their minds, controlling every nook and cranny of their selves. They were afraid.

They realized that they were facing a mighty civilization that surpassed their own by many thousands of years of evolution.

Admiral Narab's flagship cruiser was a great space warship. The huge hangar in which the afterglow ship was hidden was a small fraction of its area. To go around this huge colossus, were used special carts moving along an invisible magnetic track.

Two such carts drove up under the platform, or actually flew up, because without touching the floor, two such carts moved silently towards him. Two aliens entered one of them. The second, with a gesture invited Geo inside the next cart and stepped onto its board. Geo stepped in without fear, and his protective field was blowing away the robot directing its movement. The Tadpole programmed its ride, and to the astonishment of all the aliens, the vehicle swiftly moved towards the Command Room.

The expressions of aliens following his actions were worth this little trick. The news of this strange newcomer and his skills overtook him, reaching Admiral Narab just before his arrival.

"What nonsense are you telling me?" The admiral shouted to his aide. "Where did this intruder come from onto the ship?"

"We don't know. He probably went out of the alien ship. He has his own personal protective field and some energy that destroys our robots. He knows your name, Admiral, and he's on his way here. He programmed the route to the Command Room himself. He bypassed all security measures and will be here soon," he added, looking at the special entrance only for the narrow group of the cruiser commanders.

"Security," the Admiral shouted. "When he shows up, incapacitate him, but don't kill him, he may be useful to us," he gave the order, not accepting the information he had just received.

Four of his adjutants stood beside the transport exit, and two more beside the Admiral, who sat in his command post and watched the screen showing Geo driving towards them.

"Who the hell is running this?" He thought for a moment and, receiving no answer, reached for his ionizing ray thrower. It was the latest generation of secret weapons that only the highest commanders of spacecraft were equipped with. This was to make it easier for them to control subordinates who would have liked to rebel.

As the vehicle stopped and the door to the Command Hall opened, four of his best men lunged at Geo to overpower him. In an instant, rejected by his force field, they plunged onto the board, just below the Admiral's feet.

Geo heard a distinctive quasi-whistle, something like humpback whales singing. It was a personal form of the Tadpole laughter.

"Thank you," he sent the message to her. Seeing the rest of them reaching for their weapons, in a strong, firm voice, he said:

"Don't shoot, hide your gun, I come in peace," he repeated, looking at the Admiral. He had no doubts who this tall, dressed in a silver suit, representative of the hostile civilization was.

Sitting in the center of the room, with a series of fluid video screens above him, he shifted nervously, reaching for one of the longitudinal desks on the left side, dotted with a series of different buttons for command and control.

"I'm Geo from the Blue Planet, and you are Narab the commander of this ship," he said, looking at the four of his best men lumbering along from the board.

"Yes," the Admiral replied, surprised by his words and the fact that the mysterious stranger spoke in their language and knew who he was. The sight of his aides' defeat made him realize that he was dealing with someone who was not afraid either of him or all that was behind him. With one gesture of his outstretched hand, he calmed the two soldiers who were approaching Geo with their weapons drawn.

"Hide your weapons," he ordered.

"What are you coming with?" he asked.

Geo looked around him. He wasn't going to stand while the Admiral was sitting. It pissed him off that he was patronized by him.

"Get up when you talk to me," he said in a sharp tone. The glint in his eyes showed that he was speaking very seriously.

"Nobody will order me on my ship," the Admiral replied contemptuously.

Geo focused and angrily embraced Admiral with his force field. He lifted him and carried straight before himself. When he saw Narab waving his arms and legs helplessly in the air, he slowly began lowering him to the deck. The frightened expressions of his subordinates calmed him so much that he slowly put him on the board without releasing his grip of the force field.

"You are a commander; you should know when you can and when you cannot dictate your terms to the other party." The admiral couldn't understand how it was possible that his body wasn't listening to him and was a toy in the hands of this strange newcomer. He looked like they all, maybe only the face was different and these eyes were different from their round bulging eyes and therefore very expressive and predictable. His eyes resembled the eyes of some of the animals on their planet. They too were wild, shiny and penetrating.

Geo slowly released his grip.

The admiral responded to this gesture of goodwill pointing to a large round table on the other side of the Command Room. Nine armchairs and a liquid video-screen embedded in its table top showed that this was the place of the meeting of the ship commanders.

Geo was the first to go to the table and take the seat that undoubtedly belonged to the Admiral. One and only armchair distinguished by its style and build from the others, swayed gently as Geo sat on it.

Narab took a chair on the opposite side of the table, not letting others know that this move by Geo was insulting him. "Sit down," he said to the division commanders. Geo waited until everyone sat down at the table and then spoke:

"I'm the representative of the four civilizations. I am to give you a message from their High Clans. You are in the region of the Rebirth Nebula. Their Supreme Council and the Great Diviner have decided to come to your aid. We know about your situation and that is why we will not destroy your ships, but we will give your colonizers our Fifth Planet. The only condition is to come to the planet unarmed. Eliminate all of your warships by placing them in the Base to neutralize their warfare intended use. In addition, you must get rid of everything that can be used to start a war on the fifth planet. The fact that you are alive and were not destroyed the moment you crossed the galaxy's boundaries of the Rebirth Nebula, you owe to their steadfast and lasting longer than your civilization, the iron rule "don't kill if you don't have to".

"Why didn't they come to us themselves?" asked their chief psychogalactisist - a scientist dealing with contacts with an alien civilization.

"Their evolution is hundreds of thousands of years ahead of yours. You, too, have had no contact with any insects on your planet," Geo replied. He looked at the mixture of anger and disbelief on their faces. It was a slap in the face for those who considered themselves the navel of the cosmos. For someone who had a weapon that could destroy entire planets, such a comparison was offensive and at the same time a signal for reflection. Some commanders and scientists had long argued that there could be a civilization in space for which they themselves could be insects.

For the remainder of their population, the prevailing thesis was that they were the ones ahead of all other evolutions in the universe. And although they had already met some strange representatives of other civilizations, such as material afterglowers, they still considered themselves the invincible rulers of their galaxy.

"To get rid of the weapons, to disarm our war fleet, it is impossible," their commander responsible for the security of their colonization escapade announced irritatedly.

"The Council knows about the destruction by your Admiral Narab of the only planet in your galaxy to which you could safely transport your entire civilization. Unfortunately, your unbalanced step led to the degradation of its surface, which makes it impossible to settle it.

The time that passes here is out of sync with your planetary system. You would never return to the same reality that was when you left your galactic system. Your planet was destroyed, torn by the gravitational forces of the Great Dwarf, and fell into pieces. You have nothing to go back to."

That world - your world doesn't exist, returning, maybe you will find a planet suitable for colonization, or maybe not. So, you have no choice," Geo dispassionately told them their location.

"How do we know you're telling the truth?" Asked one of their astrophysicists.

"We can destroy all your planets and then come back," added Narab.

"You can't destroy any of the planets of the Consciousness System. You don't know what power you are dealing with. You are in a time trap. I'll convince you of that."

He turned to the large screen that showed a panorama of the sky across many hundreds of light years.

"You can present their situation to them," he said in a slightly stronger voice, looking at the screen. It's a homoexpansus species, for them only strength counts. Show them something spectacular, something that will bring them to their knees," he sent the impulse to the Tadpole.

"Their ships of war protect the Admiral's flagship and transport ships with the colonizers on board. I will move all the transport ships to the other side of the fourth moon of the fifth planet. They will be invisible to them," the Tadpole replied.

"Great, do it." The satisfaction on Geo's face didn't go unnoticed.

"The council will show its goodwill and demonstrate you, its power. It will separate all the colonizer ships from you and transfer them to the orbit of the fifth planet. They will be able to decide their own fate. They will decide for themselves whether to come back with you or stay and settle the fifth planet," he introduced them to what awaited their transport ships with the colonizers on board.

"It's impossible, it's a bluff. The transport ships are protected by our armada!" exclaimed the Admiral, simultaneously pressing the emergency button of the first stage. From that moment on, all the ships of their flotilla heard and saw what was happening in their Command Hall.

"Look," Geo said, and with the help of the Tadpole that he controlled with his second degree of consciousness, he changed the image on the screen, displaying on it a view of their entire armada and all transport ships.

People on board all the ships watched in amazement as their entire armada with transport ships of 1,200 intergalactic space units disappeared one by one. They were so amazed that neither of them reacted to the immobilization of their visor. After a while, all the space around them was empty. Only from navy ships, terrified voices reported the disappearance of their transport ships.

Geo activated a communicator that covered all ships of the alien fleet. On the advice of the Tadpole, he announced to all the commanders and crew members that they could now participate in further talks. Anyone who wanted to peacefully settle the fifth planet must have renounced violence and gotten rid of all weapons. Only then will they be transported to its surface. All the others will be sent back to your Planetary System. Your planet doesn't exist, it was destroyed by the gravitational forces of the Great Dwarf. You have little time to think. After that, the time loop will close and it will not be possible to return to your System. The time and path that you traveled to us is the effect of the space-time corridor that brought you into the orbit of the Rebirth Nebula. After the time loop closes, the distance to your constellation will be 0.5 billion light years. None of you can survive this path."

"What about robots and all the devices we need to live?" one of the commanders of the transport ship asked.

"They will be successively transported to the fifth planet. Everything but weapons and technology for aggression and killing. Your transport ships will remain in the orbit of the fifth planet and the warships will be neutralized."

"How will you transport us? Most of the colonizers reside in inco spaces. It will take many revolutions around the sun to wake up so many people."

"We will transport the entire inco cosmoses along with everything that is used to wake up. Hospitals, laboratories, halls, workshops and all the equipment you need to live on board ships. Anyone who wants to be on the fifth planet should express such a will through the deep thought and loud expression - I want to peacefully settle the fifth planet."

"And who will decide for those who sleep in the inco cosmoses?"

"We," Geo replied shortly.

The communicator roared, questions, threats, doubts, and terror mingled with each other. This was not what all those who had decided to make this trip expected. As it turned out, a one-way trip.

The Tadpole opened the Genti Corridor from the Cap on the fifth planet and began transporting all those who chose to live there. It was faster and safer that way. With a separate transport, she started to move all the inco cosmoses with all the equipment, which was not a technical difficulty, as all of them had a built-in emergency leaving system. It was enough just to direct them to the genti corridor.

The current homoexodes were in an evacuation amok. They were fed up with staying in Spartan conditions aboard shipping ships. The unbelievers and the undecided were convinced by the beautiful panorama of the planet full of greenery, water and golden sand. The Tadpole made every effort to show the image of their new place in the best possible light.

Geo turned off the image in the visor and spoke in a strong, confident voice that reached the people on all the ships:

"I'm one of you and although I live in a different part of the cosmos, on the Blue Planet, we come from the same species of homo sapiens. I don't know everything, I don't understand everything, but I'm sure that the main principle of the Inhabitants of the Consciousness System is to do good. Hello to all those who want to live in a new place in peace and harmony with all the inhabitants of the Consciousness System. I'm waiting for you on your new planet."

Get me out of here," he sent the message to the Tadpole.

"Go to the afterglowers' ship and take off. I'll open the take-off hatch for you."

"I can't fly," he said to her, bantering.

He knew that he didn't need to do anything to make the Glow go itself to the arrivals hall on the Fourth Planet of Souls.

"Don't be kidding, you don't have to do anything. I will bring you here myself," he heard her soft whistle - a sign of joy. He got up and moved toward the transport cart. Unstopped by anyone, he boarded it. The cart started moving and Geo knew his mission had just ended and it was time to head back to Iva.

The Great Debating Chamber boomed with cheers as he stepped onto the podium where the Tadpole was waiting for him. She walked over to him and hugged him with a smile on her face. "I'm proud of you," he heard.

He smelled her scent again. He felt dizzy with that strange, exciting aftertaste of something that seemed impossible to understand by his senses. This is not the smell you can find on Earth," he thought, looking at the beautiful face of the Tadpole.

She saw his excitement and the sexual eagerness radiating from him.

"My spawning is coming. And you, Geo, are the only one with whom my spawn wants to play our eternal dance of life."

"I love Iva," he replied in a weak voice.

"I know. But I also know that on your Blue Planet you can have roe with anyone who wants you. And I want to have roe with you," she replied with a disarming smile.

"How can I explain to you all the dependencies between a woman and a man in our world - it's not the same as on your planet."

"You don't have to explain anything. I'm not your other half like Iva and I will never be it."

"I know it now. And actually, I don't know what it's like on your planet, but I'd love to know - with your help," he added against his will.

"You'll find out - I promise," she added before Geo grabbed her hand.

"Let's go to repose, they can deal with the rest themselves," he said, pointing to the crowd of chatty afterglowers celebrating the end of the conflict.

Geo couldn't help but touch her body. This smell, this lure emanating from her, paralyzed his senses, putting him into some sexual trance. The Tadpole, holding his hand, led him to her apartment. Her chamber changed its original appearance. It was as for earthly imagination - more feminine and reminded him of the decor that can be seen in interior decoration magazines addressed to women.

Geo took a shower, changed into the clothes prepared by the Tadpole, and sat down to eat. They were one of the few newcomers of this system who needed material food for their life. Androgenic robots from the very beginning were perfectly aware of their material needs and guessed them in a way surprising for them. Their task was to fulfill in the best possible way their subconscious wishes that they had had on their planets.

The table was set with earthly delicacies as well as dishes that were Tadpoles' favorite food.

Geo poured wine into glasses and, handing one to the Tadpole, said:

"Let's drink to victory - your victory.

"It would have been impossible without you. No one else would not have survived the genti corridor and you persuaded them to evacuate," she replied.

Holding the glass in her slender hand, she looked at the wine shimmering with all the colors of warm purple and absorbed its slightly tart scent.

"I know that on your Blue Planet you drink such a liquid, but I have never had wine in my mouth," she whispered to him, taking a small sip.

"Drink this nectar of the gods - that's what we say for wine."

"Who is God?" She asked.

"He is the creator of the universe and everything that lives in it. You cannot see him, but he exists and is watching over us."

"It's illogical what you say," she replied taking a larger sip of wine.

"Maybe we'll talk about it another time, now wine relaxes me and soothes my senses."

"I know, I feel you are excited about the proximity of my spawning."

"I don't know what's happening to me," he confirmed with disarming frankness.

"Nothing unusual, believe me, it's just the way you react to the scent of my ether decoys. Come, I will soothe your desires," saying it, she took his hand and led him towards the water. With one movement of her other hand, she threw her dress off herself. The strong scent of her body reached Geo. It was something he had never encountered before. A fragrance that captivated his senses. Losing his temper, he nervously took off his clothes and followed her into the warm water, slowly losing track of time and the ability to control his senses. He only wanted one thing, to fuse with her body as quickly as possible.

The Tadpole gently hugged him and they plunged into the water. She was breathing freely under the water, and he had to come up from time to time to take a sip of salutary air. She then took advantage of it by getting him sexually ready. He sent her an impulse of his thoughts and desires that she fulfilled. She began to circle around him, getting closer and closer to his body. Her silky skin rubbed against him, caressed him, and her little legs hugged him in a special way, causing him to explode uncontrollably. Then, her genitals sucked in his semen, but Geo couldn't see it. Dazed by sexual play, he floated on the surface of the pool, supported by the Tadpole. When their underwater dance was over, she embraced and led him to the living room, where they both fell down on the couch, panting heavily.

After a while, Geo got roused from that numbness, full of shame and embarrassment. He was surprised that he hadn't restrained himself and hadn't resisted the sexual lures of the Tadpole.

"What was that?" He asked after a moment.

"Don't be angry, you didn't do anything wrong. On my Fish Planet, it is a way for a new life. Here I only have you, and with you I wanted to have the roe."

Geo got up. "I have to go home now, it has been a hard and exhausting time for me," he said without looking at her.

Satisfied with the sexual dance, the Tadpole only waved her leg goodbye. They both knew that this evening ended their period of sexual dependence, but didn't end the friendly relations between them.

The cause of his shallow and short sleep was the frustration and dissatisfaction he fell into after he was sexually abused by the Tadpole. He didn't know if Iva penetrated their consciousness and discovered his betrayal, or if the Tadpole herself informed Iva about their sexual brotherhood.

He wanted to get back to Earth so he concentrated and sent out the strong signal of consciousness:

"Iva, I'm coming back. The Planets of Consciousness saved. The enemy fleet neutralized. The colonizers peacefully settled their fifth planet. I have discovered something very important. I miss and I love you." Although this last message sounded a bit hesitant, it was a truth which he realized more when he tried to forget about the evening event.

The Tadpole received the message addressed to Iva and smiled. For her, love and affection for one creature didn't matter. What mattered, was spawning and extension of the species.

It was a priority on their Fish Planet. She emanated her sexuality once a year in search of a second roe with which she could mix her roe. It was her evolutionary duty that she had now fulfilled with Geo. He was still an important person for her, but it didn't affect the further relations between them. She didn't reason like Geo and Iva. The feeling of jealousy didn't exist in her consciousness.

She knew she was going to have a baby with Geo. She also knew that their child would be the beginning of a new race of Homo sapiens and that all the ways of the universe would be open to he or she.

Now they were sure that it was the Forbidden Moon of Hope that was the beginning and ending for every species of homo sapiens and every path in the universe connecting all planets to the Hope Second Moon.

Table of contents